TIMEGATES

Edited by Jack Dann & Gardner Dozois

Edited by Jack Dann & Gardner Dozois

Edited by Terri Windling

TIMEGATES

MAR 1 0 1997

EDITED BY
JACK DANN & GARDNER DOZOIS

ACE BOOKS, NEW YORK

This book is an Ace original edition,
and has never been previously published.

TIMEGATES

An Ace Book / published by arrangement with
the editors

PRINTING HISTORY
Ace edition / March 1997

All rights reserved.
Copyright © 1997 by Jack Dann and Gardner Dozois.
Cover art by Jean-Francois Podevin.
This book may not be reproduced in whole or in part,
by mimeograph or any other means, without permission.
For information address: The Berkley Publishing Group,
200 Madison Avenue, New York, NY 10016.

The Putnam Berkley World Wide Web site address is
http://www.berkley.com/berkley
Make sure to check out *PB Plug*,
the science fiction/fantasy newsletter, at
http://www.pbplug.com

ISBN: 0-441-00428-8

ACE®
Ace Books are published by The Berkley Publishing Group,
200 Madison Avenue, New York, NY 10016.
ACE and the "A" design are trademarks
belonging to Charter Communications, Inc.

PRINTED IN THE UNITED STATES OF AMERICA

10 9 8 7 6 5 4 3 2 1

*Acknowledgment is made
for permission to reprint the following material:*

"The Man Who Walked Home," by James Tiptree, Jr. Copyright © 1972 by Ultimate Publishing Co. First published in *Amazing Science Fiction Stories*, 1972. Reprinted by permission of the author's estate and the agent for the estate, Virginia Kidd.

"Air Raid," by John Varley. Copyright © 1977 by Davis Publications, Inc. First published in *Isaac Asimov's Science Fiction Magazine*, Spring 1977. Reprinted by permission of the author and the author's agent.

"The Hole on the Corner," by R.A. Lafferty. Copyright © 1967 by Damon Knight. First published in *Orbit 2* (Berkley). Reprinted by permission of the author and the author's agent, Virginia Kidd.

"Trapalanda," by Charles Sheffield. Copyright © 1987 by Davis Publications, Inc. First published in *Isaac Asimov's Science Fiction Magazine*, June 1987. Reprinted by permission of the author.

"Arachon," by Damon Knight. Copyright © 1953 by Quinn Publishing Company, Inc. First published in *World SF IF*, January 1954. Reprinted by permission of the author.

"Hole-in-the-Wall," by Bridget McKenna. Copyright © 1991 by Davis Publications, Inc. First published in *Isaac Asimov's Science Fiction Magazine*, May 1991. Reprinted by permission of the author.

"Time's Arrow," by Jack McDevitt. Copyright © 1991 by Davis Publications, Inc. First published in *Isaac Asimov's*

CONTENTS

PREFACE

It may be one of the oldest dreams of all—to step through a door and find yourself in a different time or a different place . . . or a different world. Somehow, enclosing yourself in a rattling, stuffy, claustrophobic time machine for a long flight back through the ages is just not the same. To have a gate open before you and to take one step forward and suddenly *be* Elsewhere or Elsewhen! To *stroll* between the ages or between the worlds! To step to Ancient Greece, or the far future, or to a world circling a distant star, or to the New York of the Roaring Twenties, or to the age of the dinosaurs, or on to a Civil War battlefield just before the fateful charge, or to a different reality altogether, an alterate reality where you might perhaps encounter an alternate *you* . . . just to suddenly *be* there, without having to journey through time or space, without fuss or bother, everything and everywhere no further away and no more difficult to get to than it is to step from your kitchen to your living room. Surely of all the freedoms that humankind has dreamed of for itself, there can be no freedom more complete and more liberating than *this*.

So open the pages of this anthology and let the stories here be your gates through time and space to mysterious new worlds that you thought were forever unreachable. Let the authors you'll find within these pages be your tour guides through the infinite vistas of time and space—they'll take you as far as the imagination can reach and bring you back alive!

The gates are opening before you. Go ahead, take that first step . . .

THE MAN
WHO WALKED HOME

James Tiptree, Jr.

As most of you know by now, multiple Hugo and Nebula Award-winning author James Tiptree, Jr. was actually the pseudonym of the late Dr. Alice Sheldon, a semi-retired experimental psychologist and former member of the American intelligence community, who also wrote occasionally under the name of Raccoona Sheldon. Dr. Sheldon's tragic death in 1987 put an end to "both" careers, but not before she had won two Nebula and two Hugo Awards as Tiptree, won another Nebula Award as Raccoona Sheldon, and established herself, under whatever name, as one of the very best science fiction writers of our times. As Tiptree, Dr. Sheldon published two novels, Up the Walls of the World *and* Brightness Falls From the Air, *and nine short-story collections:* Ten Thousand Light Years From Home, Warm Worlds and Otherwise, Starsongs of an Old Primate, Out of the Everywhere, Tales of the Quintana Roo, Byte Beautiful, The Starry Rift, *the posthumously published* Crown of Stars, *and the recent posthumous retrospective collection,* Her Smoke Rose Up Forever.*

In the vivid and compelling story that follows, she shows us although home may only be a step away, sometimes that step can be very hard to take . . .

Transgression! Terror! And he thrust and lost there— punched into impossibility, abandoned, never to be known now, the wrong man in the most wrong of all wrong places in that unimaginable collapse of never-to-be-reimagined mechanism—he stranded, undone, his lifeline severed, he in that nanosecond knowing his only tether parting, going

*away, the longest line to life withdrawing, winking out,
disappearing forever beyond his grasp—telescoping away
from him into the closing vortex beyond which lay his home,
his life, his only possibility of being; seeing it sucked back
into the deepest maw, melting, leaving him orphaned on
what never-to-be-known shore of total wrongness—of
beauty beyond joy, perhaps? Of horror? Of nothingness? Of
profound otherness only, only, certainly whatever it was,
that place into which he transgressed, certainly it could not
support his life there, his violent and violating aberrance;
and he, fierce, brave, crazy—clenched into one total
protest, one body-fist of utter repudiation of himself there in
that place, forsaken there—what did he do? Rejected,
exiled, hungering homeward more desperate than any lost
beast driving for its unreachable home, his home, his
HOME—and no way, no transport, no vehicle, means,
machinery, no force but his intolerable resolve aimed
homeward along that vanishing vector, that last and only
lifeline—he did, what?*

He walked.

Home.

Precisely what hashed up in the work of the major
industrial lessee of the Bonneville Particle Acceleration
Facility in Idaho was never known. Or rather, all those who
might have been able to diagnose the original malfunction
were themselves obliterated almost at once in the greater
catastrophe which followed.

The nature of this second cataclysm was not at first
understood either. All that was ever certain was that at
1153.6 of May 2, 1989 Old Style, the Bonneville laboratories and all their personnel were transformed into an intimately disrupted form of matter resembling a high-energy
plasma, which became rapidly airborne to the accompani-
ment of radiating seismic and atmospheric events.

The disturbed area unfortunately included an operational
MIRV Watchdog bomb.

In the confusions of the next hours the Earth's population
was substantially reduced, the biosphere was altered, and
the Earth itself was marked with numbers of more conven-

tional craters. For some years thereafter the survivors were existentially preoccupied and the peculiar dust bowl at Bonneville was left to weather by itself in the changing climatic cycles.

It was not a large crater; just over a kilometer in width and lacking the usual displacement lip. Its surface was covered with a finely divided substance which dried into dust. Before the rains began it was almost perfectly flat. Only in certain lights, had anyone been there to inspect it, a small surface marking or abraded place could be detected almost exactly as the center.

Two decades after the disaster a party of short brown people appeared from the south, together with a flock of somewhat atypical sheep. The crater at this time appeared as a wide shallow basin in which the grass did not grow well, doubtless from the almost complete lack of soil micro-organisms. Neither this nor the surrounding vigorous grass were found to harm the sheep. A few crude hogans went up at the southern edge and a faint path began to be traced across the crater itself, passing by the central bare spot.

One spring morning two children who had been driving sheep across the crater came screaming back to camp. A monster had burst out of the ground before them, a huge flat animal making a dreadful roar. It vanished in a flash and a shaking of the earth, leaving an evil smell. The sheep had run away.

Since this last was visibly true, some elders investigated. Finding no sign of the monster and no place in which it could hide, they settled for beating the children, who settled for making a detour around the monster-spot, and nothing more occurred for a while.

The following spring the episode was repeated. This time an older girl was present but she could add only that the monster seemed to be rushing flat out along the ground without moving at all. And there was a scraped place in the dirt. Again nothing was found; an evil-ward in a cleft stick was placed at the spot.

When the same thing happened for the third time a year later, the detour was extended and other charm-wands were

added. But since no harm seemed to come of it and the
brown people had seen far worse, sheep-tending resumed as
before. A few more instantaneous apparitions of the monster
were noted, each time in the spring.

At the end of the third decade of the new era a tall old
man limped down the hills from the south, pushing his pack
upon a bicycle wheel. He camped on the far side of the
crater, and soon found the monster-site. He attempted to
question people about it, but no one understood him, so he
traded a knife for some meat. Although he was obviously
feeble, something about him dissuaded them from killing
him, and this proved wise because he later assisted the
women to treat several sick children.

He spent much time around the place of the apparition
and was nearby when it made its next appearance. This
excited him very much, and he did several inexplicable but
apparently harmless things, including moving his camp into
the crater by the trail. He stayed on for a full year watching
the site and was close by for its next manifestation. After
this he spent a few days making a charmstone for the spot
and then left, northward, hobbling, as he had come.

More decades passed. The crater eroded and a rain-gully
became an intermittent steamlet across one edge of the
basin. The brown people and their sheep were attacked by a
band of grizzled men, after which the survivors went away
eastward. The winters of what had been Idaho was now
frost-free; aspen and eucalyptus sprouted in the moist plain.
Still the crater remained treeless, visible as a flat bowl of
grass, and the bare place at the center remained. The skies
cleared somewhat.

After another three decades a larger band of black people
with ox-drawn carts appeared and stayed for a time, but left
again when they too saw the thunderclap-monster. A few
other vagrants straggled by.

Five decades later a small permanent settlement had
grown up on the nearest range of hills, from which men
riding on small ponies with dark stripes down their spines
herded humped cattle near the crater. A herdsman's hut was
built by the streamlet, which in time became the habitation

of an olive-skinned, red-haired family. In due course one of this clan again observed the monster-flash, but these people did not depart. The stone the tall man had placed was noted and left undisturbed.

The homestead at the crater's edge grew into a group of three and was joined by others, and the trail across it became a cartroad with a log bridge over the stream. At the center of the still-faintly-discernible crater the cartroad made a bend, leaving a grassy place which bore on its center about a square meter of curiously impacted bare earth and a deeply-etched sandstone rock.

The apparition of the monster was now known to occur regularly each spring on a certain morning in this place, and the children of the community dared each other to approach the spot. It was referred to in a phrase that could be translated as "the Old Dragon." The Old Dragon's appearance was always the same; a brief, violent thunderburst which began and cut off abruptly, in the midst of which a dragon-like creature was seen apparently in furious motion on the earth although it never actually moved. Afterward there was a bad smell and the earth smoked. People who saw it from close by spoke of a shivering sensation.

Early in the second century two young men rode into town from the north. Their ponies were shaggier than the local breed and the equipment they carried included two boxlike objects which the young men set up at the monster-site. They stayed in the area a full year, observing two materializations of the Old Dragon, and they provided much news and maps of roads and trading-towns in the cooler regions to the north. They built a windmill which was accepted by the community and offered to build a lighting machine, which was refused. Then they departed with their boxes after unsuccessfully attempting to persuade a local boy to learn to operate one.

In the course of the next decades other travelers stopped by and marveled at the monster, and there was sporadic fighting over the mountains to the south. One of the armed bands made a cattle-raid into the crater hamlet. It was repulsed, but the raiders left a spotted sickness which killed many. For all this time the bare place at the crater's center remained, and the monster made his regular appearances, observed or not.

The hill-town grew and changed and the crater hamlet grew to be a town. Roads widened and linked into networks. There were gray-green conifers in the hills now, spreading down into the plain, and chirruping lizards lived in their branches.

At century's end a shabby band of skin-clad squatters with stunted milk-beasts erupted out of the west and were eventually killed or driven away, but not before the local herds had contracted a vicious parasite. Veterinaries were fetched from the market-city up north, but little could be done. The families near the crater left, and for some decades the area was empty. Finally cattle of a new strain reappeared in the plain and the crater hamlet was reoccupied. Still the bare center continued annually to manifest the monster and he became an accepted phenomenon of the area. On several occasions parties came from the distant Northwest Authority to observe it.

The crater hamlet flourished and grew into the fields where cattle had grazed and part of the old crater became the town park. A small seasonal tourist industry based on the monster-site developed. The townspeople rented rooms for the appearances and many more-or-less authentic monster-relics were on display in the local taverns.

Several cults now grew up around the monster. Some held that it was a devil or damned soul forced to appear on Earth in torment to expiate the catastrophe of two centuries back. Others believed that it, or he, was some kind of messenger whose roar portended either doom or hope according to the believer. One very vocal sect taught that the apparition registered the moral conduct of the townspeople over the past year, and scrutinized the annual apparition for changes which could be interpreted for good or ill. It was considered lucky, or dangerous, to be touched by some of the dust raised by the monster. In every generation at least one small boy would try to hit the monster with a stick, usually acquiring a broken arm and a lifelong tavern tale. Pelting the monster with stones or other objects was a popular sport, and for some years people systematically flung prayers and flowers at it. Once a party tried to net it and were left with strings and vapor. The area itself had long since been fenced off at the center of the park.

Through all this the monster made his violently enigmatic annual appearance, sprawled furiously motionless, unreachably roaring.

Only as the fourth century of the new era went by was it apparent that the monster had been changing slightly. He was now no longer on the earth but had an arm and a leg thrust upward in a kicking or flailing gesture. As the years passed he began to change more quickly until at the end of the century he had risen to a contorted crouching pose, arms outflung as if frozen in gyration. His roar, too, seemed somewhat differently pitched and the earth after him smoked more and more.

It was then widely felt that the man-monster was about to do something, to make some definitive manifestation, and a series of natural disasters and marvels gave support to a vigorous cult teaching this doctrine. Several religious leaders journeyed to the town to observe the apparitions.

However, the decades passed and the man-monster did nothing more than turn slowly in place, so that he now appeared to be in the act of sliding or staggering while pushing himself backward like a creature blown before a gale. No wind, of course, could be felt, and presently the general climate quieted and nothing came of it all.

Early in the fifth century New Calendar three survey parties from the North Central Authority came through the area and stopped to observe the monster. A permanent recording device was set up at the site, after assurances to the townfolk that no hardscience was involved. A local boy was trained to operate it; he quit when his girl left him but another volunteered. At this time nearly everyone believed that the apparition was a man, or the ghost of one. The record-machine boy and a few others, including the school mechanics teacher, referred to him as The Man John. In the next decades the roads were greatly improved; all forms of travel increased and there was talk of building a canal to what had been the Snake River.

One May morning at the end of Century Five a young couple in a smart green mule-trap came jogging up the high-road from the Sandreas Rift Range to the southwest. The girl was golden-skinned and chatted with her young husband in a language unlike that ever heard by the Man John either at the end or the beginning of his life. What she said to him has, however, been heard in every age and tongue.

"Oh Serli, I'm so glad we're taking this trip now! Next summer I'll be so busy with baby."

To which Serli replied as young husbands often have, and so they trotted up to the town's inn. Here they left trap and bags and went in search of her uncle who was expecting them there. The morrow was the day of the Man John's annual appearance, and her Uncle Laban had come from the MacKenzie History Museum to observe it and to make certain arrangements.

They found him with the town school instructor of mechanics, who was also the recorder at the monster-site. Presently Uncle Laban took them all with him to the town mayor's office to meet with various religious personages. The mayor was not unaware of tourist values, but he took Uncle Laban's part in securing the cultists' grudging assent to the MacKenzie authorities' secular interpretation of the "monster," which was made easier by the fact that they disagreed among themselves. Then, seeing how pretty the niece was, the mayor took them all home to dinner.

When they returned to the inn for the night it was abrawl with holiday makers.

"Whew," said Uncle Laban. "I've talked myself dry, sister's daughter. What a weight of holy nonsense is that Morsha female! Serli, my lad, I know you have questions. Let me hand you this to read; it's a guide book we're giving 'em to sell. Tomorrow I'll answer for it all." And he disappeared into the crowded tavern.

So Serli and his bride took the pamphlet upstairs to bed

with them, but it was not until the next morning at breakfast
that they found time to read it.

"'All that is known of John Delgano,'" read Serli with
his mouth full, "'comes from two documents left by his
brother Carl Delgano in the archives of the MacKenzie
Group in the early years after the holocaust.' Put some
honey on this cake, Mira my dove, 'Verbatim transcript
follows; this is Carl Delgano speaking.

"'I'm not an engineer or an astronaut like John. I ran an
electronics repair shop in Salt Lake City. John was only
trained as a spaceman, he never got to space, the slump
wiped all that out. So he tied up with this commercial group
who were leasing part of Bonneville. They wanted a man for
some kind of hard vacuum tests; that's all I knew about it.
John and his wife moved to Bonneville, but we all got
together several times a year, our wives were like sisters.
John had two kids, Clara and Paul.

"'The tests were all supposed to be secret, but John told
me confidentially they were trying for an anti-gravity
chamber. I don't know if it ever worked. That was the year
before.

"'Then that winter they came down for Christmas and
John said they had something new. He was really excited. A
temporal displacement, he called it; some kind of time
effect. He said the chief honcho was like a real mad
scientist. Bit ideas. He kept adding more angles every time
some other project would quit and leave equipment he could
lease. No, I don't know who the top company was—maybe
an insurance conglomerate, they had all the cash, didn't
they? I guess they'd pay to catch a look at the future; that
figures. Anyway, John was go, go, go. Katharine was
scared; that's natural. She pictured him like, you know, H.G.
Wells—walking around in some future world. John told her
it wasn't like that at all. All they'd get would be this kind of
flicker, like a second or two. All kinds of complications'—
Yes, yes, my greedy piglet, some brew for me too. This is
thirsty work!

"So . . . 'I remember I asked him, what about the Earth
moving? I mean, you could come back in a different place,

right? He said they had that all figured. A spatial trajectory. Katherine was so scared we dropped it. John told her, don't worry, I'll come home. But he didn't. Not that it makes any difference, of course; everything was wiped out. Salt Lake too. The only reason I'm here is that I went up by Calgary to see Mom, April twenty-ninth. May second it all blew. I didn't find you folks at Mackenzie until July. I guess I may as well stay. That's all I know about John, except that he was an all-right guy. If that accident started all this it wasn't his fault.

"'The second document'—In the name of love, little mother, do I have to read all this! Oh very well; but you will kiss me first, madam. Must you look so ineffable? . . . 'The second document. Dated in the year eighteen, New Style, writer by Carl'—see the old handwriting, my plump pigeon. Oh, very well, very well.

"'Written at Bonneville Crater, I have seen my brother John Delgano. When I knew I had the rad sickness I came down here to look around. Salt Lake's still hot. So I hiked up here by Bonneville. You can see the crater where the labs were; it's grassed over. It's different, it's not radioactive, my film's OK. There's a bare place in the middle. Some Indios here told me a monster shows up here every year in the spring. I saw it myself a couple of days after I got here but I was too far away to see much, except I was sure it's a man. In a vacuum suit. There was a lot of noise and dust, took me by surprise. It was all over in a second. I figure it's pretty close to the day, I mean, May second, old.

"'So I hung around a year and he showed up again yesterday. I was on the face side and I could see his face through the faceplate. It's John all right. He's hurt. I saw blood on his mouth and his suit is frayed some. He's lying on the ground. He didn't move while I could see him but the dust boiled up, like a man sliding onto base without moving. His eyes are open like he was looking. I don't understand it anyway, but I know it's John, not a ghost. He was in exactly the same position each time and there's a loud crack like thunder and another sound like a siren, very fast. And an ozone smell, and smoke, I felt a kind of shudder.

"'I know it's John there and I think he's alive. I have to leave here now to take this back while I can still walk. I think somebody should come here and see. Maybe you can help John. Signed. Carl Delgano.

"'The records were kept by the Mackenzie Group but it was not for several years—' Etcetera, first light-print, etcetera, archives, analysts, etcetera—very good! Now it is time to meet your uncle, my edible one, after we go upstairs for just a moment."

"No, Serli, I will wait for you downstairs," said Mira prudently.

When they came into the town park Uncle Leban was directing the installation of a large durite slab in front of the enclosure around the Man John's appearance-spot. The slab was wrapped in a curtain to await the official unveiling. Townspeople and tourists and children thronged the walks and a Ride-For-Good choir was singing in the bandshell. The morning was warming up fast. Vendors hawked ices and straw toys of the monster and flowers and good-luck confetti to throw at him. Another religious group stood by in dark robes; they belonged to the Repentance church beyond the park. Their pastor was directing somber glares at the crowd in general and Mira's uncle in particular.

Three official-looking strangers who had been at the inn came up and introduced themselves to Uncle Laban as observers from Alberta Central. They went on into the tent which had been erected over the enclosure, carrying with them several pieces of equipment which the town-folk eyed suspiciously.

The mechanics teacher finished organizing a squad of students to protect the slab's curtain, and Mira and Serli and Laban went on into the tent. It was much hotter inside. Benches were set in rings around a railed enclosure about twenty feet in diameter. Inside the railing the earth was bare and scuffed. Several bunches of flowers and blooming poinciana branches leaned against the rail. The only thing inside the rail was a rough sandstone rock with markings etched on it.

Just as they came in a small girl raced across the open center and was yelled at by everybody. The officials from Alberta were busy at one side of the rail, where the light-print box was mounted.

"Oh, no," muttered Mira's uncle, as one of the officials leaned over to set up a tripod stand inside the rails. He adjusted it and a huge horsetail of fine feathery filaments blossomed out and eddied through the center of the space.

"Oh *no*," Laban said again. "Why can't they let it be?"

"They're trying to pick up dust from his suit, is that right?" Serli asked.

"Yes, insane. Did you get time to read?"

"Oh yes," said Serli.

"Sort of," added Mira.

"Then you know. He's falling. Trying to check his—well, call it velocity. Trying to slow down. He must have slipped or stumbled. We're getting pretty close to when he lost his footing and started to fall. What did it? Did somebody trip him?" Laban looked from Mira to Serli, dead serious now. "How would you like to be the one who made John Delgano fall?"

"Ooh," said Mira in quick sympathy. Then she said, "Oh."

"You mean," asked Serli, "whoever made him fall caused all the, caused—"

"Possible," said Laban.

"Wait a minute," Serli frowned. "He did fall. So somebody had to do it—I mean, he has to trip or whatever. If he doesn't fall the past would all be changed, wouldn't it? No war, no—"

"Possible," Laban repeated. "God knows. All *I* know is that John Delgano and the space around him is the most unstable, improbable, highly charged area ever known on Earth and I'm damned if I think anybody should go poking sticks in it."

"Oh come now, Laban!" One of the Alberta men joined them, smiling. "Our dust-mop couldn't trip a gnat. It's just vitreous monofilaments."

"Dust from the future," grumbled Laban. "What's it going to tell you? That the future has dust in it?"

"If we could only get a trace from that thing in his hand."

"In his hand?" asked Mira. Serli started leafing hurriedly through the pamphlet.

"We've had a recording analyzer aimed at it," the Albertan lowered his voice, glancing around. "A spectroscope. We know there's something there, or was. Can't get a decent reading. It's severely deteriorated."

"People poking at him, grabbing at him," Leban muttered. "You—"

"*Ten minutes!*" shouted a man with a megaphone. "Take your places, friends and strangers."

The Repentance people were filing in at one side, intoning an ancient incantation, "mi-seri-cordia, ora pro nobis!"

The atmosphere suddenly took on tension. It was now very close and hot in the big tent. A boy from the mayor's office wiggled through the crowd, beckoning Laban's party to come and sit in the guest chairs on the second level on the "face" side. In front of them at the rail one of the Repentance ministers was arguing with an Albertan official over his right to occupy the space taken by a recorder, it being his special duty to look into the Man John's eyes.

"Can he really see us?" Mira asked her uncle.

"Blink your eyes," Laban told her. "A new scene every blink, that's what he sees. Phantasmagoria. Blink-blink-blink—for god knows how long."

"Mi-sere-re, pec-cavi," chanted the penitentials. A soprano neighed "May the red of sin pa-aa-ass from us!"

"They believe his oxygen tab went red because of the state of their souls." Laban chuckled. "Their souls are going to have to stay damned a while; John Delgano has been on oxygen reserve for five centuries—or rather, he *will be* low for five centuries more. At a half-second per year his time, that's fifteen minutes. We know from the audio trace he's still breathing more or less normally and the reserve was good for twenty minutes. So they should have their salvation about the year seven hundred, if they last that long."

"*Five minutes!* Take your seats, folks. Please sit down so everyone can see. Sit down, folks."

"It says we'll hear his voice through his suit speaker," Serli whispered. "Do you know what he's saying?"

"You get mostly a twenty-cycle howl," Laban whispered back. "The recorders have spliced up something like *ayt*, part of an old word. Take centuries to get enough to translate."

"Is it a message?"

"Who knows? Could be his word for 'date' or 'hate.' 'Too late,' maybe. Anything."

The tent was quieting. A fat child by the railing started to cry and was pulled back onto a lap. There was a subdued mumble of praying. The Holy Joy faction on the far side rustled their flowers.

"Why don't we set our clocks by him?"

"It's changing. He's on sidereal time."

"*One minute.*"

In the hush the praying voices rose slightly. From outside a chicken cackled. The bare center space looked absolutely ordinary. Over it the recorder's silvery filaments eddied gently in the breath from a hundred lungs. Another recorder could be heard ticking faintly.

For long seconds nothing happened.

The air developed a tiny hum. At the same moment Mira caught a movement at the railing on her left.

The hum developed a beat and vanished into a peculiar silence and suddenly everything happened at once.

Sound burst on them, raced shockingly up the audible scale. The air cracked as something rolled and tumbled in the space. There was a grinding, wailing roar and—

He was there.

Solid, huge—a huge man in a monster suit, his head was a dull bronze transparent globe holding a human face, dark smear of open mouth. His position was impossible, legs strained forward thrusting himself back, his arms frozen in a whirlwind swing. Although he seemed to be in a frantic forward motion nothing moved, only one of his legs buckled or sagged slightly—

—And then he was gone, utterly and completely gone in a thunderclap, leaving only the incredible afterimage in a hundred pairs of staring eyes. Air boomed, shuddering, dust roiled out mixed with smoke.

"Oh, oh my God," gasped Mira, unheard, clinging to Serli. Voices were crying out, choking. "He saw me, he saw me!" a woman shrieked. A few people dazedly threw their confetti into the empty dust-cloud; most had failed to throw at all. Children began to howl. "He *saw* me!" the woman screamed hysterically. "Red, Oh Lord have mercy!" a deep male voice intoned.

Mira heard Laban swearing furiously and looked again into the space. As the dust settled she could see that the recorder's tripod had tipped over into the center. There was a dusty mound lying against it—flowers. Most of the end of the stand seemed to have disappeared or been melted. Of the filaments nothing could be seen.

"Some damn fool pitched flowers into it. Come on, let's get out."

"Was it under, did it trip him?" asked Mira, squeezed in the crowd.

"It was still red, his oxygen thing," Serli said over her head. "No mercy this trip, eh, Laban?"

"Shsh!" Mira caught the Repentance pastor's dark glance. They jostled through the enclosure gate and were out in the sunlit park, voices exclaiming, chattering loudly in excitement and relief.

"It was terrible," Mira cried softly. "Oh, I never thought it was a real live man. There he is, he's *there*. Why can't we help him? Did we trip him?"

"I don't know; I don't think so," her uncle grunted. They sat down near the new monument, fanning themselves. The curtain was still in place.

"Did we change the past?" Serli laughed, looked lovingly at his little wife. He wondered for a moment why she was wearing such odd earrings. Then he remembered he had given them to her at that Indian pueblo they'd passed.

"But it wasn't just those Alberta people," said Mira. She

seemed obsessed with the idea. "It was the flowers really."
She wiped at her forehead.

"Mechanics or superstition," chuckled Serli. "Which is
the culprit, love or science?"

"Shsh." Mira looked about nervously. "The flowers were
love, I guess . . . I feel so strange. It's hot. Oh, thank
you." Uncle Laban had succeeded in attracting the attention
of the iced-drink vendor.

People were chatting normally now and the choir struck
into a cheerful song. At one side of the park a line of people
were waiting to sign their names in the visitors' book. The
mayor appeared at the park gate, leading a party up the
bougainvillea alley for the unveiling of the monument.

"What did it say on that stone by his foot?" Mira asked.
Serli showed her the guidebook picture of Carl's rock with
the inscription translated below: WELCOME HOME JOHN.

"I wonder if he can see it."

The mayor was about to begin his speech.

Much later when the crowd had gone away the monument
stood alone in the dark, displaying to the moon the
inscription in the language of that time and place:

ON THIS SPOT THERE APPEARS ANNUALLY THE FORM OF MAJOR JOHN
DELGANO, THE FIRST AND ONLY MAN TO TRAVEL IN TIME.

MAJOR DELGANO WAS SENT INTO THE FUTURE SOME HOURS
BEFORE THE HOLOCAUST OF DAY ZERO. ALL KNOWLEDGE OF THE
MEANS BY WHICH HE WAS SENT IS LOST, PERHAPS FOREVER. IT IS
BELIEVED THAT AN ACCIDENT OCCURRED WHICH SENT HIM MUCH
FARTHER THAN WAS INTENDED. SOME ANALYSTS SPECULATE THAT HE
MAY HAVE GONE AS FAR AS FIFTY THOUSAND YEARS AHEAD. HAVING
REACHED THIS UNKNOWN POINT MAJOR DELGANO APPARENTLY WAS
RECALLED, OR ATTEMPTED TO RETURN, ALONG THE COURSE IN SPACE
AND TIME THROUGH WHICH HE WAS SENT. HIS TRAJECTORY IS
THOUGHT TO START AT THE POINT WHICH OUR SOLAR SYSTEM WILL
OCCUPY AT A FUTURE TIME AND IS TANGENT TO THE COMPLEX HELIX
WHICH OUR EARTH DESCRIBES AROUND THE SUN.

HE APPEARS ON THIS SPOT IN THE ANNUAL INSTANTS IN WHICH HIS
COURSE INTERSECTS OUR PLANET'S ORBIT AND HE IS APPARENTLY
ABLE TO TOUCH THE GROUND IN THOSE INSTANTS. SINCE NO TRACE

OF HIS PASSAGE INTO THE FUTURE HAS BEEN MANIFESTED, IT IS
BELIEVED THAT HE IS RETURNING BY A DIFFERENT MEANS THAN HE
WENT FORWARD. HE IS ALIVE IN OUR PRESENT. OUR PAST IS HIS
FUTURE AND OUR FUTURE IS HIS PAST. THE TIME OF HIS APPEARANCES
IS SHIFTING GRADUALLY IN SOLAR TIME TO CONVERGE ON THE
MOMENT OF 1153.6 ON MAY 2ND 1989 OLD STYLE, OR DAY ZERO.

THE EXPLOSION WHICH ACCOMPANIED HIS RETURN TO HIS OWN
TIME AND PLACE MAY HAVE OCCURRED WHEN SOME ELEMENTS OF
THE PAST INSTANTS OF HIS COURSE WERE CARRIED WITH HIM INTO
THEIR OWN PRIOR EXISTENCE. IT IS CERTAIN THAT THIS EXPLOSION
PRECIPITATED THE WORLDWIDE HOLOCAUST WHICH ENDED FOREVER
THE AGE OF HARDSCIENCE.

*—He was falling, losing control, failing in his fight against
the terrible momentum he had gained, fighting with his
human legs shaking in the inhuman stiffness of his armor,
his soles charred, not gripping well now, not enough
traction to brake, battling, thrusting as the flashes came, the
punishing alternation of light, dark, light, dark, which he
had borne so long, the claps of air thickening and thinning
against his armor as he skidded through space which was
time, desperately braking as the flickers of earth hammered
against his feet—only his feet mattered now, only to slow
and stay on course—and the pull, the beacon was getting
slacker; as he came near home it was fanning out, hard to
stay centered; he was becoming, he supposed, more probable; the wound he had punched in time was healing itself.
In the beginning it had been so tight—a single ray in a
closing tunnel—he had hurled himself after it like an
electron flying to the anode, aimed surely along that
exquisitely complex single vector of possibility of life, shot
and been shot like a squeezed pip into the last clink in that
rejecting and rejected nowhere through which he, John
Delgano, could conceivably continue to exist, the hole
leading to home—had pounded down it across time, across
space, pumping with his human legs as the real Earth of that
unreal time came under him, his course as certain as the
twisting dash of an animal down its burrow, he a cosmic
mouse on an interstellar, intertemporal race for his nest*

with the wrongness of everything closing round the right-
ness of that one course, the atoms of his heart, his blood, his
every well crying Home—HOME!—as he drove himself
after that fading breath-hole, each step faster, surer, stronger,
until he raced with invincible momentum upon the rolling
flickers of Earth as a man might race a rolling log in a
torrent! Only the stars stayed constant around him from
flash to flash, he looked down past his feet at a million
strobes of Crux, of Triangulum; once at the height of his
stride he had risked a century's glance upward and seen the
Bears weirdly strung out from Polaris—But a Polaris not
the Pole Star now, he realized, jerking his eyes back to his
racing feet, thinking, I am walking home to Polaris, home!
to the strobing beat. He had ceased to remember where he
had been, the beings, people or aliens or things he had
glimpsed in the impossible moment of being where he could
not be; had ceased to see the flashes of worlds around him,
each flash different, the jumble of bodies, walls, landscapes,
shapes, colors beyond deciphering—some lasting a breath,
some changing pell-mell—the faces, limbs, things poking at
him; the nights he had pounded through, dark or lit by
strange lamps; roofed or unroofed; the day flashing sunlight, gales, dust, snow, interiors innumerable, strobe after
strobe into night again; he was in daylight now, a hall of
some kind; I am getting closer at last, he thought, the feel is
changing—but he had to slow down, to check; and that
stone near his feet, it had stayed there some time now, he
wanted to risk a look but he did not dare, he was so tired,
and he was sliding, was going out of control, fighting to kill
the merciless velocity that would not let him slow down; he
was hurt, too, something had hit him back there, they had
done something, he didn't know what back somewhere in
the kaleidoscope of faces, arms, hooks, beams, centuries of
creatures grabbing at him—and his oxygen was going,
never mind, it would last—it had to last, he was going
home, home! And he had forgotten now the message he had
tried to shout, hoping it could be picked up somehow, the
important thing he had repeated; and the thing he had
carried, it was gone now, his camera was gone too,

something had torn it away—but he was coming home! Home! If only he could kill this momentum, could stay on the failing course, could slip, scramble, slide, somehow ride this avalanche down to home, to home—and his throat said Home!—said Kate, Kate! And his heart shouted, his lungs almost gone now, as his legs fought, fought and failed, as his feet gripped and skidded and held and slid, as he pitched, flailed, pushed, strove in the gale of timerush across space, across time, at the end of the longest path ever; the path of John Delgano, coming home.

AIR RAID

John Varley

John Varley appeared on the SF scene in 1975, and by the end of 1976—in what was a meteoric rise to prominence even for a field known for meteoric rises—he was already being recognized as one of the hottest new writers of the seventies. His books include the novels Ophiuchi Hotline, Titan, Wizard, *and* Demon, *and the collections* The Persistence of Vision, The Barbie Murders, Picnic on Nearside, *and* Blue Champagne. *His most recent book is a major new novel,* Steel Beach. *He has won two Nebulas and two Hugos for his short fiction.*

In the jazzy and jolting little shocker that follows, he shows us that it doesn't matter how *bad you think you have it, there's always someone who has it worse. And who'd be willing to* switch . . .

"**I** *was jerked* awake by the silent alarm vibrating my skull. It won't shut down until you sit up, so I did. All around me in the darkened bunkroom the Snatch Team members were sleeping singly and in pairs. I yawned, scratched my ribs, and patted Gene's hairy flank. He turned over. So much for a romantic send-off.

Rubbing sleep from my eyes, I reached to the floor for my leg, strapped it on and plugged it in. Then I was running down the rows of bunks toward Ops.

The situation board glowed in the gloom. Sun-Belt Airlines Flight 128, Miami to New York, September 15, 1979. We'd been looking for that one for three years. I should have been happy, but who can afford it when you wake up?

Liza Boston muttered past me on the way to Prep. I

muttered back, and followed. The lights came on around the mirrors, and I groped my way to one of them. Behind us, three more people staggered in. I sat down, plugged in, and at last I could lean back and close my eyes.

They didn't stay closed for long. Rush! I sat up straight as the sludge I use for blood was replaced with supercharged go-juice. I looked around me and got a series of idiot grins. There was Liza, and Pinky and Dave. Against the far wall Cristabel was already turning slowly in front of the airbrush, getting a caucasian paint job. It looked like a good team.

I opened the drawer and started preliminary work on my face. It's a bigger job every time. Transfusion or no, I looked like death. The right ear was completely gone now. I could no longer close my lips; the gums were permanently bared. A week earlier, a finger had fallen off in my sleep. And what's it to you, bugger?

While I worked, one of the screens around the mirror glowed. A smiling young woman, blonde, high brow, round face. Close enough. The crawl line read *Mary Katrina Sondergard, born Trenton, New Jersey, age in 1979: 25.* Baby, this is your lucky day.

The computer melted the skin away from her face to show me the bone structure, rotated it, gave me cross-sections. I studied the similarities with my own skull, noted the differences. Not bad, and better than some I'd been given.

I assembled a set of dentures that included the slight gap in the upper incisors. Putty filled out my cheeks. Contact lenses fell from the dispenser and I popped them in. Nose plugs widened my nostrils. No need for ears; they'd be covered by the wig. I pulled a blank plastiflesh mask over my face and had to pause while it melted in. It took only a minute to mold it to perfection. I smiled at myself. How nice to have lips.

The delivery slut clunked and dropped a blonde wig and a pink outfit into my lap. The wig was hot from the styler. I put it on, then the pantyhose.

"Mandy? Did you get the profile on Sondergard?" I didn't look up; I recognized the voice.

"Roger."

"We've located her near the airport. We can slip you in before take-off, so you'll be the joker."

I groaned, and looked up at the face on the screen. Elfreda Baltimore-Louisville, Director of Operational Teams: lifeless face and tiny slits for eyes. What can you do when all the muscles are dead?

"Okay." You take what you get.

She switched off, and I spent the next two minutes trying to get dressed while keeping my eyes on the screens. I memorized names and faces of crew members plus the few facts known about them. Then I hurried out and caught up with the others. Elapsed time from the first alarm: twelve minutes and seven seconds. We'd better get moving.

"Goddam Sun-Belt," Cristabel groused, hitching at her bra.

"At least they got rid of the high heels," Dave pointed out. A year earlier we would have been teetering down the aisles on three-inch platforms. We all wore short pink shifts with blue and white stripes, diagonally across the front, and carried matching shoulder bags. I fussed trying to get the ridiculous pillbox cap pinned on.

We jogged into the dark Operations Control Room and lined up at the gate. Things were out of our hands now. Until the gate was ready, we could only wait.

I was first, a few feet away from the portal. I turned away from it; it gives me vertigo. I focused instead on the gnomes sitting at their consoles, bathed in yellow lights from their screens. None of them looked back at me. They don't like us much. I don't like them, either. Withered, emaciated, all of them. Our fat legs and butts and breasts are a reproach to them, a reminder that Snatchers eat five times their ration to stay presentable for the masquerade. Meantime we continue to rot. One day I'll be sitting at a console. One day I'll be *built in* to a console, with all my guts on the outside and nothing left of my body but stink. The hell with them.

I buried my gun under a clutter of tissues and lipsticks in my purse. Elfreda was looking at me.

"Where is she?" I asked.

"Motel room. She was alone from 10 PM to noon on flight day."

Departure time was 1:15. She cut it close and would be in a hurry. Good.

"Can you catch her in the bathroom? Best of all, in the tub?"

"We're working on it." She sketched a smile with a fingertip drawn over lifeless lips. She knew how I liked to operate, but she was telling me I'd take what I got. It never hurts to ask. People are at their most defenseless stretched out and up to their necks in water.

"Go!" Elfreda shouted. I stepped through, and things started to go wrong.

I was faced the wrong way, stepping *out* of the bathroom door and facing the bedroom. I turned and spotted Mary Katrina Sondergard through the haze of the gate. There was no way I could reach her without stepping back through. I couldn't even shoot without hitting someone on the other side.

Sondergard was at the mirror, the worst possible place. Few people recognize themselves quickly, but she'd been looking right at herself. She saw me and her eyes widened. I stepped to the side, out of her sight.

"What the hell is . . . hey? Who the hell . . ." I noted the voice, which can be the trickiest thing to get right.

I figured she'd be more curious than afraid. My guess was right. She came out of the bathroom, passing through the gate as if it wasn't there, which it wasn't, since it only has one side. She had a towel wrapped around her.

"Jesus Christ! What are you doing in my—" Words fail you at a time like that. She knew she ought to say something, but what? *Excuse me, haven't I seen you in the mirror?*

I put on my best stew smile and held out my hand.

"Pardon the intrusion. I can explain everything. You see, I'm—" I hit her on the side of the head and she staggered and went down hard. Her towel fell to the floor. "—working my way through college." She started to get up, so I caught her under the chin with my artificial knee. She stayed down.

"Standard fuggin' *oil!*" I hissed, rubbing my injured knuckles. But there was no time. I knelt beside her, checked her pulse. She'd be okay, but I think I loosened some front teeth. I paused a moment. Lord, to look like that with no makeup, no prosthetics! She nearly broke my heart.

I grabbed her under the knees and wrestled her to the gate. She was a sack of limp noodles. Somebody reached through, grabbed her feet, and pulled. *So long, love! How would you like to go on a long voyage?*

I sat on her rented bed to get my breath. There were car keys and cigarettes in her purse, genuine tobacco, worth its weight in blood. I lit six of them, figuring I had five minutes of my very own. The room filled with sweet smoke. They don't make 'em like that anymore.

The Hertz sedan was in the motel parking lot. I got in and headed for the airport. I breathed deeply of the air, rich in hydrocarbons. I could see for hundreds of yards into the distance. The perspective nearly made me dizzy, but I live for those moments. There's no way to explain what it's like in the pre-meck world. The sun was a fierce yellow ball through the haze.

The other stews were boarding. Some of them knew Sondergard so I didn't say much, pleading a hangover. That went over well, with a lot of knowing laughs and sly remarks. Evidently it wasn't out of character. We boarded the 707 and got ready for the goats to arrive.

It looked good. The four commandos on the other side were identical twins for the women I was working with. There was nothing to do but be a stewardess until departure time. I hoped there would be no more glitches. Inverting a gate for a joker run into a motel room was one thing, but in a 707 at twenty thousand feet . . .

The plane was nearly full when the woman that Pinky would impersonate sealed the forward door. We taxied to the end of the runway, then we were airborne. I started taking orders for drinks in first.

The goats were the usual lot, for 1979. Fat and sassy, all of them, and as unaware of living in a paradise as a fish is of the sea. *What would you think, ladies and gents, of a trip to the future? No? I can't say I'm surprised. What if I told you this plane is going to—*

My arm beeped as we reached cruising altitude. I consulted the indicator under my Lady Bulova and glanced at one of the restroom doors. I felt a vibration pass through the plane. *Damn it, not so soon.*

The gate was in there. I came out quickly, and motioned for Diana Gleason—Dave's pigeon—to come to the front.

"Take a look at this," I said with a disgusted look. She started to enter the restroom, stopped when she saw the green glow. I planted a boot on her fanny and shoved. Perfect. Dave would have a chance to hear her voice before popping in. Though she'd be doing little but screaming when she got a look around . . .

Dave came through the gate, adjusting his silly little hat. Diana must have struggled.

"Be disgusted," I whispered.

"What a mess," he said as he came out of the restroom. It was a fair imitation of Diana's tone, though he'd missed the accent. It wouldn't matter much longer.

"What is it?" It was one of the stews from tourist. We stepped aside so she could get a look, and Dave shoved her through. Pinky popped out very quickly.

"We're minus on minutes," Pinky said. "We lost five on the other side."

"Five?" Dave-Diana squeaked. I felt the same way. We had a hundred and three passengers to process.

"Yeah. They lost control after you pushed my pigeon through. It took that long to re-align."

You get used to that. Time runs at different rates on each side of the gate, though it's always sequential, past to future. Once we'd started the snatch with me entering Sondergard's room, there was no way to go back any earlier on either side. Here, in 1979, we had a rigid ninety-four minutes to get everything done. On the other side, the gate could never be maintained longer than three hours.

"When you left, how long was it since the alarm went in?"

"Twenty-eight minutes."

It didn't sound good. It would take at least two hours just customizing the wimps. Assuming there was no more slippage on 79-time, we might just make it. But there's *always* slippage. I shuddered, thinking about riding it in.

"No time for any more games, then," I said. "Pink, you go back to tourist and call both of the other girls up here. Tell 'em to come one at a time, and tell 'em we've got a problem. You know the bit."

"Biting back the tears. Got you." She hurried aft. In no time the first one showed up. Her friendly Sun-Belt Airlines smile was stamped on her face, but her stomach would be churning. *Oh God, this is it!*

I took her by the elbow and pulled her behind the curtains in front. She was breathing hard.

"Welcome to the twilight zone," I said, and put the gun to her head. She slumped, and I caught her. Pinky and Dave helped me shove her through the gate.

"Fug! The rotting thing's flickering."

Pinky was right. A very ominous sign. But the green glow stabilized as we watched, with who-knows-how-much slippage on the other side. Cristabel ducked through.

"We're plus thirty-three," she said. There was no sense talking about what we were all thinking: things were going badly.

"Back to tourist," I said. "Be brave, smile at everyone, but make it just a little bit too good, got it?"

"Check," Cristabel said.

We processed the other quickly, with no incident. Then there was no time to talk about anything. In eighty-nine minutes Flight 128 was going to be spread all over a mountain whether we were finished or not.

Dave went into the cockpit to keep the flight crew out of our hair. Me and Pinky were supposed to take care of first class, then back up Cristabel and Liza in tourist. We used the standard "coffee, tea, or milk" gambit, relying on our speed and their inertia.

I leaned over the first two seats on the left.

"Are you enjoying your flight?" Pop, pop. Two squeezes

on the trigger, close to the heads and out of sight of the rest of the goats.

"Hi, folks. I'm Mandy. Fly me." Pop, pop.

Halfway to the galley, a few people were watching us curiously. But people don't make a fuss until they have a lot more to go on. One goat in the back row stood up, and I let him have it. By now there were only eight left awake. I abandoned the smile and squeezed off four quick shots. Pinky took care of the rest. We hurried through the curtains, just in time.

There was an uproar building in the back of tourist, with about sixty percent of the goats already processed. Cristabel glanced at me, and I nodded.

"Okay, folks," she bawled. "I want you to be quiet. Calm down and listen up. *You*, fathead, *pipe down* before I cram my foot up your ass sideways."

The shock of hearing her talk like that was enough to buy us a little time, anyway. We had formed a skirmish line across the width of the plane, guns out, steadied on seat backs, aimed at the milling, befuddled group of thirty goats.

The guns are enough to awe all but the most foolhardy. In essence, a standard-issue stunner is just a plastic rod with two grids about six inches apart. There's not enough metal in it to set off a hijack alarm. And to people from the Stone Age to about 2190 it doesn't look any more like a weapon than a ballpoint pen. So Equipment Section jazzes them up in a plastic shell to real Buck Rogers blasters, with a dozen knobs and lights that flash and a barrel like the snout of a hog. Hardly anyone ever walks into one.

"We are in great danger, and time is short. You must all do exactly as I tell you, and you will be safe."

You can't give them time to think, you have to rely on your status as the Voice of Authority. The situation is just *not* going to make sense to them, no matter how you explain it.

"Just a minute, I think you owe us—"

An airborne lawyer. I made a snap decision, thumbed the fireworks switch on my gun, and shot him.

The gun made a sound like a flying saucer with hemorrhoids, spit sparks and little jets of flame, and extended a green laser finger to his forehead. He dropped.

All pure kark, of course. But it sure is impressive.

And it's damn risky, too. I had to choose between a panic if the fathead got them to thinking, and a possible panic from the flash of the gun. But when a 20th gets to talking about his "rights" and what he is "owed," things can get out of hand. It's infectious.

It worked. There was a lot of shouting, people ducking behind seats, but no rush. We could have handled it, but we needed some of them conscious if we were ever going to finish the Snatch.

"Get up. Get *up*, you *slugs!*" Cristabel yelled. "He's stunned, nothing worse. But I'll *kill* the next one who gets out of line. Now *get to your feet* and do what I tell you. *Children first! Hurry,* as fast as you can, to the front of the plane. Do what the stewardess tells you. Come on, kids, *move!*"

I ran back into first class just ahead of the kids, turned at the open restroom door, and got on my knees.

They were petrified. There were five of them—crying, some of them, which always chokes me up—looking left and right at dead people in the first class seats, stumbling, near panic.

"Come on, kids," I called to them, giving my special smile. "Your parents will be along in just a minute. Everything's going to be all right, I promise you. Come on."

I got three of them through. The fourth balked. She was determined not to go through that door. She spread her legs and arms and I couldn't push her through. I will *not* hit a child, never. She raked her nails over my face. My wig came off, and she gaped at my bare head. I shoved her through.

Number five was sitting in the aisle, bawling. He was maybe seven. I ran back and picked him up, hugged him and kissed him, and tossed him through. God, I needed a rest, but I was needed in tourist.

"You, you, you, and you. Okay, you too. Help him, will you?" Pinky had a practiced eye for the ones that wouldn't be any use to anyone, even themselves. We herded them toward the front of the plane, then deployed ourselves along the left side where we could cover the workers. It didn't take long to prod them into action. We had them dragging the limp bodies forward as fast as they could go. Me and Cristabel were in tourist, with the others up front.

Adrenaline was being catabolized in my body now; the rush of action left me and I started to feel very tired. There's an unavoidable feeling of sympathy for the poor dumb goats that starts to get me about this stage of the game. Sure, they were better off, sure they were going to die if we didn't get them off the plane. But when they saw the other side they were going to have a hard time believing it.

The first ones were returning for a second load, stunned at what they'd just seen: dozens of people being put into a cubicle that was crowded when it was empty. One college student looked like he'd been hit in the stomach. He stopped by me and his eyes pleaded.

"Look, I want to *help* you people, just . . . what's going *on*? Is this some new kind of rescue? I mean, are we going to crash——"

I switched my gun to prod and brushed it across his cheek. He gasped, and fell back.

"Shut your fuggin' mouth and get moving, or I'll kill you." It would be hours before his jaw was in shape to ask any more stupid questions.

We cleared tourist and moved up. A couple of the work gang were pretty damn pooped by then. Muscles like horses, all of them, but they can hardly run up a flight of stairs. We let some of them go through, including a couple that were at least fifty years old. *Je*-zuz. Fifty! We got down to a core of four men and two women who seemed strong, and worked them until they nearly dropped. But we processed everyone in twenty-five minutes.

The portapak came through as we were stripping off our clothes. Cristabel knocked on the door to the cockpit and Dave came out, already naked. A bad sign.

"I had to cork 'em," he said. "Bleeding Captain just *had* to make his Grand March through the plane. I tried *everything*."

Sometimes you have to do it. The plane was on autopilot, as it normally would be at this time. But if any of us did anything detrimental to the craft, changed the fixed course of events in any way, that would be it. All that work for nothing, and Flight 128 inaccessible to us for all Time. I don't know sludge about time theory, but I know the practical angles. We can do things in the past only at times and in places where it won't make any difference. We have to cover our tracks. There's flexibility; once a Snatcher left her gun behind and it went in with the plane. Nobody found it, or if they did, they didn't have the smoggiest idea of what it was, so we were okay.

Flight 128 was mechanical failure. That's the best kind; it means we don't have to keep the pilot unaware of the situation in the cabin right down to ground level. We can cork him and fly the plane, since there's nothing he could have done to save the flight anyway. A pilot-error smash is almost impossible to Snatch. We mostly work mid-air, bombs, and structural failures. If there's even one survivor, we can't touch it. It would not fit the fabric of space-time, which is immutable (though it can stretch a little), and we'd all just fade away and appear back in the ready-room.

My head was hurting. I wanted that portapak very badly.

"Who has the most hours on a 707?" Pinky did, so I sent her to the cabin, along with Dave, who could do the pilot's voice for air traffic control. You have to have a believable record in the flight recorder, too. They trailed two long tubes from the portapak, and the rest of us hooked in up close. We stood there, each of us smoking a fistful of cigarettes, wanting to finish them but hoping there wouldn't be time. The gate had vanished as soon as we tossed our clothes and the flight crew through.

But we didn't worry long. There's other nice things about Snatching, but nothing to compare with the rush of plugging into a portapak. The wake-up transfusion is nothing but fresh blood, rich in oxygen and sugars. What we were getting now was an insane brew of concentrated adrenaline, super-saturated hemoglobin, methedrine, white lightning,

TNT, and Kickapoo joyjuice. It was like a firecracker in your heart; a boot in the box that rattled your sox.

"I'm growing hair on my chest," Cristabel said solemnly. Everyone giggled.

"Would someone hand me my eyeballs?"

"The blue ones, or the red ones?"

"I think my ass just fell off."

We'd heard them all before, but we howled anyway. We were strong, *strong,* and for one golden moment we had no worries. Everything was hilarious. I could have torn sheet metal with my eyelashes.

But you get hyper on that mix. When the gage didn't show, and didn't show, and *didn't sweetjeez show* we all started milling. This bird wasn't going to fly all that much longer.

Then it did show, and we turned on. The first of the wimps came through, dressed in the clothes taken from a passenger it had been picked to resemble.

"Two thirty-five elapsed upside time," Cristabel announced.

"Je-zuz."

It is a deadening routine. You grab the harness around the wimp's shoulders and drag it along the aisle, after consulting the seat number painted on its forehead. The paint would last three minutes. You seat it, strap it in, break open the harness and carry it back to toss through the gate as you grab the next one. You have to take it for granted they've done the work right on the other side: fillings in the teeth, fingerprints, the right match in height and weight and hair color. Most of those things don't matter much, especially on Flight 128, which was a crash-and-burn. There would be bits and pieces, and burned to a crisp at that. But you can't take chances. Those rescue workers are pretty thorough on the parts they *do* find; the dental work and fingerprints especially are important.

I hate wimps. I really hate 'em. Every time I grab the harness of one of them, if it's a child, I wonder if it's Alice. *Are you my kid, you vegetable, you slug, you slimy worm?* I joined the Snatchers right after the brain bugs ate the life

out of my baby's head. I couldn't stand to think she was
the last generation, that the last humans there would ever be
would live with nothing in their heads, medically dead by
standards that prevailed even in 1979, with computers
working their muscles to keep them in tone. You grow up,
reach puberty still fertile—one in a thousand—rush to get
pregnant in your first heat. Then you find out your mom or
pop passed on a chronic disease bound right into the genes,
and none of your kids will be immune. I *knew* about the
para-leprosy; I grew up with my toes rotting away. But this
was too much. What do you do?

Only one in ten of the wimps had a customized face. It
takes time and a lot of skill to build a new face that will
stand up to a doctor's autopsy. The rest came pre-mutilated.
We've got millions of them; it's not hard to find a good
match in the body. Most of them would stay breathing, too
dumb to stop, until they went in with the plane.

The plane jerked hard. I glanced at my watch. Five
minutes to impact. We should have time. I was on my last
wimp. I could hear Dave frantically calling the ground. A
bomb came through the gate, and I tossed it into the cockpit.
Pinky turned on the pressure sensor on the bomb and came
running out, followed by Dave. Liza was already through. I
grabbed the limp dolls in stewardess costume and tossed
them to the floor. The engine fell off and a piece of it came
through the cabin. We started to depressurize. The bomb
blew away part of the cockpit (the ground crash crew would
read it—we hoped—that part of the engine came through
and killed the crew: no more words from the pilot on the
flight recorder) and we turned, slowly, left and down. I was
lifted toward the hole in the side of the plane, but I managed
to hold onto a seat. Cristabel wasn't so lucky. She was
blown backwards.

We started to rise slightly, losing speed. Suddenly it was
uphill from where Cristabel was lying in the aisle. Blood
oozed from her temple. I glanced back; everyone was gone,
and three pink-suited wimps were piled on the floor. The
plane began to stall, to nose down, and my feet left the floor.

"Come on, Bel!" I screamed. The gate was only three feet

away from me, but I began pulling myself along to where she floated. The plane bumped, and she hit the floor. Incredibly, it seemed to wake her up. She started to swim toward me, and I grabbed her hand as the floor came up to slam us again. We crawled as the plane went through its final death agony, and we came to the door. The gate was gone.

There wasn't anything to say. We were going in. It's hard enough to keep the gate in place on a plane that's moving in a straight line. When a bird gets to corkscrewing and coming apart, the math is fearsome. So I've been told.

I embraced Cristabel and held her bloodied head. She was groggy, but managed to smile and shrug. You take what you get. I hurried into the restroom and got both of us down on the floor. Back to the forward bulkhead, Cristabel between my legs, back to front. Just like in training. We pressed our feet against the other wall. I hugged her tightly and cried on her shoulder.

And it was there. A green glow to my left. I threw myself toward it, dragging Cristabel, keeping low as two wimps were thrown headfirst through the gate above our heads. Hands grabbed and pulled us through. I clawed my way a good five yards along the floor. You can leave a leg on the other side and I didn't have one to spare.

I sat up as they were carrying Cristabel to Medical. I patted her arm as she went by on the stretcher, but she was passed out. I wouldn't have minded passing out myself.

For a while, you can't believe it all really happened. Sometimes it turns out it *didn't* happen. You come back and find out all the goats in the holding pen have softly and suddenly vanished away because the continuum won't tolerate the changes and paradoxes you've put into it. The people you've worked so hard to rescue are spread like tomato surprise all over some goddam hillside in Carolina and all you've got left is a bunch of ruined wimps and an exhausted Snatch Team. But not this time. I could see the goats milling around in the holding pen, naked and more bewildered than ever. And just starting to be *really* afraid.

Elfreda touched me as I passed her. She nodded, which

meant well-done in her limited repertoire of gestures. I shrugged, wondering if I cared, but the surplus adrenaline was still in my veins and I found myself grinning at her. I nodded back.

Gene was standing by the holding pen. I went to him, hugged him. I felt the juices start to flow. *Damn it, let's squander a little ration and have us a good time*.

Someone was beating on the sterile glass wall of the pen. She shouted, mouthing angry words at us. *Why? What have you done to us?* It was Mary Sondergard. She implored her bald, one-legged twin to make her understand. She thought she had problems. God, was she pretty. I hated her guts.

Gene pulled me away from the wall. My hands hurt, and I'd broken off all my fake nails without scratching the glass. She was sitting on the floor now, sobbing. I heard the voice of the briefing officer on the outside speaker.

". . . Centauri 3 is hospitable, with an Earth-like climate. By that, I mean *your* Earth, not what it has become. You'll see more of that later. The trip will take five years, shiptime. Upon landfall, you will be entitled to one horse, a plow, three axes, two hundred kilos of seed grain . . ."

I leaned against Gene's shoulder. At their lowest ebb, this very moment, they were so much better than us. I had maybe ten years, half of that as a basketcase. They are our best, our very brightest hope. Everything is up to them.

". . . that no one will be forced to go. We wish to point out again, not for the last time, that you would all be dead without our intervention. There are things you should know, however. You cannot breathe our air. If you remain on Earth, you can never leave this building. We are not like you. We are the result of a genetic winnowing, a mutation process. We are the survivors, but our enemies have evolved along with us. They are winning. You, however, are immune to the diseases that afflict us . . ."

I winced, and turned away.

". . . the other hand, if you emigrate you will be given a chance at a new life. It won't be easy, but as Americans you should be proud of your pioneer heritage. Your ancestors survived, and so will you. It can be a rewarding experience, and I urge you . . ."

Sure. Gene and I looked at each other and laughed. *Listen to this, folks. Five percent of you will suffer nervous breakdowns in the next few days, and never leave. About the same number will commit suicide, here and on the way. When you get there, sixty to seventy percent will die in the first three years. You will die in childbirth, be eaten by animals, bury two out of three of your babies, starve slowly when the rains don't come. If you live, it will be to break your back behind a plow, sunup to dusk. New Earth is Heaven, folks!*

God, how I wish I could go with them.

THE HOLE
ON THE CORNER

R. A. Lafferty

R. A. Lafferty started writing in 1960, at the relatively advanced age (for a new writer, anyway) of 48, and in the years before his retirement in 1987, he published some of the freshest and funniest short stories ever written in the genre, as well as a string of vivid and unforgettable books such as the novels Past Master, The Devil Is Dead, The Reefs of Earth, Okla Hannali, The Fall of Rome, Arrive at Easterwine, *and* The Flame Is Green, *and landmark collections such as* Nine Hundred Grandmothers, Strange Doings, Does Anyone Else Have Something Further to Add?, Golden Gate and Other Stories, *and* Ringing the Changes. *Lafferty won the Hugo Award in 1973 for his story "Eurema's Dam," and in 1990 received the World Fantasy Award, the prestigious Life Achievement Award. His most recent books are the collections* Lafferty in Orbit *and* Iron Star.

In the shaggy, strange, and very funny story that follows, he takes us along with a man on his way home on an ordinary day who finds that everything there is exactly the same as it's always been—except for being completely different, *of course . . .*

Homer Hoose came home that evening to the golden cliché: the un-noble dog who was a personal friend of his; the perfect house where just to live was a happy riot; the loving and unpredictable wife; and the five children—the perfect number (four more would have been too many, four less would be too few).

The dog howled in terror and bristled up like a hedge-hog. Then it got a whiff of Homer and recognized him; it licked his heels and gnawed his knuckles and made him welcome. A good dog, though a fool. Who wants a smart dog!

Homer had a little trouble with the doorknob. They don't have them in all the recensions, you know; and he had that off-the-track feeling tonight. But he figured it out (you don't pull it, you turn it), and opened the door.

"Did you remember to bring what I asked you to bring this morning, Homer?" the loving wife Regina inquired.

"What did you ask me to bring this morning, quickheat blueberry biscuit of my heart?" Homer asked.

"If *I'd* remembered, I'd have phrased it different when I asked if you remembered," Regina explained. "But I know I told you to bring something, old ketchup of my soul. Homer! Look at me, Homer! You look different tonight! DIFFERENT!! *You're not my Homer, are you!* Help! Help! There's a monster in my house!! Help, help! Shriek!"

"It's always nice to be married to a wife who doesn't understand you," Homer said. He enfolded her affectionately, bore her down, trod on her with large friendly hooves, and began (as it seemed) to devour her.

"Where'd you get the monster, Mama?" son Robert asked as he came in. "What's he got your whole head in his mouth for? Can I have one of the apples in the kitchen? What's he going to do, kill you, Mama?"

"Shriek, shriek," said Mama Regina. "Just one apple, Robert, there's just enough to go around. Yes, I think he's going to kill me. Shriek!"

Son Robert got an apple and went outdoors.

"Hi, Papa, what's you doing to Mama?" daughter Fregona asked as she came in. She was fourteen, but stupid for her age. "Looks to me like you're going to kill her that way. I thought they peeled people before they swallowed them. Why! You're not Papa at all, are you? You're some monster. I thought at first you were my papa. You look just like him except for the way you look."

"Shriek, shriek," said Mama Regina, but her voice was muffled.

They had a lot of fun at their house.

• • •

Homer Hoose came home that evening to the golden cliché:
the u.n.d.; the p.h.; and l. and u.w.; and the f.c. (four more
would have been too many).

The dog waggled all over him happily, and son Robert
was chewing an apple core on the front lawn.

"Hi, Robert," Homer said, "what's new today?"

"Nothing, Papa. Nothing ever happens here. Oh yeah,
there's a monster in the house. He looks kind of like you.
He's killing Mama and eating her up."

"Eating her up, you say, son? How do you mean?"

"He's got her whole head in his mouth."

"Droll, Robert, mighty droll," said Homer, and he went in
the house.

One thing about the Hoose children: a lot of times they
told us the bald-headed truth. There *was* a monster there. He
was killing and eating the wife Regina. This was no mere
evening antic. It was something serious.

Homer the man was a powerful and quick-moving fellow.
He fell on the monster with judo chops and solid body
punches; and the monster let the woman go and confronted
the man.

"What's with it, you silly oaf?" the monster snapped. "If
you've got a delivery, go to the back door. Come punching
people in here, will you? Regina, do you know who this
silly simpleton is?"

"Wow, that was a pretty good one, wasn't it, Homer?"
Regina gasped as she came from under, glowing and
gulping. "Oh, him? Gee, Homer, I think he's my husband.
But how can he be, if you are? Now the two of you have got
me so mixed up that I don't know which one of you is my
Homer."

"Great goofy Gestalten! You don't mean I look like him?"
howled Homer the monster, near popping.

"My brain reels," moaned Homer the man. "Reality melts
away. Regina! Exorcise this nightmare if you have in some
manner called it up! I knew you shouldn't have been fooling
around with that book."

"Listen, mister reely-brains," wife Regina began on Homer

the man. "You learn to kiss like he does before you tell me which one to exorcise. All I ask is a little affection. And this I didn't find in a book."

"How we going to know which one is Papa? They look just alike," daughters Clara-Belle, Anna-Belle, and Maudie-Belle came in like three little chimes.

"Hell-hipping horrors!" roared Homer the man. "How are you going to know—? He's got green skin."

"There's nothing wrong with green skin as long as it's kept neat and oiled," Regina defended.

"He's got tentacles instead of hands," said Homer the man.

"Oh boy, I'll say!" Regina sang out.

"How we going to know which one is Papa when they look just alike?" the five Hoose children asked in chorus.

"I'm sure there's a simple explanation to this, old chap," said Homer the monster. "If I were you, Homer—and there's some argument whether I am or not—I believe I'd go to a doctor. I don't believe we both need to go, since our problem's the same. Here's the name of a good one," said Homer the monster, writing it out.

"Oh, I know him," said Homer the man when he read it. "But how did you know him? He isn't an animal doctor. Regina, I'm going over to the doctor to see what's the matter with me, or you. Try to have this nightmare back in whatever corner of your under-id it belongs when I come back."

"Ask him if I keep taking my pink medicine," Regina said.

"No, not him. It's the head doctor I'm going to."

"Ask him if I have to keep on dreaming those pleasant dreams," Regina said. "I sure do get tired of them. I want to get back to the other kind. Homer, leave the coriander seed when you go." And she took the package out of his pocket. "You did remember to bring it. My other Homer forgot."

"No, I didn't," said Homer the monster. "You couldn't remember what you told me to get. Here, Regina."

"I'll be back in a little while," said Homer the man. "The doctor lives on the corner. And you, fellow, if you're real, keep your plankton-picking polypusses off my wife till I get back."

Homer Hoose went up the street to the house of Dr. Corte on the corner. He knocked on the door, and then opened it and went in without waiting for an answer. The doctor was sitting there, but he seemed a little bit dazed.

"I've got a problem, Dr. Corte," said Homer the man. "I came home this evening, and I found a monster eating my wife—as I thought."

"Yes, I know," said Dr. Corte. "Homer, we got to fix that hole on the corner."

"I didn't know there was a hole there, Doctor. As it happened, the fellow wasn't really swallowing my wife, it was just his way of showing affection. Everybody thought the monster looked like me, and Doctor, it has green skin and tentacles. When I began to think it looked like me too, I came here to see what was wrong with me, or with everybody else."

"I can't help you, Hoose. I'm a psychologist, not a contingent-physicist. Only one thing to do; we got to fix that hole on the corner."

"Doctor, there's no hole in the street on this corner."

"Wasn't talking about a hole in the street. Homer, I just got back from a visit of my own that shook me up. I went to an analyst who analyzes analysts. 'I've had a dozen people come to see me with the same sort of story,' I told him. 'They all come home in the evenings; and everything is different, or themselves are different; or they find that they are already there when they get there. What do you do when a dozen people come in with the same nonsense story, Dr. Diebel?' I asked him.

" 'I don't know, Corte,' he said to me. 'What do I do when *one* man comes in a dozen times with the same nonsense story, all within one hour, and he a doctor too?' Dr. Diebel asked me.

" 'Why, Dr. Diebel?' I asked. 'What doctor came to you like that?'

" 'You,' he said. 'You've come in here twelve times in the last hour with the same dish of balderhash; you've come in each time looking a little bit different; and each time you act as if you hadn't seen me for a month. Dammit, man,' he said, 'you must have passed yourself going out when you came in.'

"'Yes, that *was* me, wasn't it?' I said. 'I was trying to think who he reminded me of. Well, it's a problem, Dr. Diebel,' I said. 'What are you going to do about it?'

"'I'm going to the analyst who analyzes the analysts who analyze the analysts,' he said. 'He's tops in the field.' Dr. Diebel rushed out then; and I came back to my office here. You came in just after that. I'm not the one to help you. But, Homer, we got to do something about that hole on the corner!"

"I don't understand the bit about the hole, Doctor," Homer said. "But—has a bunch of people been here with stories like mine?"

"Yes, every man in this block has been in with an idiot story, Homer, except—Why, everybody except old double-domed Diogenes himself! Homer, that man who knows everything has a finger in this up to the humerus. I saw him up on the power poles the other night, but I didn't think anything of it. He likes to tap the lines before they come to his meter. Saves a lot of power that way, and he uses a lot of it in his laboratory. But he was setting up the hole on the corner. That's what he was doing. Let's get him and bring him to your house and make him straighten it out."

"Sure, a man who knows everything ought to know about a hole on the corner, Doctor. But I sure don't see any hole anywhere on this corner."

The man who knew everything was named Diogenes Pontifex. He lived next door to Homer Hoose, and they found him in his back yard wrestling with his anaconda.

"Diogenes, come over to Homer's with us," Dr. Corte insisted. "We've got a couple of questions that might be too much even for you."

"You touch my pride there," Diogenes sang out. "When psychologists start using psychology on you, it's time to give in. Wait a minute till I pin this fellow."

Diogenes put a chancery on the anaconda, punched the

thing's face a few times, then pinned it with a double bar-arm and body lock, and left it writhing there. He followed them into the house.

"Hi, Homer," Diogenes said to Homer the monster when they had come into the house. "I see there's two of you here at the same time now. No doubt that's what's puzzling you."

"Dr. Corte, did Homer ask you if I could stop dreaming those pleasant dreams?" wife Regina asked. "I sure do get tired of them. I want to go back to the old flesh-crawlers."

"You should be able to do so tonight, Regina," said Dr. Corte. "Now then, I'm trying to bait Diogenes here into telling us what's going on. I'm sure he knows. And if you would skip the first part, Diogenes, about all the other scientists in the world being like little boys alongside of you, it would speed things up. I believe that this is another of your experiments like—Oh no! Let's not even think about the last one!

"Tell us, Diogenes, about the hole on the corner, and what falls through it. Tell us how some people come home two or three times within as many minutes, and find themselves already there when they get there. Tell us how a creature that staggers the imagination can seem so like an old acquaintance after a moment or two that one might not know which is which. I am not now sure which of these Homers it was who came to my office several moments ago, and with whom I returned to this house. They look just alike in one way, and in another they do not."

"My Homer always was funny looking," Regina said.

"They appear quite different if you go by the visual index," Diogenes explained. "But nobody goes by the visual index except momentarily. Our impression of a person or a thing is much more complex, and the visual element in our appraisal is small. Well, one of them is Homer in gestalt two, and the other is Homer in gestalt nine. But they are quite distinct. Don't ever get the idea that such are the same persons. That would be silly."

"And Lord spare us that!" said Homer the man. "All right, go into your act, Diogenes."

"First, look at me closely, all of you," Diogenes said.

"Handsome, what? But note my clothing and my complexion and my aspect.

"Then to the explanations: it begins with my Corollary to Phelan's Corollary on Gravity. I take the opposite alternate of it. Phelan puzzled that gravity should be so weak on all worlds but one. He said that the gravity of that one remote world was typical, and that the gravity of all other worlds was atypical and the result of a mathematical error. But I, from the same data, deduce that the gravity of our own world is not too weak, but too strong. It is about a hundred times as strong as it should be."

"What do you compare it to when you decide it is too strong?" Dr. Corte wanted to know.

"There's nothing I can compare it to, Doctor. The gravity of *every* body that I am able to examine is from eighty to a hundred times too strong. There are two possible explanations: either my calculations of theories are somehow in error—unlikely—or there are, in every case, about a hundred bodies, solid and weighted, occupying the same place at the same time. *Old Ice Cream Store Chairs! Tennis Shoes in October! The Smell of Slippery Elm! County-Fair Barkers with Warts on Their Noses! Horned Toads in June!*"

"I was following you pretty good up to the Ice Cream Store Chairs," said Homer the monster.

"Oh. I tied that part in, and the tennis shoes too," said Homer the man. "I'm pretty good at following this cosmic theory business. What threw me was the slippery elm. I can't see how it especially illustrates a contingent theory of gravity."

"The last part was an incantation," said Diogenes. "Do you remark anything different about me now?"

"You're wearing a different suit now, of course," said Regina, "but there's nothing remarkable about that. Lots of people change to different clothes in the evening."

"You're darker and stringier," said Dr. Corte. "But I wouldn't have noticed any change if you hadn't told us to look for it. Actually, if I didn't know that you were Diogenes, there wouldn't be any sane way to identify Diogenes in you.

You don't look a thing like you, but still I'd know you anywhere."

"I was first a gestalt two. Now I'm a gestalt three for a while," said Diogenes. "Well, first we have the true case that a hundred or so solid and weighty bodies are occupying the same space that our earth occupies, and at the same time. This in itself does violence to conventional physics. But now let us consider the characteristics of all these cohabiting bodies. Are they occupied and peopled? Will it then mean that a hundred or so persons are occupying at all times the same space that each person occupies? Might not this idea do violence to conventional psychology? Well, I have proved that there are at least eight other persons occupying the same space occupied by each of us, and I have scarcely begun proving. *Stark White Sycamore Branches! New-Harrowed Earth! (New harrow, old earth.) Cow Dung Between Your Toes in July! Pitchers'-Mound Clay in the Old Three-Eye League! Sparrow Hawks in August!*"

"I fell off the harrow," said wife Regina. "I got the sycamore branches bit, though."

"I got clear down to the sparrow hawks," said Homer the monster.

"Do you remark anything different about me this time?" Diogenes asked.

"You have little feathers on the backs of your hands where you used to have little hairs," said Homer the man, "and on your toes. You're barefoot now. But I wouldn't have noticed any of it if I hadn't been looking for something funny."

"I'm a gestalt four now," said Diogenes. "My conduct is likely to become a little extravagant."

"It always was," said Dr. Corte.

"But not so much as if I were a gestalt five," said Diogenes. "As a five, I might take a Pan-like leap onto the shoulders of young Fregona here, or literally walk barefoot through the hair of the beautiful Regina as she stands there. Many normal gestalt twos become gestalt fours or fives in their dreams. It seems that Regina does.

"I found the shadow, but not the substance, of the whole

situation in the psychology of Jung. Jung served me as the second element in this, for it was the errors of Phelan and Jung in widely different fields that set me on the trail of the truth. What Jung really says is that each of us is a number of persons in depth. This I consider silly. There is something about such far-out theories that repels me. The truth is that our counterparts enter into our unconsciousness and dreams only by accident, as being most of the time in the same space that we occupy. But we are all separate and independent persons. And we may, two or more of us, be present in the same frame at the same time, and then in a near, but not the same, place. Witness the gestalt two and the gestalt nine Homers here present.

"I've been experimenting to see how far I can go with it, and the gestalt nine is the furthest I have brought it so far. I do not number the gestalten in the order of their strangeness to our own norm, but in the order in which I discovered them. I'm convinced that the concentric and congravitic worlds and people complexes number near a hundred, however."

"Well, there *is* a hole on the corner, isn't there?" Dr. Corte asked.

"Yes, I set it up there by the bus stop as a convenient evening point of entry for the people of this block," said Diogenes. "I've had lots of opportunity to study the results these last two days."

"Well, just how *do* you set up a hole on the corner?" Dr. Corte persisted.

"Believe me, Corte, it took a lot of imagination," Diogenes said. "I mean it literally. I drew so deeply on my own psychic store to construct the thing that it left me shaken, and I have the most manifold supply of psychic images of any person I know. I've also set up magnetic amplifiers on both sides of the street, but it is my original imagery that they amplify. I see a never-ending field of study in this."

"Just what is the incantation stuff that takes you from one gestalt to another?" Homer the monster asked.

"It is only one of dozens of possible modes of entry, but I sometimes find it the easiest," said Diogenes. "It is

Immediately Remembered, or the Verbal Ramble. It is the Evocation—an intuitive or charismatic entry. I often use it in the Bradmont Motif—named by me from two as-aff writers in the twentieth century."

"You speak of it as if . . . well, isn't *this* the twentieth century?" Regina asked.

"This the twentieth? Why, you're right! I guess it is," Diogenes agreed. "You see, I carry on experiments in other fields also, and sometimes I get my times mixed. All of you, I believe, do sometimes have moments of peculiar immediacy and vividness. It seems then as if the world were somehow fresher in that moment, as though it were a new world. And the explanation is that, to you, it *is* a new world. You have moved, for a moment into a different gestalt. There are many accidental holes or modes of entry, but mine is the only contrived one I know of."

"There's a discrepancy here," said Dr. Corte. "If the persons are separate, how can you change from one to another?"

"I do not change from one person to another," said Diogenes. "There have been three different Diogenes lecturing you here in series. Fortunately, my colleagues and I, being of like scientific mind, work together in close concert. We have made a successful experiment in substitution acceptance on you here this evening. Oh, the ramifications of this thing! The aspects to be studied. I will take you out of your narrow gestalt-two world and show you worlds upon worlds."

"You talk about the gestalt-two complex that we normally belong to," said wife Regina, "and about others up to gestalt nine, and maybe a hundred. Isn't there a gestalt one? Lots of people start counting at one."

"There is a number one, Regina," said Diogenes. "I discovered it first and named it, before I realized that the common world of most of you was of a similar category. But I do not intend to visit gestalt one again. It *is* turgid and dreary beyond tolerating. One instance of its mediocrity will serve. The people of gestalt one refer to their world as the 'everyday world.' Retch quietly, please. May the lowest of us never fall so low! *Persimmons After First Frost! Old Barbershop Chairs! Pink Dogwood Blossoms in the Third Week of November! Mural Cigarette Advertisements!!"*

Diogenes cried out the last in mild panic, and he seemed disturbed. He changed into another fellow a little bit different, but the new Diogenes didn't like what he saw either.

"Smell of Sweet Clover!" he cried out. *"St. Mary's Street in San Antonio! Model Airplane Glue! Moon Crabs in March!* It won't work! The rats have run out on me! Homer and Homer, grab that other Homer there! I believe he's a gestalt six, and they sure are mean."

Homer Hoose wasn't particularly mean. He had just come home a few minutes late and had found two other fellows who looked like him jazzing his wife Regina. And those two mouth men, Dr. Corte and Diogenes Pontifex, didn't have any business in his house when he was gone either.

He started to swing. You'd have done it too.

Those three Homers were all powerful and quick-moving fellows, and they had a lot of blood in them. It was soon flowing, amid the crashing and breaking-up of furniture and people—ocher-colored blood, pearl-gray blood, one of the Homers even had blood of a sort of red color. Those boys threw a real riot!

"Give me that package of coriander seed, Homer," wife Regina said to the latest Homer as she took it from his pocket. "It won't hurt to have three of them. Homer! Homer! Homer! All three of you! Stop bleeding on the rug!"

Homer was always a battler. So was Homer. And Homer.

*"Stethoscopes and Moonlight and Memory—*ah—*in Late March,"* Dr. Corte chanted. "Didn't work, did it? I'll get out of here a regular way. Homers, boys, come up to my place, one at a time, and get patched up when you're finished. I have to do a little regular medicine on the side nowadays."

Dr. Corte went out the door with the loopy run of a man not in very good condition.

"Old Hairbreadth Harry Comic Strips! Congress Street in Houston! Light Street in Baltimore! Elizabeth Street in Sydney! Varnish on Old Bar-Room Pianos! B-Girls Named

Dotty! I believe it's easier just to make a dash for my house next door," Diogenes rattled off. And he did dash out with the easy run of a man who is in good condition.

"I've had it!" boomed one of the Homers—and we don't know which one—as he was flung free from the donny-brook and smashed into a wall. "Peace and quiet is what a man wants when he comes home in the evening, not this. Folks, I'm going out and up to the corner again. Then I'm going to come home all over again. I'm going to wipe my mind clear of all this. When I turn back from the corner I'll be whistling "Dixie" and I'll be the most peaceful man in the world. But when I get home, I bet neither of you guys had better have happened at all."

And Homer dashed up to the corner.

Homer Hoose came home that evening to the g.c.—everything as it should be. He found his house in order and his wife Regina alone.

"Did you remember to bring the coriander seed, Homer, like gossamer of my fusus?" Regina asked him.

"Ah, I remembered to get it, Regina, but I don't seem to have it in my pocket now. I'd rather you didn't ask me where I lost it. There's something I'm trying to forget, Regina, I didn't come home this evening before this, did I?"

"Not that I remember, little dolomedes sexpunctatus."

"And there weren't a couple other guys here who looked just like me only different?"

"No, no, little cobby. I love you and all that, but nothing else could look like you. Nobody has been here but you. Kids! Get ready for supper! Papa's home!"

"Then it's all right," Homer said. "I was just daydreaming on my way home, and all that stuff never happened. Here I am in the perfect house with my wife Regina, and the kids'll be underfoot in just a second. I never realized how wonderful it was. AHHHHNNN!!! YOU'RE NOT REGINA!!"

"But of course I am, Homer. Lycosa Regina is my species name. Well, come, come, you know how I enjoy our evenings together."

She picked him up, lovingly broke his arms and legs for

easier handling, spread him out on the floor, and began to devour him.

"No, no, you're not Regina," Homer sobbed. "You look just like her, but you also look like a giant monstrous arachnid. Dr. Corte was right, we got to fix that hole on the corner."

"That Dr. Corte doesn't know what he's talking about," Regina munched. "He says I'm a compulsive eater."

"What's you eating Papa again for, Mama?" daughter Fregona asked as she came in. "You know what the doctor said."

"It's the spider in me," said Mama Regina. "I wish you'd brought the coriander seed with you, Homer. It goes so good with you."

"But the doctor says you got to show a little restraint, Mama," daughter Fregona cut back in. "He says it becomes harder and harder for Papa to grow back new limbs so often at his age. He says it's going to end up by making him nervous."

"Help! help!" Homer screamed. "My wife is a giant spider and is eating me up. My legs and arms are already gone. If only I could change back to the first nightmare! *Night-Charleys under the Bed at Grandpa's House on the Farm! Rosined Cord to the Make Bull-Roarers on Hallowe'en! Pig Mush in February! Cobwebs on Fruit Jars in the Cellar!* No, no, not that! things never work when you need them. That Diogenes fools around with too much funny stuff."

"All I want is a little affection," said Regina, talking with her mouth full.

"Help, help," said Homer as she ate him clear up to his head. "Shriek, shriek!"

TRAPALANDA

Charles Sheffield

One of the best contemporary "hard science" writers, British-born Charles Sheffield is a theoretical physicist who has worked on the American space program and is currently chief scientist of the Earth Satellite Corporation. Sheffield is also the only person who has ever served as president of both the American Astronautical Society and the Science Fiction Writers of America. He won the Hugo Award in 1994 for his story, "Georgia on My Mind." His books include the bestselling non-fiction title Earthwatch, *the novels* Sight of Proteus, The Web Between the Worlds, Hidden Variables, My Brother's Keeper, Between the Strokes of Night, The Nimrod Hunt, Trader's World, Proteus Unbound, Summertide, Divergence, Transcendence, Cold As Ice, Brother To Dragons, *and* The Mind Pool, *and the collections* Erasmus Magister, The McAndrew Chronicles, *and* Dancing With Myself. *His most recent books are the novels* Godspeed *and* The Ganymede Club, *and a new collection,* Georgia on My Mind and Other Places. *He lives in Silver Spring, Maryland.*

Here he takes us to the wild border country between Chile and Argentina, to the wind-swept barrens of Patagonia, for an encounter with a very strange and frightening object— one that will forever change the lives of those who come in contact with it.

John Kenyon Martindale seldom did things the usual way. Until a first-class return air ticket and a check for $10,000 arrived at my home in Lausanne I did not know he existed. The enclosed note said only: "For consulting services of Klaus Jacobi in New York, June 6–7." It was typed on his letterhead and initialed, JKM. The check was drawn on the

Riggs Bank of Washington, D.C. The tickets were for Geneva–New York on June 5, with an open return.

I did not need work. I did not need money. I had no particular interest in New York, and a trans-Atlantic telephone call to John Kenyon Martindale revealed only that he was out of town until June 5. Why would I bother with him? It is easy to forget what killed the cat.

The limousine that met me at Kennedy Airport drove to a stone mansion on the East River, with a garden that went right down to the water's edge. An old woman with the nose, chin, and hairy moles of a storybook witch opened the door. She took me upstairs to the fourth floor, while my baggage disappeared under the house with the limousine. The mansion was amazingly quiet. The elevator made no noise at all, and when we stepped out of it the deeply carpeted floors of the corridor were matched by walls thick with oriental tapestries. I was not used to so much silence. When I was ushered into a long, shadowed conservatory filled with flowering plants and found myself in the presence of a man and woman, I wanted to shout. Instead I stared.

Shirley Martindale was a brunette, with black hair, thick eyebrows, and a flawless, creamy skin. She was no more than five feet three, but full-figured and strongly built. In normal company she would have been a center of attention; with John Kenyon Martindale present, she was ignored.

He was of medium height and slender build, with a wide smiling mouth. His hair was thin and wheat-colored, combed straight back from his face. Any other expression he might have had was invisible. From an inch below his eyes to two inches above them, a flat, black shield extended across his whole face. Within that curved strip of darkness colored shadows moved, little darting points and glints of light that flared red and green and electric blue. They were hypnotic, moving in patterns that could be followed but never quite predicted, and they drew and held the attention. They were so striking that it took me a few moments to realize that John Kenyon Martindale must be blind.

He did not act like a person without sight. When I came

into the room he at once came forward and confidently shook my hand. His grip was firm, and surprisingly strong for so slight a man.

"A long trip," he said, when the introductions were complete. "May I offer a little refreshment?"

Although the witch was still standing in the room, waiting, he mixed the drinks himself, cracking ice, selecting bottles, and pouring the correct measures slowly but without error. When he handed a glass to me and smilingly said "There! How's that?" I glanced at Shirley Martindale and replied, "It's fine; but before we start the toasts I'd like to learn what we are toasting. Why am I here?"

"No messing about, eh? You are very direct. Very Swiss—even though you are not one." He turned his head to his wife, and the little lights twinkled behind the black mask. "What did I tell you, Shirley? This is the man." And then to me. "You are here to make a million dollars. Is that enough reason?"

"No. Mr. Martindale, it is not. It was not money that brought me here. I have enough money."

"Then perhaps you are here to become a Swiss citizen. Is that a better offer?"

"Yes. If you can pay in advance." Already I had an idea what John Martindale wanted of me. I am not psychic, but I can read and see. The inner wall of the conservatory was papered with maps of South America.

"Let us say, I will pay half in advance. You will receive five hundred thousand dollars in your account before we leave. The remainder, and the Swiss citizenship papers, will be waiting when we return from Patagonia."

"We? Who are 'we'?"

"You and I. Other guides if you need them. We will be going through difficult country, though I understand that you know it better than anyone."

I looked at Shirley Martindale, and she shook her head decisively. "Not me, Klaus. Not for one million dollars, not for ten million dollars. This is all John's baby."

"Then my answer must be no." I sipped the best pisco sour I had tasted since I was last in Peru, and wondered where he had learned the technique. "Mr. Martindale, I retired four years ago to Switzerland. Since then I have not set foot in Argentina, even though I still carry those citizenship papers. If you want someone to lead you through the *echter Rand* of Patagonia, there must now be a dozen others more qualified than I. But that is beside the point. Even when I was in my best condition, even when I was so young and cocky that I thought nothing could kill me or touch me—even then I would have refused to lead a blind man to the high places that you display on your walls. With your wife's presence and her assistance to you for personal matters, it might barely be possible. Without her—have you any idea at all what conditions are like there?"

"Better than most people." He leaned forward. "Mr. Jacobi, let us perform a little test. Take something from your pocket, and hold it up in front of you. Something that should be completely unfamiliar to me."

I hate games, and this smacked of one; but there was something infinitely persuasive about that thin, smiling man. What did I have in my pocket? I reached in, felt my wallet, and slipped out a photograph. I did not look at it, and I was not sure myself what I had selected. I held it between thumb and forefinger, a few feet away from Martindale's intent face.

"Hold it very steady," he said. Then, while the points of light twinkled and shivered, "It is a picture, a photograph of a woman. It is your assistant, Helga Korein. Correct?"

I turned it to me. It was a portrait of Helga, smiling into the camera. "You apparently know far more about me than I know of you. However, you are not quite correct. It is a picture of my wife, Helga Jacobi. I married her four years ago, when I retired. You are not blind?"

"Legally, I am completely blind and have been since my twenty-second year, when I was foolish enough to drive a racing car into a retaining wall." Martindale tapped the black shield. "Without this, I can see nothing. With it, I am neither blind nor seeing. I receive charge-coupled diode inputs directly to my optic nerves, and I interpret them. I see neither at the wavelengths nor with the resolution provided by the human eye, nor is what I reconstruct anything like the images that I remember from the time before I became blind; but I see. On another occasion I will be happy to tell you all that I know about the technology. What you need to know tonight is that I will be able to pull my own weight on any journey. I can give you that assurance. And now I ask again: will you do it?"

It was, of course, curiosity that killed the cat. Martindale had given me almost no information as to where he wanted to go, or when, or why. But something was driving John Martindale, and I wanted to hear what it was.

I nodded my head, convinced now that he would see my movement. "We certainly need to talk in detail; but for the moment let us use that fine old legal phrase, and say there is agreement in principle."

There is agreement in principle. With that sentence, I destroyed my life.

Shirley Martindale came to my room last night. I was not surprised. John Martindale's surrogate vision was a miracle of technology, but it had certain limitations. The device could not resolve the fleeting look in a woman's eye, or the millimeter just to a lower lip. I had caught the signal in the first minute.

We did not speak until it was done and we were lying side by side in my bed. I knew it was not finished. She had not relaxed against me. I waited. "There is more than he told you," she said at last.

I nodded. "There is always more. But he was quite right about that place. I have felt it myself, many times."

As South America narrows from the great equatorial swell of the Amazon Basin, the land becomes colder and more broken. The great spine of the Andean cordillera loses height as one travels south. Ranges that tower to twenty-three thousand feet in the tropics dwindle to a modest twelve thousand. The land is shared between Argentina and Chile, and along their border, beginning with the chill depths of Lago Buenos Aires (sixty miles long, ten miles wide; bigger than anything in Switzerland), a great chain of mountain lakes straddles the frontier, all the way south to Tierra del Fuego and the flowering Chilean city of Puntas Arenas.

For fourteen years, the Argentina-Chile borderland between latitude 46 and 50 South had been my home, roughly from Lago Buenos Aires to Lago Argentina. It had become closer to me than any human, closer even than Helga. The east side of the Andes in this region is a bitter, parched desert, where gale-force winds blow incessantly three hundred and sixty days of the year. They come from the snowbound slopes of the mountains, freezing whatever they touch. I knew the country and I loved it, but Helga had persuaded me that it was not a land to which a man could retire. The buffeting wind was an endless drain, too much for old blood. Better, she said, to leave in early middle age, when a life elsewhere could still be shaped.

When the time came for us to board the aircraft that would take me away to Buenos Aires and then to Europe, I wanted to throw away my ticket. I am not a sentimental man, but only Helga's presence allowed me to leave the Kingdom of the Winds.

Now John Martindale was tempting me to return there, with more than money. At one end of his conservatory-study stood a massive globe, about six feet across. Presumably it dated from the time before he had acquired his artificial eyes, because it differed from all other globes I had ever seen in one important respect; namely, it was a relief globe. Oceans were all smooth surface, while mountain ranges of the world stood out from the surface of the flattened sphere. The degree of relief had been exaggerated, but everything was in proportion. Himalayan and Karakoram ranges projected a few tenths of an inch more than the Rockies and the Andes, and they in turn were a little higher than the Alps or the volcanic ranges of Indonesia.

When my drink was finished Martindale had walked me across to that globe. He ran his finger down the backbone of the Americas, following the continuous mountain chains from their beginning in Alaska, through the American Rockies, through Central America, and on to the rising Andes and northern Chile. When he finally came to Patagonia his fingers slowed and stopped.

"Here," he said. "It begins here."

His fingertip was resting on an area very familiar to me. It was right on the Argentina-Chile border, with another of the cold mountain lakes at the center of it. I knew the lake as Lago Pueyrredon, but as usual with bodies of water that straddle the border there was a different name—Lago Cochrane—in use on the Chilean side. The little town of Paso Roballo, where I had spent a dozen nights in a dozen years, lay just to the northeast.

If I closed my eyes I could see the whole landscape that lay beneath his finger. To the east it was dry and dusty, sustaining only thornbush and tough grasses on the dark surface of old volcanic flows; westward were the tall flowering grasses and the thicketed forests of redwood, cypress, and Antarctic beech. Even in the springtime of late November there would be snow on the higher ground, with snow-fed lake waters lying black as jet under a Prussian-blue sky.

I could see all this, but it seemed impossible that John Martindale could do so. His blind skull must hold a different vision.

"*What* begins here?" I asked, and wondered again how much he could receive through arrays of inorganic crystal.

"The anomalies. This region has weather patterns that defy all logic and all models."

"I agree with that, from personal experience. That area has the most curious pattern of winds of any place in the world." It had been a long flight and a long day, and by this time I was feeling a little weary. I was ready to defer discussion of the weather until tomorrow, and I wanted time to reflect on our "agreement in principle." I continued, "However, I do not see why those winds should interest you."

"I am a meteorologist. Now wait a minute." His sensor array must have caught something of my expression. "Do not jump to a wrong conclusion. Mine was a perfect profession for a blind man. Who can see the weather? I was ten times as sensitive as a sighted person to winds, to warmth, to changes in humidity and barometric pressure. What I could not see was cloud formations, and those are consequences rather than causes. I could deduce their appearance from other variables. Eight years ago I began to develop my own computer models of weather patterns, analyzing the interaction of snows, winds, and topography. Five years ago I believed that my method was completely general and completely accurate. Then I studied the Andean system; and in one area—only one—it failed." He tapped the globe. "Here. Here there are winds with no sustaining source of energy. I can define a circulation pattern and locate a vortex, but I cannot account for its existence."

"The area you show is known locally as the Kingdom of the Winds."

"I know. I want to go there."

And so did I.

When he spoke I felt a great longing to return, to see again the *altiplano* of the eastern Andean slopes and hear the banshee music of the western wind. It was all behind me. I had sworn to myself that Argentina existed only in my past, that the Patagonian spell was broken forever. John Martindale was giving me a million dollars and Swiss citizenship, but more than that he was giving me an *excuse*. For four years I had been unconsciously searching for one.

I held out my glass. "I think, Mr. Martindale, that I would like another drink."

Or two. Or three.

Shirley Martindale was moving by my side now, running her hand restlessly along my arm. "There is more. He wants to understand the winds, but there is more. He hopes to find Trapalanda."

She did not ask me if I had heard of it. No one who spends more than a week in central Patagonia can be ignorant of Trapalanda. For three hundred yeas, explorers have searched for the "City of the Caesars." *Trapalanda*, the Patagonian version of El Dorado. Rumor and speculation said that Trapalanda would be found at about 47 degrees South, at the same latitude as Paso Roballo. Its fabled treasure-houses of gold and gemstones had drawn hundreds of men to their death in the high Andes. People did not come back, and say, "I sought Trapalanda, and I failed to find it." They did not come back at all. I was an exception.

"I am disappointed," I said. "I had thought your husband to be a wiser man."

"What do you mean?"

"Everyone wants to find Trapalanda. Four years of my life went into the search for it, and I had the best equipment and the best knowledge. I told your husband that there were a dozen better guides, but I was lying. I know that country better than any man alive. He is certain to fail."

"He believes that he has special knowledge. And you are going to do it. You are going to take him there. For Trapalanda."

She knew better than I. Until she spoke, I did not know what I would do. But she was right. Forget the "agreement in principle." I would go.

"You want me to do it, don't you?" I said. "But I do not understand *your* reasons. You are married to a very wealthy man. He seems to have as much money as he can ever spend."

"John is curious, always curious. He is like a little boy. He is not doing this for money. He does not care about money."

She had not answered my implied question. I had never asked for John Kenyon Martindale's motives. I had been looking for *her* reasons why he should go. Then it occurred to me that her presence, here in my bed, told me all I needed to know. He would go to the Kingdom of the Winds. If he found what he was looking for, it would bring enormous wealth. Should he fail to return, Shirley Martindale would be a free and very wealthy widow.

"Sex with your husband is not good?" I asked.

"What do you think? I am here, am I not?" Then she relented. "It is worse than not good, it is terrible. It is as bad with him as it is exciting with you. John is a gentle, thoughtful man, but I need someone who takes me and does not ask or explain. You are a strong man, and I suspect that you are a cold, selfish man. Since we have been together, you have not once spoken my name, or said a single word of affection. You do not feel it is necessary to pretend to commitments. And you are sexist. I noticed John's reactions when you said. 'I married Helga.' He would always say it differently, perhaps 'Shirley and I got married.'" Her hands moved from my arm, and were touching me more intimately. She sighed. "I do not mind your attitude. What John finds hard to stand, I *need*. You saw what you did to me here, without one word. You make me shiver."

I turned to bring our bodies into full contact. "And John?" I said. "Why did he marry you?" There was no need to ask why she had married him.

"What do you think," she said. "Was it my wit, my looks, my charm? Give me your hand." She gently moved my fingers along her face and breasts. "It was five years ago. John was still blind. We met, and when we said goodnight he felt my cheek." Her voice was bitter. "He married me for my pelt."

The texture was astonishing. I could feel no roughness, no blemish, not even the most delicate of hairs. Shirley Martindale had the warm, flawless skin of a six-month-old baby. It was growing warm under my touch.

Before we began she raised herself high above me, propping herself on straight arms. "Helga. What is she like? I cannot imagine her."

"You will see," I said. "Tomorrow I will telephone Lausanne and tell her to come to New York. She will go with us to Trapalanda."

Trapalanda. Had I said that? I was very tired, I had meant to say Patagonia.

I reached up to touch her breasts. "No talk now," I said. "No more talk." Her eyes were as black as jet, as dark as mountain lakes. I dived into their depths.

Shirley Martindale did not meet Helga; not in New York, not anywhere, not ever. John Kenyon Martindale made his position clear to me the next morning as we walked together around the seventh floor library. "I won't allow her to stay in this house," he said. "It's not for my sake or yours, and certainly not for Shirley's. It is for her sake. I know how Shirley would treat her."

He did not seem at all annoyed, but I stared at the blind black mask and revised my ideas about how much he could see with his CCD's and fiber optic bundles.

"Did she tell you last night why I am going to Patagonia?" he asked, as he picked out a book and placed it in the hopper of an iron pot-bellied stove with electronic aspirations.

I hesitated, and told the truth. "She said you were seeking Trapalanda."

He laughed. "I wanted to go to Patagonia. The easiest way to do it without an argument from Shirley was to hold out a fifty billion dollar bait. The odd thing, though, is that she is quite right. I am seeking Trapalanda." And he laughed again, more heartily than anything he had said would justify.

The black machine in front of us made a little purr of contentment, and a pleasant woman's voice began to read aloud. It was a mathematics text on the foundations of geometry. I had noticed that although Martindale described himself as a meteorologist, four-fifths of the books in the library were mathematics and theoretical physics. There were too many things about John Martindale that were not what they seemed.

"Shirley's voice," he said, while we stood by the machine and listened to a mystifying definition of the intrinsic curvature of a surface. "And a very pleasant voice, don't you think, to have whispering sweet epsilons in your ear? I borrowed it for use with this optical character recognition equipment, before I got my eyes."

"I didn't think there was a machine in the world that could do that."

"Oh, yes." He switched it off, and Shirley halted in mid-word. "This isn't even state-of-the-art any more. It was, when it was made, and it cost the earth. Next year it will be an antique, and they'll give this much capability out in cereal packets. Come on, let's go and join Shirley for a pre-lunch aperitif."

If John Martindale were angry with me or with his wife, he concealed it well. I realized that the mask extended well beyond the black casing.

Five days later we flew to Argentina. When Martindale mentioned his idea of being in the Kingdom of the Winds in time for the winter solstice, season of the anomaly's strongest showing, I dropped any thoughts of a trip back to Lausanne. I arranged for Helga to pack what I needed and meet us in Buenos Aires. She would wait at Ezeiza Airport without going into the city proper, and we would fly farther south at once. Even if our travels went well, we would need luck as well as efficiency to have a week near Paso Roballo before solstice.

It amused me to see Martindale searching for Helga in the airport arrival lounge as we walked off the plane. He had seen her photograph, and I assured him that she would be there. He could not find her. Within seconds, long before it was possible to see her features, I had picked her out. She was staring down at a book on her lap. Every fifteen seconds her head lifted for a rapid radar-like scan of the passenger lounge, and returned to the page. Martindale did not notice until we were at her side.

I introduced them. Helga nodded but did not speak. She stood up and led the way. She had rented a four-seater plane on open charter, and in her usual efficient way she had arranged for our luggage to be transferred to it.

Customs clearance, you ask? Let us be realistic. The Customs Office in Argentina is no more corrupt than that of, say, Bolivia or Ecuador; that is quite sufficient. Should John Martindale be successful in divining the legendary treasures of Trapalanda, plenty of hands would help to remove them illegally from the country.

Helga led the way through the airport. She was apparently not what he had expected of my wife, and I could see him studying her closely. Helga stood no more than five feet two, to my six-two, and her thin body was not quite straight. Her left shoulder dipped a bit, and she favored her left leg a trifle as she walked.

Since I was the only one with a pilot's license I sat

forward in the copilot's chair, next to Owen Davies. I had used Owen before as a by-the-day hired pilot. He knew the Kingdom of the Winds, and he respected it. He would not take risks. In spite of his name he was Argentina born—one of the many Welshmen who found almost any job preferable to their parents' Argentinian sheep-farming. Martindale and Helga sat behind us, side-by-side in the back, as we flew to Comodora Rivadavia on the Atlantic coast. It was the last real airfield we would see for a while unless we dipped across the Chilean border to Cochrane. I preferred not to try that. In the old days, you risked a few machine-gun bullets from frontier posts. Today it is likely to be a surface-to-air missile.

We would complete our supplies in Comodoro Rivadavia, then use dry dust airstrips the rest of the way. The provisions were supposed to be waiting for us. While Helga and Owen were checking to make sure that the delivery included everything we had ordered, Martindale came up to my side.

"Does she never talk?" he said. "Or is it just my lack of charm?" He did not sound annoyed, merely puzzled.

"Give her time." I looked to see what Owen and Helga were doing. They were pointing at three open chests of supplies, and Owen was becoming rather loud.

"You noticed how Helga walks, and how she holds her left arm?"

The black shield dipped down and up, making me suddenly curious as to what lay behind it. "I even tried to hint at a question in that direction," he said. "Quite properly she ignored it."

"She was not born that way. When Helga walked into my office nine years ago, I assumed that I was looking at some congenital condition. She said nothing, nor did I. I was looking for an assistant, someone who was as interested in the high border country as I was, and Helga fitted. She was only twenty-one years old and still green, but I could tell she was intelligent and trainable."

"Biddable," Martindale said. "Sorry, go on."

"You have to be fit to wander around in freezing temperatures at ten thousand feet," I said. "As part of Helga's

condition of employment, she had to take a full physical.
She didn't want to. She agreed only when she saw that the
job depended on it. She was in excellent shape and passed
easily; but the doctor—quite improperly—allowed me to
look at her X-rays."

Were the eyebrows raised, behind that obsidian visor?
Martindale cocked his head to the right, a small gesture of
inquiry. Helga and Owen Davies were walking our way.

"She was put together like a jigsaw puzzle. Almost every
bone in her arms and legs showed marks of fracture and
healing. Her ribs, too. When she was small she had been
what these enlightened times call 'abused.' Tortured. As a
very small child, Helga learned to keep quiet. The best thing
she could hope for was to be ignored. You saw already how
invisible she can be."

"I have never heard you angry before," he said. "You
sound like her father, not her husband." His tone was calm,
but something new hid behind that mask. "And is that," he
continued, "why in New York—"

He was interrupted. "Tomorrow," said Owen from behind
him. "He says he'll have the rest then. I believe him. I told
him he's a fat idle bastard, and if we weren't on our way by
noon I'd personally kick the shit out of him."

Martindale nodded at me. Conversation closed. We headed
into town for Alberto McShane's bar and the uncertain
pleasures of nightlife in Comodora Rivadavia. Martindale
didn't give up. All the way there he talked quietly to Helga.
He may have received ten words in return.

It had been five years. Alberto McShane didn't blink
when we walked in. He took my order without comment,
but when Helga walked past him he reached out his good
arm and gave her a big hug. She smiled like the sun. She
was home. She had hung around the *Guanaco* bar since she
was twelve years old, an oil brat brought here in the boom
years. When her parents left, she stayed. She hid among the
beer barrels in McShane's cellar until the plane took off.
Then she could relax for the first time in her life. Poverty
and hard work were luxury after what she had been through.

The decor of the bar hadn't changed since last time. The

bottle of dirty black oil (the first one pumped at Comodoro Rivadavia, if you believe McShane) hung over the bar, and the same stuffed guanaco and rhea stood beside it. McShane's pet armadillo, or its grandson, ambled among the tables looking for beer heel-taps.

I knew our search plans, but Helga and Owen Davies needed briefing. Martindale took Owen's 1:1,000,000 scale ONC's, with their emendations and local detail in Owen's careful hand, added to them the 1:250,000 color photomaps that had been made for him in the United States, and spread the collection out to cover the whole table.

"From here, to here," he said. His fingers tapped the map near Laguna del Sello, then moved south and west until they reached Lago Belgrano.

Owen studied them for a few moments. "All on this side of the border," he said. "That's good. What do you want to do there?"

"I want to land. Here, and here, and here." Martindale indicated seven points, on a roughly north-south line.

Owen Davies squinted down, assessing each location. "Lago Gio, Paso Roballo, Lago Posadas. Know 'em all. Tough landing at two, and that last point is in the middle of the Perito Morena National Park; but we can find a place." He looked up, not at Martindale but at me. "You're not in the true high country, though. You're twenty miles too far east. What do you want to do when you get there?"

"I want to get out, and look west," said Martindale. "After that, I'll tell you where we have to go."

Owen Davies said nothing more, but when we were at the bar picking up more drinks he gave me a shrug. *Too far east*, it said. *You're not in the high country. You won't find Trapalanda there, where he's proposing to land. What's the story?*

Owen was an honest man and a great pilot, who had made his own failed attempt at Trapalanda (sometimes I thought that was true of everyone who lived below 46 degrees South). He had found it hard to believe that anyone could succeed where he had not, but he couldn't resist the lure.

"He knows something he's not telling us," I said. "He's keeping information to himself. Wouldn't you?"

Owen nodded. Barrels of star rubies and tones of platinum and gold bars shone in his dark Welsh eyes.

When he returned to the table John Martindale had made his breakthrough. Helga was talking and bubbling with laughter. "How did you *do* that," she was saying. "He's untouchable. What did you *do* to him?" McShane's armadillo was sitting on top of the table, chewing happily at a piece of apple. Martindale was rubbing the ruffle of horny plates behind its neck, and the armadillo was pushing itself against his hand.

"He thinks I'm one of them,." Martindale touched the black screen across his eyes. "See? We've both got plates. I'm just one of the family." His face turned up to me. I read satisfaction behind his mask. *And should I do to your wife, Klaus, what you did to mine?* it said. *It would be no more than justice.*

Those were not Martindale's thoughts. I realized that. They were mine. And that was the moment when my liking for John Kenyon Martindale began to tilt toward resentment.

At ground level, the western winds skim off the Andean slopes at seventy knots or more. At nine thousand feet, they blow at less than thirty. Owen was an economy-minded pilot. He flew west at ten thousand until we were at the preferred landing point, then dropped us to the ground in three sickening sideslips.

He had his landing already planned. Most of Patagonia is built of great level slabs, rising like terraces from the high coastal cliffs on the Atlantic Ocean to the Andean heights in the west. The exception was in the area we were exploring. Volcanic eruptions there have pushed great layers of basalt out onto the surface. The ground is cracked and irregular, and scarred by the scouring of endless winds. It takes special skill to land a plane when the wind speed exceeds the landing air-speed, and Owen Davies had it. We showed an airspeed of over a hundred knots when we touched down, light as a dust mote, and rolled to a perfect landing. "Good enough," said Owen.

He had brought us down on a flat strip of dark lava, at three o'clock in the afternoon. The sun hung low on the northwest horizon, and we stepped out into the teeth of a cold and dust-filled gale. The wind beat and tugged and pushed our bodies, trying to blow us back to the Atlantic. Owen, Helga, and I wore goggles and helmets against the driving clouds of grit and sand.

Martindale was bare-headed. He planted a GPS transponder on the ground to confirm our exact position, and faced west. With his head tilted upward and his straw-colored hair blowing wild, he made an adjustment to the side of his visor, then nodded. "It is there," he said. "I knew it must be."

We looked, and saw nothing. "What is there?" said Helga.

"I'll tell you in a moment. Note these down. I'm going to read off heights and headings." Martindale looked at the sun and the compass. He began to turn slowly from north to south. Every fifteen degrees he stopped, stared at the featureless sky, and read off a list of numbers. When he was finished he nodded to Owen. "All right. We can do the next one now."

"You mean that's it? *The whole thing?* All you're going to do is stand there?" Owen is many good things, but he is not diplomatic.

"That's it—for the moment." Martindale led the way back to the aircraft.

I could not follow. Not at once. I had lifted my goggles and was peering with wind-teared eyes to the west. The land there fell upward to the dark-blue twilight sky. It was the surge of the Andes, less than twenty miles away, rolling up in long, snow-capped breakers. I walked across the tufts of bunch grass and reached out a hand to steady myself on an isolated ten-foot beech tree. Wind-shaped and stunted it stood, trunk and branches curved to the east, hiding its head from the deadly western wind. It was the only one within sight.

This was my Patagonia, the true, the terrible.

I felt a gentle touch on my arm. Helga stood there,

waiting. I patted her hand in reply, and she instinctively recoiled. Together we followed Martindale and Davies back to the aircraft.

"I found what I was looking for," Martindale said, when we were all safely inside. The gale buffeted and rocked the craft, resenting our presence. "It's no secret now. When the winds approach the Andes from the Chilean side, they shed all the moisture they have picked up over the Pacific; and they accelerate. The energy balance equation is the same everywhere in the world. It depends on terrain, moisture, heating, and atmospheric layers. The same equation everywhere—except that *here*, in the Kingdom of the Winds, something goes wrong. The winds pick up so much speed that they are thermodynamically impossible. There is a mechanism at work, pumping energy into the moving air. I knew it before I left New York City; and I knew what it must be. There had to be a long, horizontal line-vortex, running north to south and transmitting energy to the western wind. But that too was impossible. First, then, I had to confirm that the vortex existed." He nodded vigorously. "It does. With my vision sensors I can see the patterns of compression and rarefaction. In other words, I can see direct evidence of the vortex. With half a dozen more readings, I will pinpoint the exact origin of its energy source."

"But what's all that got to do with finding . . ." Owen trailed off and looked at me guiltily. I had told him what Martindale was after, but I had also cautioned him never to mention it.

"With finding Trapalanda?" finished Martindale. "Why, it has everything to do with it. There must be one site, a specific place where the generator exists to power the vortex line. Find that, and we will have found Trapalanda."

Like God, Duty, or Paradise, Tarpalanda means different things to different people. I could see from the expression on Owen's face that a line vortex power generator was not *his* Trapalanda, no matter what it meant to Martindale.

I had allowed six days; it took three. On the evening of June 17, we sat around the tiny table in the aircraft's rear cabin.

There would be no flying tomorrow, and Owen had produced a bottle of *usquebaugh australis*; "southern whiskey," the worst drink in the world.

"On foot," John Martindale was saying. "Now it has to be on foot—and just in case, one of us will stay at the camp in radio contact."

"Helga," I said. She and Martindale shook heads in unison. "Suppose you have to carry somebody out?" she said. "I can't do that. It must be you or Owen."

At least she was taking this seriously, which Owen Davies was not. He had watched with increasing disgust while Martindale made atmospheric observations at seven sites. Afterward he came to me secretly. "We're working for a madman," he said. "We'll find no treasure. I'd almost rather work for Diego."

Diego Luria—"Mad Diego"—believed that the location of Trapalanda could be found by a correct interpretation of the Gospel according to Saint John. He had made five expeditions to the altiplano, four of them with Owen as pilot. It was harder on Owen than you might think, since Diego sometimes said that human sacrifice would be needed before Trapalanda could be discovered. They had found nothing; but they had come back, and that in itself was no mean feat.

Martindale had done his own exact triangulation, and pinpointed a place on the map. He had calculated UTM coordinates accurate to within twenty meters. They were not promising. When we flew as close as possible to his chosen location we found that we were looking at a point halfway up a steep rock face, where a set of broken waterfalls cascaded down a near-vertical cliff.

"I am sure," he said, in reply to my implied question. "The data-fit residuals are too small to leave any doubt." He tapped the map, and looked out of the aircraft window at the distant rock face. "Tomorrow. You and Helga, and I will go. You, Owen, you stay here and monitor our transmission frequency. If we are off the air for more than twelve hours, come and get us."

He was taking this *too* seriously. Before the light faded I went outside again and trained my binoculars on the rock face. According to Martindale, at that location was a power generator that could modify the flow of winds along two hundred and fifty miles of mountain range. I saw nothing but the blown white spray of falls and cataracts, and a grey highland fox picking its way easily up the vertical rock face.

"Trust me." Martindale had appeared suddenly at my side. "I can *see* those wind patterns when I set my sensors to function at the right wavelengths. What's your problem?"

"Size." I turned to him. "Can you make your sensors provide telescopic images?"

"Up to three-inch effective aperture."

"Then take a look up there. You're predicting that we'll find a machine which produces tremendous power——"

"Many gigawatts."

"——more power than a whole power station. And there is nothing there, nothing to see. That's impossible."

"Not at all." The sun was crawling along the northern horizon. The thin daylight lasted for only eight hours, and already it was fading. John Kenyon Martindale peered off westward and shook his head. He tapped his black visor. "You've had a good look at this," he said. "Suppose I had wanted to buy something that could do what this does, say, five years ago. Do you know what it would have weighed?"

"*Weighed?*" I shook my head.

"At least a ton. And ten years ago, it would have been impossible to build, no matter how big you allowed it to be. In another ten years, this assembly will fit easily inside a prosthetic eye. The way is toward miniaturization, higher energy densities, more compact design. I expect the generator to be small." He suddenly turned again to look right into my face. "I have a question for you, and it is an unforgivably personal one. Have you ever consummated your marriage with Helga?"

He had not anticipated my lunge at him, and he backed away rapidly. "Do not misunderstand me," he said. "Helga's extreme aversion to physical contact is obvious. If it is total, there are New York specialists who can probably help her. I have influence there."

I looked down at my hands as they held the binoculars. They were trembling. "It is—total," I said.

"You knew that—and yet you married her. Why?"

"Why did you marry *your* wife, knowing you would be cuckolded?" I was lashing out, not expecting an answer.

"Did she tell you it was for her skin?" His voice was weary, and he was turning away as he spoke. "I'm sure she did. Well, I will tell you. I married Shirley—because she wanted me to."

Then I was standing alone in the deepening darkness. Shirley Martindale had warned me, back in New York. He was like a child, curious about everything. Including me, including Helga, including me and Helga.

Damn you, John Martindale. I looked at the bare hillside, and prayed that Trapalanda would somehow swallow him whole. Then I would never again have to endure that insidious, probing voice, asking the unanswerable.

The plane had landed on the only level piece of ground in miles. Our destination was a mile and a half away, but it was across some formidable territory. We would have to descend a steep scree, cross a quarter mile of boulders until we came to a fast-moving stream, and follow that water-course upward, until we were in the middle of the waterfalls themselves.

The plain of boulders showed the translucent sheen of a thin ice coating. The journey could not be done in poor light. We would wait until morning, and leave promptly at ten.

Helga and I went to bed early, leaving Martindale with his calculations and Owen Davies with his *usquebaugh australis*. At a pinch the aircraft would sleep four, but Helga and I slept outside in a small reinforced tent brought along for the purpose. The floor area was five feet by seven. We had pitched the tent in the lee of the aircraft, where the howl of the wind was muted. I listened to Helga's breathing, and knew after half an hour that she was still awake.

"Think we'll find anything?" I said softly.

"I don't know." And then, after maybe one minute. "It's not that. It's you, Klaus."

"I've never been better."

"That's the problem. I've seen you, these last few days. You love it here. I should never have taken you away."

"I'm not complaining."

"That's part of the problem, too. You never complain. I wish you would." I heard her turn to face me in the dark, and for one second I imagined a hand was reaching out towards it. It was an illusion. She went on, "When I said I wanted to leave Patagonia and live in Europe, you agreed without an argument. But your heart has always been here."

"Oh, well, I don't know . . ." The lie stuck in my throat.

"And there's something else. I wasn't going to tell you, because I was afraid that you would misunderstand. But I will tell you. John Martindale tried to touch me."

I stirred, began to sit up, and felt the rough canvas against my forehead. Outside, the wind gave a sudden scream around the tent. "You mean he tried to—to—"

"No. He reached out and tried to touch the back of my hand. That was all. I don't know why he did it, but I think it was just curiosity. He watches everything, and he has been watching us. I pulled my hand away before he got near. But it made me think of you. I have not been a wife to you, Klaus. You've done your best, and I've tried my hardest but it hasn't improved at all. Be honest with yourself, you know it hasn't. So if you want to stay here when his work is finished . . ."

I hated to hear her sound so confused and lost. "Let's not discuss it now," I said.

In other words, I can't bear to talk about it.

We had tried so hard at first, with Helga gritting her teeth at every gentle touch. When I finally realized that the sweat on her forehead and the quiver in her thin limbs was a hundred percent fear and zero percent arousal, I stopped trying. After that we had been happy—or at least, I had. I had not been faithful physically, but I could explain that well enough. And then, with this trip and the arrival on the scene of John Kenyon Martindale, the whole relationship

between Helga and me felt threatened. And I did not know
why.

"We ought to get as much sleep as we can tonight," I said,
after another twenty seconds or so. "Tomorrow will be a
tough day."

She said nothing, but she remained awake for a long, long
time.

And so, of course, did I.

The first quarter mile was easy, a walk down a gently
sloping incline of weathered basalt. Owen Davies had
watched us leave with an odd mixture of disdain and greed
on his face. We were not going to find anything, he was
quite sure of that—but on the other hand, if by some
miracle we *did* and he was not there to see it . . .

We carried minimal packs. I thought it would be no more
than a two-hour trek to our target point, and we had no
intention of being away overnight.

When we came to the field of boulders I revised my
estimate. Every square millimeter of surface was coated
with the thinnest and most treacherous layer of clear ice. In
principle its presence was impossible. With an atmosphere
of this temperature and dryness, that ice should have
sublimed away.

We picked our way carefully across, concentrating on
balance far more than progress. The wind buffeted us,
always at the worst moments. It took another hour and a half
before we were at the bottom of the waterfalls and could see
how to tackle the rock face. It didn't look too bad. There
were enough cracks and ledges to make the climb fairly
easy.

"That's the spot," said Martindale. "Right in there."

We followed his pointing finger. About seventy feet
above our heads one of the bigger waterfalls came cascading its way out from the cliff for a thirty-foot vertical drop.

"The waterfall?" said Helga. Her tone of voice said more
than her words. *That's supposed to be a generator of two
hundred and fifty miles of gale-force winds?* she was saying.
Tell me another one.

"Behind it." Martindale was walking along the base of the cliff, looking for a likely point where he could begin the climb. "The coordinates are actually *inside* the cliff. Which means we have to look *behind* the waterfall. And that means we have to come at it from the side."

We had brought rock-climbing gear with us. We did not need it. Martindale found a diagonal groove that ran at an angle of thirty degrees up the side of the cliff, and after following it to a vertical chimney, we found another slanting ledge running the other way. Two more changes of route, neither difficult, and we were on a ledge about two feet wide that ran up to the right behind our waterfall.

Two feet is a lot less when you are seventy feet up and walking a rock ledge slippery with water. Even here, the winds plucked restlessly at our clothes. We roped ourselves together, Martindale leading, and inched our way forward. When we were a few feet from the waterfall Martindale lengthened the rope between him and me, and went on alone behind the cascading water.

"It's all right." He had to shout to be heard above the crash of water. "It gets easier. The ledge gets wider. It runs into a cave in the face of the cliff. Come on."

We were carrying powerful electric flashlights, and we needed them. Once we were in behind the screen of water, the light paled and dwindled. We shone the lights toward the back of the cave. We were standing on a flat area, maybe ten feet wide and twelve feet deep. So much for Owen's dream of endless caverns of treasure; so much for my dreams, too, though they had been a lot less grandiose than his.

Standing about nine feet in from the edge of the ledge stood a dark blue cylinder, maybe four feet long and as thick as man's thigh. It was smooth-surfaced and uniform, with no sign of controls or markings on its surface. I heard Martindale grunt in satisfaction.

"Bingo," he said. "that's it."

"The whole thing?"

"Certainly. Remember what I said last night, about advanced technology making this smaller? There's the source of the line-vortex—the power unit for the whole

Kingdom of the Winds." He took two steps towards it, and as he did so Helga cried out, "Look out!"

The blank wall at the back of the cave had suddenly changed. Instead of damp grey stone, a rectangle of striated darkness had formed, maybe seven feet high and five feet wide.

Martindale laughed in triumph, and turned back to us. "Don't move for the moment. But don't worry, this is exactly what I hoped we might find. I suspected something like this when I first saw that anomaly. The winds are just an accidental by-product—like an eddy. The equipment here must be a little bit off in its tuning. But it's still working, no doubt about that. Feel the inertial dragging?"

I could feel something, a weak but persistent force drawing me toward the dark rectangle. I leaned backward to counteract it and looked more closely at the opening. As my eyes adjusted I realized that it was not true darkness there. Faint blue lines of luminescence started in from the edges of the aperture and flew rapidly toward a vanishing point at the center. There they disappeared, while new blue threads came into being at the outside.

"Where did the opening come from?" said Helga. "It wasn't there when we came in."

"No. It's a portal. I'm sure it only switches on when it senses the right object within range." Martindale took another couple of steps forward. Now he was standing at the very edge of the aperture, staring through at something invisible to me.

"What is it?" I said. In spite of Martindale's words I too had taken a couple of steps closer, and so had Helga.

"A portal—a gate to some other part of the Universe, build around a gravitational line singularity." He laughed, and his voice sounded half an octave lower in pitch. "Somebody left it here for us humans, and it leads to the stars. You wanted Trapalanda? This is it—the most priceless discovery in the history of the human race."

He took one more step forward. His moving leg stretched out forever in front of him, lengthening and lengthening. When his foot came down, the leg looked fifty yards long and it dwindled away to the tiny, distant speck of his foot. He lifted his back foot from the ground, and as he leaned forward his whole body rippled and distorted, stretching away from me. Now he looked his usual self—but he was a hundred yards away, carried with one stride along a tunnel that ran as far as the eye could follow.

Martindale turned, and reached out his hand. A long arm zoomed back towards us, still attached to that distant body, and a normal-sized right hand appeared out of the aperture.

"Come on." The voice was lower again in tone, and strangely slowed. "Both of you. Don't you want to see the rest of the Universe? Here's the best chance that you will ever have."

Helga and I took another step forward, staring in to the very edge of the opening. Martindale reached out his left hand too, and it hurtled toward us, growing rapidly, until it was there to be taken and held. I took another step, and I was within the portal itself. I felt normal, and I was aware of that force again, tugging us harder toward the tunnel. Suddenly I was gripped by an irrational and irresistible fear. I had to get away. I turned to move back from the aperture, and found myself looking at Helga. She was thirty yards away, drastically diminished, standing in front of a tiny wall of falling water.

One more step would have taken me outside again to safety, clear of the aperture and its persistent, tugging field. But as I was poised to take that step, Helga acted. She closed her eyes and took a long, trembling step forward. I could see her mouth moving, almost as though in prayer. And then the action I could not believe: she leaned forward to grasp convulsively at John Martindale's outstretched hand.

I heard her gasp, and saw her shiver. Then she was taking another step forward. And another.

"Helga!" I changed my direction and blundered after her along that endless tunnel. "This way. I'll get us out."

"No." She had taken another shivering step, and she was still clutching Martindale's hand. "No, Klaus." Her voice was breathless. "He's right. This is the biggest adventure ever. It's worth everything."

"Don't be afraid," said a hollow, booming voice. It was Martindale, and now all I could see of him was a shimmering silhouette. The man had been replaced by a sparkling outline. "Come on, Klaus. It's almost here."

The tugging force was stronger, pulling on every cell of my body. I looked at Helga, a shining outline now like John Martindale. They were dwindling, vanishing. They were gone. I wearily turned around and tried to walk back the way we had come. Tons of weight hung on me, wreathed themselves around every limb. I was trying to drag the whole world up an endless hill. I forced my legs to take one small step, then another. It was impossible to see if I was making progress. I was surrounded by that roaring silent pattern of rushing blue lines, all going in the opposite direction from me, every one doing its best do drag me back.

I inched along. Finally I could see the white of the waterfall ahead. It was growing in size, but at the same time it was losing definition. My eyes ached. By the time I took the final step and fell on my face on the stone floor of the cave, the waterfall was no more than a milky haze and a sound of rushing water.

Owen Davies saved my life, what there is of it. I did my part to help him. I wanted to live when I woke up, and weak as I was, and half-blind, I managed to crawl down that steep rock face. I was dragging myself over the icy boulders when he found me. My clothes were shredding, falling off my body, and I was shivering and weeping from cold and fear. He wrapped me in his own jacket and helped me back to the aircraft.

Then he went off to look for John Martindale and Helga. He never came back. I do not know to this day if he found and entered the portal, or if he came to grief somewhere on the way.

I spent two days in the aircraft, knowing that I was too sick and my eyes were too bad to dream of flying anywhere.

My front teeth had all gone, and I ate porridge or biscuits soaked in tea. Three more days, and I began to realize that if I did not fly myself, I was not going anywhere. On the seventh day I managed a faltering, incompetent takeoff and flew northeast, peering at the instruments of my newly purblind eyes. I made a crash landing at Comodora Rivadavia, was dragged from the wreckage, and flown to a hospital in Bahia Blanca. They did what they could for me, which was not too much. By the time I was beginning to have some faint idea what had happened to my body, and as soon as the hospital was willing to release me I took a flight to Buenos Aires, and on at once to Geneva's Lakeside Hospital. They removed the cataracts from my eyes. Three weeks later I could see again without that filmy mist over everything.

Before I left the hospital I insisted on a complete physical. Thanks to John Martindale's half-million deposit, money was not going to be a problem. The doctor who went over the results with me was about thirty years old, a Viennese Jew who had been practicing for only a couple of years. He looked oddly similar to one of my cousins at that age. "Well, Mr. Jacobi," he said (after a quick look at his dossier to make sure of my name), "there are no organic abnormalities, no cardiovascular problems, only slight circulation problems. You have some osteo-arthritis in your hips and your knees. I'm delighted to tell you that you are in excellent overall health for your age."

"If you didn't know," I said, "how old would you think I am?"

He looked again at his crib sheet, but found no help there. I had deliberately left out my age at the place where the hospital entry form required it. "Well," he said. He was going to humor me. "Seventy-six?"

"Spot on," I said.

I had the feeling that he had knocked a couple of years off his estimate, just to make me feel good. So let's say my biological age was seventy-eight or seventy-nine. When I flew with John Martindale to Buenos Aires, I had been one month short of my forty-fourth birthday.

At that point I flew to New York, and went to John Kenyon Martindale's house. I met with Shirley—briefly. She did not recognize me, and I did not try to identify myself. I gave my name as Owen Davies. In John's absence, I said, I was interested in contacting some of the mathematician friends that he had told me I would like to meet. Could she remember the names of any of them, so I could call them even before John came back? She looked bored, but she came back with a telephone book and produced three names. One was in San Francisco, one was in Boston, and the third was here in New York, at the Courant Institute.

He was in his middle twenties, a fit-looking curly haired man with bright blue eyes and a big smile. The thing that astonished him about my visit, I think, was not the subject matter. It was the fact that I made the visit. He found it astonishing that a spavined antique like me would come to his office to ask about this sort of topic in theoretical physics.

"What you are suggesting is not just *permitted* in today's view of space and time, Mr. Davies," he said. "It's absolutely *required*. You can't do something to *space*—such as making an instantaneous link between two places, as you have been suggesting—without at the same time having profound effects on *time*. Space and time are really a single entity. Distances and elapsed times are intimately related, like two sides of the same coin."

"And the line-vortex generator?" I said. I had told him far less about this, mainly because all I knew of it had been told to us by John Martindale.

"Well, if the generator in some sense approximated an infinitely long, rapidly rotating cylinder, then yes. General relativity resists that very peculiar things would happen there. There could be global causality violations—'before' and 'after' getting confused, cause and effect becoming mixed up, that sort of thing. God knows what time and space look like near the line singularity itself. But don't misunderstand me. Before any of these things could happen, you would have to be dealing with a huge-system, something many times as massive as the Sun."

I resisted the urge to tell him he was wrong. Apparently he did not accept John Martindale's unshakable confidence in the idea that with better technology came increase in capability *and* decrease in size. I stood up and leaned on my cane. My left hip was a little dodgy and became tired if I walked too far. "You've been very helpful."

"Not at all." He stood up, too, and said, "Actually, I'm going to be giving a lecture at the Institute on these subjects in a couple of weeks. If you'd like to come . . ."

I noted down the time and place, but I knew I would not be there. It was three months to the day since John Martindale, Helga, and I had climbed the rock face and walked behind the waterfall. Time—my time—was short. I had to head south again.

The flight to Argentina was uneventful. Comodora Rivadavia was the same as always. Now I am sitting in Alberto McShane's bar, drinking one last beer (all that my digestion today will permit) and waiting for the pilot. McShane did not recognize me, but the armadillo did. It trundled to my table, and sat looking at me. *Where's my friend John Martindale?* it was saying.

Where indeed? I will tell you soon. The plane is ready. We are going to Trepalanda.

It will take all my strength, but I think I can do it. I have added equipment that will help me to cross the icy field of boulders and ascend the rock face. It is September. The weather will be warmer, and the going easier. If I close my eyes I can see the portal now, behind the waterfall, its black depths and shimmering blue streaks rushing away toward the vanishing point.

Thirty-five years. That is what the portal owes me. It sucked them out of my body as I struggled back against the gravity gradient. Maybe it is impossible to get them back. I don't know. My young mathematician friend insisted that time is infinitely fluid, with no more constraints on movement through it than there are on travel through space. I don't know, but I want my thirty-five years. If I die in the attempt, I will be losing little.

I am terrified of that open gate, with its alien twisting of the world's geometry. I am more afraid of it than I have ever been of anything. Last time I failed, and I could not go through it. But I will go through it now.

This time I have something more than Martindale's scientific curiosity to drive me on. It is not thoughts of danger or death that fill my mind as I sit here. I have that final image of Helga, reaching out and taking John Martindale's hand in hers. Reaching out, to grasp his hand, voluntarily. I love Helga, I am sure of that, but I cannot make sense of my other emotions: fear, jealousy, resentment, hope, excitement. She was *touching* him. Did she do it because she wanted to go through the portal, wanted it so much that every fear was insignificant? Or had she, after thirty years, finally found someone whom she could touch without cringing and loathing?

The pilot has arrived. My glass is empty. Tomorrow I will know.

ARACHON

Damon Knight

Crime may have it's own rewards, but, as the wry and elegant little story that follows suggests, it definitely also has it's own risks as well . . .

A multitalented professional whose career as writer, editor, critic, and anthologist spans almost fifty years, Damon Knight has long been a major shaping force in the development of modern science fiction. He wrote the first important book of SF criticism, In Search of Wonder, *and won a Hugo Award for it. He was the founder of the Science Fiction Writers of America, co-founder of the prestigious Milford Writer's Conference, and, with his wife, writer Kate Wilhelm, is still deeply involved in the operation of the* Clarion *workshop for new young writers, which was modeled after the Milford Conference. He was the editor of* Orbit, *the longest running original anthology series in the history of American science fiction, and has also produced important works of genre history, such as* The Futurians *and* Turning Points, *as well as dozens of influential reprint anthologies. Knight has also been highly influential as a writer and may well be one of the finest short story writers ever to work in the genre. His books include the novels* A For Anything, The Other Foot, Hell's Pavement, The Man in the Tree, CV, *and* A Reasonable World, *and the collections* Rule Golden and Other Stories, Turning On, Far Out, The Best of Damon Knight, *and the recent* One Side Laughing. *His most recent book is the novel* Why Do Birds. *Knight lives with his family in Eugene, Oregon.*

The body was never found. And for that reason alone, there was no body to find.

It sounds like inverted logic—which, in a sense, it

is—but there's no paradox involved. It was a perfectly orderly and explicable event, even though it could only have happened to a Castellare.

Odd fish, the Castellare brothers. Sons of a Scots-Englishwoman and an expatriate Italian, born in England, educated on the Continent, they were at ease anywhere in the world and at home nowhere.

Nevertheless, in their middle years, they had become settled men. Expatriates like their father, they lived on the island of Ischia, off the Neapolitan coast, in a palace—*quattrocento*, very fine, with peeling cupids on the walls, a multitude of rats, no central heating and no neighbors.

They went nowhere; no one except their agents and their lawyers came to them. Neither had ever married. Each, at about the age of thirty, had given up the world of people for an inner world of more precise and more enduring pleasures. Each was an amateur—a fanatical, compulsive amateur.

They had been born out of their time.

Peter's passion was virtu. He collected relentlessly, it would not be too much to say savagely; he collected as some men hunt big game. His taste was catholic, and his acquisitions filled the huge rooms of the palace and half the vaults under them—paintings, statuary, enamels, porcelain, glass, crystal, metalwork. At fifty, he was a round little man with small, sardonic eyes and a careless patch of pinkish goatee.

Harold Castellare, Peter's talented brother, was a scientist. An amateur-scientist. He belonged in the nineteenth century, as Peter was a throwback to a still earlier epoch. Modern science is largely a matter of teamwork and drudgery, both impossible concepts to a Castellare. But Harold's intelligence was in its own way as penetrating and original as a Newton's or a Franklin's. He had done respectable work in physics and electronics, and had even, at his lawyer's insistence, taken out a few patents. The income from these, when his own purchases of instruments and equipment did not consume it, he gave to his brother, who accepted it without gratitude or rancor.

Harold, at fifty-three, was sparse and shrunken, sallow and spotted, with a bloodless, melancholy countenance: on his upper lip grew a neat hedge of pink-and-salt mustache, the companion piece and antithesis of his brother's goatee.

On a certain May morning, Harold had an accident.

Goodyear dropped rubber on a hot stove; Archimedes took a bath; Becquerel left a piece of uranium ore in a drawer with a photographic plate. Harold Castellare, working patiently with an apparatus which had so far consumed a great deal of current without producing anything more spectacular than some rather unusual corona effects, sneezed convulsively and dropped an ordinary bar magnet across two charged terminals.

Above the apparatus a huge, cloudy bubble sprang into being.

Harold, getting up from his instinctive crouch, blinked at it in profound astonishment. As he watched, the cloudiness abruptly disappeared and he was looking *through* the bubble at a section of tessellated flooring that seemed to be about three feet above the real floor. He could also see the corner of a carved wooden bench, and on the bench a small, oddly shaped stringed instrument.

Harold swore fervently to himself, made agitated notes, and then began to experiment. He tested the sphere cautiously with an electroscope, with a magnet, with a Geiger counter. Negative. He tore a tiny bit of paper from his notepad and dropped it toward the sphere. The paper disappeared; he couldn't see where it went.

Speechless, Harold picked up a meter stick and thrust it delicately forward. There was no feeling of contact; the rule went into and through the bubble as if the latter did not exist. Then it touched the stringed instrument, with a solid click. Harold pushed. The instrument slid over the edge of the bench and struck the floor with a hollow thump and jangle.

Staring at it, Harold suddenly recognized its tantalizing familiar shape.

Recklessly he let go the meter stick, reached in and picked the fragile thing out of the bubble. It was solid and cool in his fingers. The varnish was clear, the color of the wood glowing through it. It looked as if it might have been made yesterday.

Peter owned one almost exactly like it, except for preservation—a viola d'amore of the seventeenth century.

Harold stooped to look through the bubble horizontally. Gold and rust tapestries hid the wall, fifty feet away, except for an ornate door in the center. The door began to open; Harold saw a flicker of umber.

Then the sphere went cloudy again. His hands were empty; the viola d'amore was gone. And the meter stick, which he had dropped inside the sphere, lay on the floor at his feet.

"Look at that," said Harold simply.

Peter's eyebrows went up slightly. "What is it, a new kind of television?"

"No, no. Look here." The viola d'amore lay on the bench, precisely where it had been before. Harold reached into the sphere and drew it out.

Peter started. "Give me that." He took it in his hands, rubbed the smoothly finished wood. He stared at his brother. "By God and all the saints," he said. "Time travel."

Harold snorted impatiently. "My dear Peter, 'time' is a meaningless word taken by itself, just as 'space' is."

"But, barring that, time travel."

"If you like, yes."

"You'll be quite famous."

"I expect so."

Peter looked down at the instrument in his hands. "I'd like to keep this, if I may."

"I'd be very happy to let you, but you can't."

As he spoke the bubble went cloudy; the viola d'amore was gone like smoke.

"There, you see?"

"What sort of devil's trick is that?"

"It goes back. . . . Later you'll see. I had that thing out once before, and this happened. When the sphere became transparent again, the viol was where I had found it."

"And your explanation for this?"

Harold hesitated. "None. Until I can work out the appropriate mathematics—"

"Which may take you some time. Meanwhile, in layman's language—"

Harold's face creased with the effort and interest of translation. "Very roughly, then—I should say it means that events are conserved. Two or three centuries ago—"

"Three. Notice the sound holes."

"Three centuries ago, then, at this particular time of day, someone was in that room. If the viola was gone, he or she would have noticed the fact. That would constitute an alteration of events already fixed; therefore it doesn't happen. For the same reason, I conjecture, we can't see into the sphere, or—" he probed at it with a fountain pen—"I thought not—or reach into it to touch anything; that would also constitute an alteration. And anything we put into the sphere while it is transparent comes out again when it becomes opaque. To put it very crudely, we cannot alter the past."

"But it seems to me that we did alter it. Just now, when you took the viol out, even if no one of that time saw it happen."

"This," said Harold, "is the difficulty of using language as a means of exact communication. If you had not forgotten all your calculus . . . However. It may be postulated (remembering of course that everything I say is a lie, because I say it in English) that an event which doesn't influence other events is not an event. In other words—"

"That, since no one saw you take it, it doesn't matter whether you took it or not. A rather dangerous precept, Harold; you would have been burned at the stake for that at one time."

"Very likely. But it can be stated in another way, or indeed, in an infinity of ways which only seem to be different. If someone, let us say God, were to remove the moon as I am talking to you, using zero duration, and substitute an exact replica made of concrete and plaster of Paris, with the same mass, albedo and so on as the genuine moon, it would make no measurable difference in the universe as we perceive it—and therefore we cannot certainly say that it hasn't happened. Nor, I may add, does it make any difference whether it has or not."

"'When there's no one about on the quad,'" said Peter.

"Yes. A basic and, as a natural consequence, a meaningless problem of philosophy. Except," he added, "in this one particular manifestation."

He stared at the cloudy sphere. "You'll excuse me, won't you, Peter? I've got to work on this."

"When will you publish, do you suppose?"

"Immediately. That's to say, in a week or two."

"Don't do it till you've talked it over with me, will you? I have a notion about it."

Harold looked at him sharply. "Commercial?"

"In a way."

"No," said Harold. "This is not the sort of thing one patents or keeps secret, Peter."

"Of course. I'll see you at dinner, I hope?"

"I think so. If I forget, knock on the door, will you?"

"Yes. Until then."

"Until then."

At dinner, Peter asked only two questions.

"Have you found any possibility of changing the time your thing reaches—from the seventeenth century to the eighteenth, for example, or from Monday to Tuesday?"

"Yes, as a matter of fact. Amazing. It's lucky that I had a rheostat already in the circuit; I wouldn't dare turn the current off. Varying the amperage varies the time set. I've had it up to what I think was Wednesday of last week—at any rate, my smock was lying over the workbench where I left it, I remember, Wednesday afternoon. I pulled it out. A curious sensation, Peter—I was wearing the same smock at the time. And then the sphere went opaque and of course the smock vanished. That must have been myself, coming into the room."

"And the future?"

"Yes. Another funny thing. I've had it forward to various

times in the near future, and the machine itself is still there, but nothing's been done to it—none of the things I'm thinking I might do. That might be because of the conservation of events, again, but I rather think not. Still farther forward there are cloudy areas, blanks; I can't see anything that isn't in existence now, apparently, but here, in the next few days, there's nothing of that.

"It's as if I were going away. Where do you suppose I'm going?"

Harold's abrupt departure took place between midnight and morning. He packed his own grip, it would seem, left unattended, and was seen no more. It was extraordinary, of course, that he should have left at all, but the details were in no way odd. Harold had always detested what he called "the tyranny of the valet." He was, as everyone knew, a most independent man.

On the following day Peter made some trifling experiments with the time-sphere. From the sixteenth century he picked up a scent bottle of Venetian glass; from the eighteenth, a crucifix of carved rosewood; from the nineteenth, when the palace had been the residence of an Austrian count and his Italian mistress, a hand-illuminated copy of De Sade's *La Nouvelle Justine*, very curiously bound in human skin.

They all vanished, naturally, within minutes or hours— all but the scent bottle. This gave Peter matter for reflection. There had been half a dozen flickers of cloudiness in the sphere just futureward of the bottle; it ought to have vanished, but it hadn't. But then, he had found it on the floor near a wall with quite a large rat hole in it.

When objects disappeared unaccountably, he asked himself, was it because they had rolled into rat holes, or because some time fisher had picked them up when they were in a position to do so?

He did not make any attempt to explore the future. That afternoon he telephoned his lawyers in Naples and gave them instructions for a new will. His estate, including his half of the jointly owned Ischia property, was to go to the

Italian government on two conditions: (1) that Harold
Castellare should make a similar bequest of the remaining
half of the property and (2) that the Italian government
should turn the palace into a national museum to house
Peter's collection, using the income from his estate for its
administration and for further acquisitions. His surviving
relatives—two cousins in Scotland—he cut off with a
shilling each.

He did nothing more until after the document had been
brought out to him, signed and witnessed. Only then did he
venture to look into his own future.

Events were conserved, Harold had said—meaning,
Peter very well understood, events of the present and future
as well as of the past. But was there only one pattern in
which the future could be fixed? Could a result exist before
its cause had occurred?

The Castellare motto was *Audentes fortuna juvat*—into
which Peter, at the age of fourteen, had interpolated the
word *"prudentesque"*: "Fortune favors the bold—and the
prudent."

Tomorrow: no change; the room he was looking at was so
exactly like this one that the time sphere seemed to vanish.
The next day: a cloudy blur. And the next, and the next . . .

Opacity, straight through to what Peter judged, by the
distance he had moved the rheostat handle, to be ten years
ahead. Then, suddenly, the room was a long marble hall
filled with display cases.

Peter smiled wryly. If you were Harold, obviously you
could not look ahead and see Peter working in your
laboratory. And if you were Peter, equally obviously, you
could not look ahead and know whether the room you saw
was an improvement you yourself were going to make, or
part of a museum established after your death, eight or nine
years from now, or . . .

No. Eight years was little enough, but he could not even
be sure of that. It would, after all, be seven years before
Harold could be declared legally dead. . . .

Peter turned the vernier knob slowly forward. A flicker,
another, a long series. Forward faster. Now the flickering

melted into a grayness; objects winked out of existence and were replaced by others in the showcases; the marble darkened and lightened again; darkened and lightened, darkened and remained dark. He was, Peter judged, looking at the hall as it would be some five hundred years in the future. There was a thick film of dust on every exposed surface; rubbish and the carcass of some small animal had been swept carelessly into a corner.

The sphere clouded.

When it cleared, there was an intricate trail of footprints in the dust, and two of the showcases were empty.

The footprints were splayed, trifurcate, and thirty inches long.

After a moment's deliberation Peter walked around the workbench and leaned down to look through the sphere from the opposite direction. Framed in the nearest of the four tall windows was a scene of picture-postcard banality: the sun-silvered bay and the foreshortened arc of the city, with Vesuvio faintly fuming in the background. But there was something wrong about the colors, even grayed as they were by distance.

Peter went and got his binoculars.

The trouble was, of course, that Naples was green. Where the city ought to have been, a rankness had sprouted. Between the clumps of foliage he could catch occasional glimpses of gray-white that might equally well have been boulders or the wreckage of buildings. There was no movement. There was no shipping in the harbor.

But something rather odd was crawling up the side of the volcano. A rust-orange pipe, it appeared to be, supported on hairline struts like the legs of a centipede, and ending without rhyme or reason just short of the top.

While Peter watched, it turned slowly blue.

One day further forward: now all the display cases had been looted; the museum, it would seem, was empty.

Given, that in five centuries the world, or at any rate the department of Campania, has been overrun by a race of Somethings, the human population being killed or driven

out in the process; and that the conquerors take an interest
in the museum's contents, which they have accordingly
removed.

Removed where, and why?

This question, Peter conceded, might have a thousand
answers, nine hundred and ninety-nine of which would
mean that he had lost his gamble. The remaining answer
was: to the vaults, for safety.

With his own hands Peter built a hood to cover the
apparatus on the workbench and the sphere above it. It was
unaccustomed labor; it took him the better part of two days.
Then he called in workmen to break a hole in the stone
flooring next to the interior wall, rig a hoist, and cut the
power cable that supplied the time-sphere loose from its
supports all the way back to the fuse box, leaving him a
single flexible length of cable more than a hundred feet
long. They unbolted the workbench from the floor, attached
casters to its legs, lowered it into the empty vault below, and
went away.

Peter unfastened and removed the hood. He looked into
the sphere.

Treasure.

Crates, large and small, racked in rows into dimness.

With pudgy fingers that did not tremble, he advanced the
rheostat. A cloudy flicker, another, a leaping blur of them as
he moved the vernier faster—and then there were no more,
to the limit of the time-sphere's range.

Two hundred years, Peter guessed—A.D. 2700 to 2900 or
thereabout—in which no one would enter the vault. Two
hundred years of "unliquidated time."

He put the rheostat back to the beginning of that
uninterrupted period. He drew out a small crate and prized
it open.

Chessmen, ivory with gold inlay, Florentine, fourteenth
century. Superb.

Another, from the opposite rack.

T'ang figurines, horses and men, ten to fourteen inches
high. Priceless.

• • •

The crates would not burn, Tomaso told him. He went down to the kitchen to see, and it was true. The pieces lay in the roaring stove untouched. He fished one out with a poker; even the feathery splinters of the unplaned wood had not ignited.

It made a certain extraordinary kind of sense. When the moment came for the crates to go back, any physical scrambling that had occurred in the meantime would have no effect; they would simply put themselves together as they had been before, like Thor's goats. But burning was another matter; burning would have released energy which could not be replaced.

That settled one paradox, at any rate. There was another that nagged at Peter's orderly mind. If the things he took out of that vault, seven hundred-odd years in the future, were to become part of the collection bequeathed by him to the museum, preserved by it, and eventually stored in the vault for him to find—then precisely where had they come from in the first place?

It worried him. Peter had learned in life, as his brother had in physics, that one never gets anything for nothing.

Moreover, this riddle was only one of his perplexities, and that not among the greatest. For another example, there was the obstinate opacity of the time-sphere whenever he attempted to examine the immediate future. However often he tried it, the result was always the same: a cloudy blank, all the way forward to the sudden unveiling of the marble gallery.

It was reasonable to expect the sphere to show nothing at times when he himself was going to be in the vault, but this accounted for only five or six hours out of every twenty-four. Again, presumably, it would show him no changes to be made by himself, since foreknowledge would make it possible for him to alter his actions. But he laboriously cleared one end of the vault, put up a screen to hide the rest and made a vow—which he kept—not to alter the clear space or move the screen for a week. Then he tried again—with the same result.

The only remaining explanation was that sometime during the next ten years something was going to happen which he would prevent if he could; and the clue to it was there, buried in that frustrating, unbroken blankness.

As a corollary, it was going to be something which he *could* prevent if only he knew what it was . . . or even when it was supposed to happen.

The event in question, in all probability, was his own death. Peter therefore hired nine men to guard him, three to a shift—because one man alone could not be trusted, two might conspire against him, whereas three, with the very minimum of effort, could be kept in a state of mutual suspicion. He also underwent a thorough medical examination, had new locks installed on every door and window, and took every other precaution ingenuity could suggest. When he had done all these things, the next ten years were as blank as before.

Peter had more than half expected it. He checked through his list of safeguards once more, found it good, and thereafter let the matter rest. He had done all he could; either he would survive the crisis or he would not. In either case, events were conserved; the time-sphere could give him no forewarning.

Another man might have found his pleasure blunted by guilt and fear; Peter's was whetted to a keener edge. If he had been a recluse before, now he was an eremite; he grudged every hour that was not given to his work. Mornings he spent in the vault, unpacking his acquisitions; afternoons and evenings, sorting, cataloguing, examining and—the word is not too strong—gloating. When three weeks had passed in this way, the shelves were bare as far as the power cable would allow him to reach in every direction, except for crates whose contents were undoubtedly too large to pass through the sphere. These, with heroic self-control, Peter had left untouched.

And still he had looted only a hundredth part of that incredible treasure house. With grappling hooks he could have extended his reach by perhaps three of four yards, but at the risk of damaging his prizes; and in any case this would have been no solution but only a postponement of the problem. There was nothing for it but to go through the sphere himself and unpack the crates while on the other "side" of it.

Peter thought about it in a fury of concentration for the rest of the day. So far as he was concerned, there was no question that the gain would be worth any calculated risk; the problem was how to measure the risk and if possible reduce it.

Item: He felt a definite uneasiness at the thought of venturing through that insubstantial bubble. Intuition was supported, if not by logic, at least by a sense of the dramatically appropriate. Now, if ever, would be the time for his crisis.

Item: Common sense did not concur. The uneasiness had two symbols. One was the white face of his brother Harold just before the water closed over it; the other was a phantasm born of those gigantic, splayed footprints in the dust of the gallery. In spite of himself, Peter had often found himself trying to imagine what the creatures that made them must look like, until his visualization was so clear that he could almost swear he had seen them.

Towering monsters they were, with crested ophidian heads and great unwinking eyes; and they moved in a strutting glide, nodding their heads, like fanatic barnyard fowl.

But, taking these premonitory images in turn: first, it was impossible that he should ever be seriously inconvenienced by Harold's death. There were no witnesses, he was sure; he had struck the blow with a stone; stones also were the weights that had dragged the body down, and the rope was an odd length Peter had picked up on the shore. Second, the three-toed Somethings might be as fearful as all the world's bogies put together; it made no difference, he could never meet them.

Nevertheless, the uneasiness persisted. Peter was not satisfied; he wanted a lifeline. When he found it, he wondered that he had not thought of it before.

He would set the time-sphere for a period just before one of the intervals of blankness. That would take care of accidents, sudden illnesses, and other unforeseeable contingencies. It would also insure him against one very real and not at all irrational dread: the fear that the mechanism which generated the time-sphere might fail while he was on the other side. For the conservation of events was not a condition created by the sphere but one which limited its operation. No matter what happened, it was impossible for him to occupy the same place-time as any future or past observer; therefore, when the monster entered that vault, Peter would not be there any more.

There was, of course, the scent bottle to remember. Every rule has its exception; but in this case, Peter thought, the example did not apply. A scent bottle could roll into a rat hole; a man could not.

He turned the rheostat carefully back to the last flicker of grayness; past that to the next, still more carefully. The interval between the two, he judged, was something under an hour: excellent.

His pulse seemed a trifle rapid, but his brain was clear and cool. He thrust his head into the sphere and sniffed cautiously. The air was stale and had a faint, unpleasant odor, but it was breathable.

Using a crate as a stepping stool, he climbed to the top of the workbench. He arranged another crate close to the sphere to make a platform level with its equator. And seven and a half centuries in the future, a third crate stood on the floor directly under the sphere.

Peter stepped into the sphere, dropped, and landed easily, legs bending to take the shock. When he straightened, he was standing in what to all appearances was a large circular hole in the workbench; his chin was just above the top of the sphere.

He lowered himself, half squatting, until he had drawn his head through and stepped down from the crate.

He was in the future vault. The sphere was a brightly luminous thing that hung unsupported in the air behind him, its midpoint just higher than his head. The shadows it cast spread black and wedge-shaped in every direction, melting into obscurity.

Peter's heart was pounding miserably. He had an illusory stifling sensation, coupled with the idiotic notion that he ought to be wearing a diver's helmet. The silence was like the pause before a shout.

But down the aisles marched the crated treasures in their hundreds.

Peter set to work. It was difficult, exacting labor, opening the crates where they lay, removing the contents and nailing the crates up again, all without disturbing the positions of the crates themselves, but it was the price he had to pay for his lifeline. Each crate was in a sense a microcosm, like the vault itself—a capsule of unliquidated time. But the vault's term would end some fifty minutes from now, when crested heads nodded down three aisles; those of the crates' interiors, for all that Peter knew to the contrary, went on forever.

The first crate contained lacework porcelain; the second, shakudō sword hilts; the third, an exquisite fourth-century Greek ornament in *repoussé* bronze, the equal in every way of the Siris bronzes.

Peter found it almost physically difficult to set the thing down, but he did so; standing on his platform crate in the future with his head projecting above the sphere in the present—like (again the absurd thought!) a diver rising from the ocean—he laid it carefully beside the others on the workbench.

Then down again, into the fragile silence and the gloom. The next crates were too large, and those just beyond were doubtful. Peter followed his shadow down the aisle. He had almost twenty minutes left: enough for one more crate, chosen with care, and an ample margin.

Glancing to his right at the end of the row, he saw a door. It was a heavy door, rivet-studded, with a single iron step below it. There had been no door there in Peter's time; the whole plan of the building must have been altered. *Of course!* he realized suddenly. If it had not, if so much as a single tile or lintel had remained of the palace as he knew it, then the sphere could never have let him see or enter this particular here-and-now, this—what would Harold have called it?—this nexus in spacetime.

For if you saw any now-existing thing as it was going to appear in the future, you could alter it in the present—carve your initials in it, break it apart, chop it down—which was manifestly impossible, and therefore . . .

And therefore the first ten years were necessarily blank when he looked into the sphere, not because anything unpleasant was going to happen to him, but because in that time the last traces of the old palace had not yet been eradicated.

There was no crisis.

Wait a moment, though! Harold had been able to look into the near future. . . . But—of course—Harold had been about to die.

In the dimness between himself and the door he saw a rack of crates that looked promising. The way was uneven; one of the untidy accumulations of refuse that seemed to be characteristic of the Somethings lay in windows across the floor. Peter stepped forward carefully—but not carefully enough.

Harold Castellare had had another accident—and again, if you choose to look at it in that way, a lucky one. The blow stunned him; the old rope slipped from the stones; flaccid, he floated where a struggling man might have drowned. A fishing boat nearly ran him down, and picked him up instead. He was suffering from a concussion, shock, exposure, asphyxiation and was more than three quarters dead. But he was still alive when he was delivered, an hour later, to a hospital in Naples.

There were, of course, no identifying papers, labels or monograms in his clothing—Peter had seen to that—and for the first week after his rescue Harold was quite genuinely unable to give any account of himself. During the second week he was mending but uncommunicative, and at the end of the third, finding that there was some difficulty about gaining his release in spite of his physical recovery, he affected to regain his memory, gave a circumstantial but entirely fictitious identification and was discharged.

To understand this as well as all his subsequent actions, it is only necessary to remember that Harold was a Castellare. In Naples, not wishing to give Peter any unnecessary anxiety, he did not approach his bank for funds but cashed a check with an incurious acquaintance, and predated it by four weeks. With part of the money so acquired he paid his hospital bill and rewarded his rescuers. Another part went for new clothing and for four days' residence in an inconspicuous hotel, while he grew used to walking and dressing himself again. The rest, on his last day, he spent in the purchase of a discreetly small revolver and a box of cartridges.

He took the last boat to Ischia and arrived at his own front door a few minutes before eleven. It was a cool evening, and a most cheerful fire was burning in the central hall.

"Signor Peter is well, I suppose," said Harold, removing his coat.

"Yes, Signor Harold. He is very well, very busy with his collection."

"Where is he? I should like to speak to him."

"He is in the vaults, Signor Harold. But . . ."

"Yes?"

"Signor Peter sees no one when he is in the vaults. He has given strict orders that no one is to bother him, Signor Harold, when he is in the vaults."

"Oh, well," said Harold. "I daresay he'll see me."

It was a thing something like a bear trap, apparently, except that instead of two semicircular jaws it had four segments that snapped together in the middle, each with a shallow, sharp tooth. The pain was quite unendurable.

Each segment moved at the end of a thin arm, cunningly hinged so that the ghastly thing would close over whichever of the four triggers you stepped on. Each arm had a spring too powerful for Peter's muscles. The whole affair was connected by a chain to a staple solidly embedded in the concrete floor; it left Peter free to move some ten inches in any direction. Short of gnawing off his own leg, he thought sickly, there was very little he could do about it.

The riddle was, what could the thing possibly be doing here? There were rats in the vaults, no doubt, now as in his own time, but surely nothing larger. Was it conceivable that even the three-toed Somethings would set an engine like this to catch a rat?

Lost inventions, Peter thought irrelevantly, had a way of being rediscovered. Even if he suppressed the time-sphere during his lifetime and it did not happen to survive him, still there might be other time-fishers in the remote future—not here, perhaps, but in other treasure houses of the world. And that might account for the existence of this metal-jawed horror. Indeed, it might account for the vault itself—a better man-trap—except that it was all nonsense; the trap could only be full until the trapper came to look at it. Events, and the lives of prudent time-travelers, were conserved.

And he had been in the vault for almost forty minutes. Twenty minutes to go, twenty-five, thirty at the most, then the Somethings would enter and their entrance would free him. He had his lifeline; the knowledge was the only thing that made it possible to live with the pain that was the center of his universe just now. It was like going to the dentist, in the bad old days before procaine; it was very bad, sometimes, but you knew that it would end.

He cocked his head toward the door, holding his breath. A distant thud, another, then a curiously unpleasant squeaking, then silence.

But he had heard them. He knew they were there. It couldn't be much longer now.

Three men, two stocky, one lean, were playing cards in the passageway in front of the closed door that led to the vault staircase. They got up slowly.

"Who is he?" demanded the shortest one.

Tomaso clattered at him in furious Sicilian; the man's face darkened, but he looked at Harold with respect.

"I am now," stated Harold, "going down to see my brother."

"No, Signor," said the shortest one positively.

"You are impertinent," Harold told him.

"Yes, Signor."

Harold frowned. "You will not let me pass?"

"No, Signor."

"Then go and tell my brother I am here."

The shortest one said apologetically but firmly that there were strict orders against this also; it would have astonished Harold very much if he had said anything else.

"Well, at least I suppose you can tell me how long it will be before he comes out?"

"Not long, Signor. One hour, no more."

"Oh, very well, then," said Harold pettishly, turning half away. He paused. "One thing more," he said, taking the gun out of his pocket as he turned, "put your hands up and stand against the wall there, will you?"

The first two complied slowly. The third, the lean one, fired through his coat pocket, just like the gangsters in the American movies.

It was not a sharp sensation at all, Harold was surprised to find; it was more as if someone had hit him in the side with a cricket bat. The racket seemed to bounce interminably from the walls. He felt the gun jolt in his hand as he fired back, but couldn't tell if he had hit anybody. Everything seemed to be happening very slowly, and yet it was astonishingly hard to keep his balance. As he swung around he saw the two stocky ones with their hands half inside their jackets, and the lean one with his mouth open, and Tomaso with bulging eyes. Then the wall came at him and he began to swim along it, paying particular attention to the problem of not dropping one's gun.

As he weathered the first turn in the passageway the roar broke out afresh. A fountain of plaster stung his eyes; then he was running clumsily, and there was a bedlam of shouting behind them.

Without thinking about it he seemed to have selected the laboratory as his destination; it was an instinctive choice, without much to recommend it logically. In any case, he realized halfway across the central hall, he was not going to get there.

He turned and squinted at the passageway entrance; saw a blur move and fired at it. It disappeared. He turned again awkwardly, and had taken two steps nearer an armchair which offered the nearest shelter, when something clubbed him between the shoulderblades. One step more, knees buckling, and the wall struck him a second, softer blow. He toppled, clutching at the tapestry that hung near the fireplace.

When the three guards, whose names were Enrico, Alberto and Luca, emerged cautiously from the passage and approached Harold's body, it was already flaming like a Viking's in its impromptu shroud; the dim horses and men and falcons of the tapestry were writhing and crisping into brilliance. A moment later an uncertain ring of fire wavered toward them across the carpet.

Although the servants came with fire extinguishers and with buckets of water from the kitchen, and although the fire department was called, it was all quite useless. In five minutes the whole room was ablaze; in ten, as windows burst and walls buckled, the fire engulfed the second story. In twenty a mass of flaming timbers dropped into the vault through the hole Peter had made in the floor of the laboratory, utterly destroying the time-sphere apparatus and reaching shortly thereafter, as the authorities concerned were later to agree, an intensity of heat entirely sufficient to consume a human body without leaving any identifiable trace. For that reason alone, there was no trace of Peter's body to be found.

The sounds had just begun again when Peter saw the light from the time-sphere turn ruddy and then wink out like a snuffed candle.

In the darkness, he heard the door open.

HOLE-IN-THE-WALL

Bridget McKenna

Here's a mordant cautionary tale that reminds us that even in the meanest of surroundings, a shabby little hole-in-the-wall diner, say, it's always best to be respectful and polite. You never know who you're going to run into, after all—or just where they'll be popping in from . . .

Bridget McKenna has made many short fiction sales to Asimov's Science Fiction, *as well as sales to* The Magazine of Fantasy and Science Fiction, Pulphouse, Tomorrow, *and elsewhere. She lives in Ahwahnee, California.*

Morton Grimes knew it was going to be of those cases even before he walked inside the diner. Pulling the file from his portfolio, he scanned the application: Ladislaw Tomacheski—a communist name, for starters, and Grimes was no fool when it came to commies. He never missed an episode of "I Led Three Lives." Flicking a thread from his coatsleeve, he opened the screen door and went inside.

The place seemed clean enough on the inside, but Grimes knew how clean a restaurant could look to the uneducated eye and still be a pesthole; knew all the places dirt could hide, breeding bacteria and foul smells. He shuddered as he bent down to check a red-upholstered stool, running his hand down the chrome column, bending low to see the interstices around the plate that bolted the stool to the linoleum. It all looked clean enough, but then, this place was operating on the temporary Ed Crawford had awarded last week. Give him a few more months to get sloppy, like they all did when they forgot Morton Grimes was watching.

"Can I help you with something? Maybe you lose something down there?" A heavily accented voice spoke from above him.

Grimes stood up quickly, rapping his head on the underside of the counter. Pain clouded his vision as he steadied himself with the chrome-studded seat of the stool and straightened his legs cautiously. "Mr. Tomacheski, I presume?" he said to the field of white before him which was slowly beginning to focus into a large beefy man a full head taller than he, in kitchen whites and apron.

"Tomacheski," the figure said, extending a huge hand.

Grimes tried to grasp it with the ends of his fingers, but the hand engulfed his and squeezed, pumping his arm up and down like an oil rig. He pulled loose and reached into his pocket for a card. "Morton Grimes. Health Department Officer."

"Oh, yes. You came to grant my A-card! How do you do, Mr. Grimes!" The arm-pumping began all over again. "An unfortunate name for a man in your profession, yes?"

Grimes stiffened. "An A-placard is not given lightly, Mr. Tomacheski. I'll be making an extensive inspection of your premises." Oh, indeed, I will, you Red bastard. The accent was definitely Russian, Grimes thought. This guy wasn't even trying to sound like an American. Of course that could mean he wasn't really a communist, since if he was, he probably wouldn't sound so much like one. Well, he could decide about that later, he had an inspection to do.

". . . Of course we weren't expecting you until Wednesday," the Russian was saying.

"Bacteria don't make appointments, Mr. Tomacheski. A Health Department Officer is empowered to inspect a business at any time."

"Of course. Well, where would you like to begin?"

"Let's begin with the exterior of the premises. On the application here, it says that the name of the business is 'Tomacheski's Hole in the Wall.' You would not appear to be doing business under that name."

"But yes, of course. That's the name. What it says right there on the paper."

"Yet," Grimes continued, warming up now, "there is no sign outside to that effect. There is only *that*."

He pointed out the front window at the sign, which said only EAT, but said it so brightly that even in broad daylight it was sending coruscating pink and green waves through the glass bricks that made up most of the front wall.

"This is a little place, Mr. Grimes." He put two huge hands close together to show how small. "The name is too big for the building. But EAT is what people come here to do, yes? So the sign says the important thing. Excuse me, but this is a concern of the Health Department, this sign business?"

"Not exactly, Mr. Tomacheski, but the Department doesn't operate in a vacuum. We have an understanding with other branches of city and county government to report possible violations of any nature."

"Well, the sign has been approved by the county, Mr. Grimes. Now, where would you like to begin?"

"With the kitchen." Grimes pushed ahead of the big man in the narrow space between the counter stools and the booths and walked into the back of the diner. "Well, here's your first problem right here," he said, pulling out a notepad and his Parker. "Peeling paint on the wall of the, uh . . ." He peered around the corner. "Ladies' Room. Peeling paint is a serious health hazard in a food service establishment. Lead, you know."

The paint seemed to melt and run even as Grimes looked at it. He put his finger to the wall to determine the degree of flaking. A hot tingling ran up his arm to the elbow and he pulled away, shaking his hand. "What have you got here, Tomacheski? Loose wiring in this wall? I think the Fire Department will want to know about this."

"They were here yesterday, Mr. Grimes, and the wiring is good in this building. The paint is good too, I think. I saw this same thing yesterday morning, and I think it is only a trick of the light. Look." He pointed at the wall. The spot was gone.

Grimes touched the wall lightly with an index finger. No shock. No paint. He stood there for a moment, feeling puzzled and not liking it. Then he turned on his heel and pushed through the swinging doors into the kitchen with Tomacheski following close behind. A row of high windows illuminated the room with a fine morning light. Grimes marched into the cooking area and stopped dead in his tracks. Tomacheski pulled up, but too late to avoid bumping Grimes, who was propelled forward into the arms of the very Negro whose presence in the kitchen had alarmed him so.

"You all right, Mister?" the Negro asked, setting him back on his feet.

Grimes pulled away from the man's grasp and brushed off his clothes. "I'm fine," he croaked. "Fine." He stared for a moment at the black face, the white cap and apron, then spun around to face Tomacheski. "We need to talk. Out there." He walked back through the kitchen doors and into the dining room.

"You weren't in the kitchen very long, Mr. Grimes. You sure you saw everything you need to see?"

"I'm scarcely finished with my inspection, Mr. Tomacheski. In fact, you might say I'm just getting started." He pointed back the way they had come. "Mr. Tomacheski, there's a Negro in your kitchen." He folded his arms across his chest and waited for the other man's reply.

Tomacheski blinked, furrowed his brow, and blinked again. "Yes."

"Well, who is he, and what is he doing there?" Grimes could hear his voice climbing a bit, like it always did when his blood pressure went up. He could definitely feel it going up now.

"He's Leon Duffy and he washes dishes, and I'm training him to cook so maybe he won't have to wash dishes the rest of his life." He cocked his head slightly, narrowed his eyes at Grimes. "Is there a problem you have with this arrangement between Mr. Duffy and myself?"

"Just this, Mr. Tomacheski, there are a lot of men—white men—out of work in this country despite Mr. Eisenhower's best efforts. We have an understanding in this town about Negroes, about selling property to them, and about encouraging them to settle here by giving them jobs that could go to white men. Do you take my meaning?"

"Not entirely, Mr. Grimes, but I don't speak the language so well yet. This is a law, this thing about not hiring Negroes?"

"Not exactly a law, Mr. Tomacheski — an understanding."

"There are a lot of these 'understandings' around here, yes?"

"Exactly. And they help keep things running smoothly with very little unpleasantness. That's the way we like it. When you grasp the way things work here, things will run smoothly for you, too." He reached into his portfolio and withdrew a shiny new A-placard with the seal of the Health Department emblazoned in gold in the center of the A. He smiled up at Tomacheski, waiting.

"Curse me for an ignorant immigrant, Mr. Grimes, but I don't understand your 'understanding.' Every night, except for Saturday when I go see a movie, I study the U.S. Constitution for my citizenship test. Nowhere do I find it written that I can't train a dishwasher to be a cook."

Grimes could have sworn that Tomacheski was deliberately avoiding his point. He felt the beginnings of a tension headache crawling up his neck to the back of his skull. He closed his eyes for a moment and took a careful breath. "He'll have to have a blood test, a skin Tuberculin test, and a lung X-ray in order to obtain a food worker's permit. Without a food worker's permit, he cannot work in your kitchen. And to obtain such a permit, he will have to go through my department."

"Oh, he has these things already. He paid for all those tests last week."

His vacation. Crawford had done it while he was away on vacation. The headache arrived in full force. Grimes slipped the A-placard back and pulled out a different one — sun-faded, flyspecked, and marked with a large blue letter B. "My inspection reveals serious nonconformance with Health Department standards. You will remove your temporary permit and display this B-placard until my next inspection."

"But you haven't inspected anything yet!" Tomacheski protested. "This is terribly unfair, Mr. Grimes. You know I deserve an A-card. This restaurant is spotless. You could eat off this floor!"

Grimes glanced at the red and white linoleum, then up at Tomacheski. "County regulations require you to display this card until the premises have been inspected again." He smiled briefly and turned to leave. That should take care of the Negro business.

Tomacheski followed him to the door. "Well, when is the next inspection?"

"You'll have to call for an appointment, but I'll warn you right now, I'm a very busy man. I may not be able to make it back for, oh . . . sixty days."

"No customers will want to come to a B-card restaurant. In sixty days I could be closed down!"

Grimes tucked his portfolio up under his arm. "Business is uncertain in the best of times, Mr. Tomacheski. Perhaps the next proprietor at this location will prove more amenable to the way we do things around here. Good day." He walked out onto the sidewalk. The screen door clicked shut—a lovely sound.

He arrived back at the department in the early afternoon. There was a message from Crawford. He left the day's files on his desk and walked down the hall to Crawford's office.

"Come in," Crawford called from the other side of the door. Grimes walked in and stood before the hopelessly cluttered desk of the Chief Health Officer. He doubted Ed Crawford had seen the surface of his desk in months. "You asked to see me, Ed?"

"Yeah, Mort. What exactly is this Tomacheski business? Did you actually perform an inspection on his premises today, or didn't you?"

So. The Russian had gone over his head. "There are serious problems at that place, Ed."

"You have samples? Is the lab starting cultures?"

"This isn't exactly something you can culture, Ed." He crossed his hands behind his back, tapped his toe on the floor.

Crawford looked up at him expectantly. "Well?"

"This guy Tomacheski has a Negro working for him. As a cook."

"Oh, yes. That would be the fellow who was in here getting tests last week. Don't see too many Negroes applying for food cards around here. Came out clean as a whistle, though." He shuffled through a stack of file folders, scattering loose papers across the desk.

Grimes went on tapping, a little harder now. "Ed, you're a newcomer around here, relatively speaking, and if you'll pardon my saying so, you haven't gone out of your way to fit in—join up—you know what I mean, I guess. But there are things we do in this town and things we don't do. Encouraging Negroes to live and work here is one of the things we just don't do." He nodded sagely, certain that Crawford would understand.

"Let me tell you what I do, Mort," Crawford said, rising from his chair. "I enforce the health regulations and protect the health standards of this county. I do not decide who will live or work here, and neither do you. It's simply not our job." He handed Grimes a sheet of paper. "You have an appointment at ten A.M. tomorrow to conduct a genuine Health Department inspection of Tomacheski's Hole in the Wall and grant or withhold his A-placard based on the results of that inspection. Is that clear?"

Grimes took the appointment slip and left the office. On his way back down the hall he reduced the paper to a tight, sweaty ball in his fist, and lobbed it at a wastebasket. It missed.

Tomacheski met him at the front door. "We've got a little problem back in the kitchen, Mr. Grimes. I don't know if this would be such a good time for your inspection."

Grimes beamed. "You made an appointment. Tomacheski—I'm keeping it." He advanced down the row of stools. Tomacheski retreating before his burning righteousness. "Just what is the nature of your problem?"

"You remember that funny spot on the Ladies' Room wall?"

"Yes, what about it?"

"Well it came back this morning, only worse."

"Probably comes from using cheap paint. I won't be able to pass you if there's any peeling. Lead, you know."

"I'm afraid it's worse than just paint." Tomacheski stopped retreating just outside the kitchen doors.

"Well? Don't just stand there. What happened?"

"It sort of opened up."

"The door to the Ladies' Room?"

"Not exactly. Sort of a hole. Where you thought the paint was bad."

"And?" Grimes was running short of patience with this ignorant commie, or not-commie, whatever he was.

"He's in the kitchen." Tomacheski pushed open the doors with his back and gestured Grimes inside, never taking his eyes from Grimes' face.

Grimes strode into the kitchen. What he saw inside nearly made him stride out again. The Negro was still there, of course, but Grimes scarcely noticed him next to the filthy, louse-ridden Indian sitting on a bench under the window and slurping soup from a Buffalo China cup. Grimes clutched his portfolio under his arm and struggled to control his voice. "What is *that* doing here?"

"That's what I was trying to explain. This hole opened up, you know, on the wall of the Ladies' Room, and he sort of fell through"

"He was in the Ladies' Room?" Grimes could feel his voice rising in step with his blood pressure. *"What was he doing in the Ladies' Room?"*

Tomacheski and the Negro were staring at him in amazement. The Indian had pulled his blanket up over his head and was peeking out with one frightened eye. Grimes stood in one spot and trembled, imagining the bacteria count on one square inch of that skin. He put two fingers on his left wrist and felt his pulse. Not good. This bastard Tomacheski was going to be the death of him. He turned toward the Russian, took two deep breaths and let them out slowly. "What," he repeated in a voice dripping control like icicles, "was this Indian doing in the Ladies' Room?"

"I don't think he was in the Ladies' Room, exactly. You

see, the wall started looking funny again, like it did yesterday and the day before, only this time it got worse, and it turned into a kind of a hole, and there was a great snowstorm on the other side."

"A blizzard," interjected Duffy. "And there was all this snow blowing in on the floor, and all this cold wind, like to froze us both."

"Duffy tells the truth. It was like some other place in there. And then we saw someone walking toward us, and this poor fellow stumbles into the hallway."

"Well, why didn't you push him right back through? He's a walking health hazard!"

"Because he was half-starved and half-frozen to death!" bellowed Tomacheski.

"And also because the hole closed up right after that," Duffy added. "Then it was just the wall again. Wasn't nothin' we could do after that. I think we're stuck with this guy."

"No," Tomacheski said, "I don't think so. What time were you here yesterday, Mr. Grimes?"

"Nine A.M."

"You're sure of that?"

Grimes snorted. "Of course I'm sure."

"And that's when you saw the wall not looking just right. And the morning before that I saw it, too. I'm sure it was about the same time. I thought it was the light, remember? I think that if we just wait around until nine o'clock tomorrow morning . . ."

"Tomorrow morning!"

"Yeah!" said Duffy. "If the hole opens up again tomorrow morning we could put this guy back where he belongs, and everything could get back to normal around here."

"And in the meantime," added Tomacheski, "We could get together some food and warm clothes. Maybe some boots. . . ." He placed his foot next to the Indian's, comparing sizes.

"Mr. Tomacheski, you will take that . . . person to the Social Welfare Department *now* if you want to retain your permit to operate a restaurant." He turned and pushed through the swinging doors, knuckles white around the handle of his portfolio.

Tomacheski followed him into the dining area. "Mr. Crawford promised you would make an inspection."

Grimes turned at the door. "You will be open for business in less than two hours, and in your kitchen there is a filthy, infested savage not six feet from where food is being prepared."

"There's a little porch out back. I'll put him out there. He can't go to the Welfare, Mr. Grimes, he needs to go home."

Grimes said nothing, but fixed the Russian with his gaze.

"You come back tomorrow," Tomacheski said. "You come back and see for yourself. The hole will come back. And then he will go. But not before that, because I've been cold, Mr. Grimes, and I've been hungry, and I've got a home I can never go back to, and I won't do that to nobody."

Grimes looked up at the Russian and anger burned in his breast, clean and bright. "I'll be back at nine tomorrow morning with the Chief Health Officer. Enjoy your day, Mr. Tomacheski. It will be your last doing business in this county." He walked out and slammed the screen behind him.

Grimes adjusted his hat and knocked on Ed Crawford's door.

"Come on in, Mort."

"Ed, it's ten minutes till nine. Aren't you coming to Tomacheski's with me?"

"Yeah, Mort. You go on ahead. I'll be along in a couple of minutes in my car. I've got some things to straighten up here." He indicated a particularly tall pile on the desk.

"Well, hurry, Ed . . . please. This is important."

"Just a few minutes, Mort. I'll meet you there."

The door was open, and Grimes walked in without knocking. He could hear voices coming from the back.

"I think it's starting. Look there."

"Yeah, there it goes. Get him ready, now."

Grimes hurried back to the hallway. Duffy and Tomacheski stood on either side of the Indian with bags of provisions. They were all staring at the Ladies' Room wall, where a widening hole was forming from churning whiteness that boiled out of . . . Grimes steadied himself on Tomacheski's arm and looked away for a moment.

"You see, Mr. Grimes?" Tomacheski was shouting over the roar that was emanating from the hole. "It was true, what I said. This hole goes somewhere. Look!"

The hole was about five feet tall now, and lengthening, but on the other side was not a raging blizzard, but a narrow alley between two tall buildings. The scent of rubber and auto exhaust drifted through. A whistle sounded in the distance, and they could hear shouts and running footsteps. A balding man in a shabby suit rounded the corner of a building and ran straight for them, a blue-coated policeman in hot pursuit. Grimes yelped as the man ran through the wall, bowled him over, and slammed through the kitchen doors.

Duffy and Tomacheski hurried into the kitchen. The Indian looked down at Grimes and said something in its barbaric language that sounded vaguely sympathetic. The hole closed as rapidly as it had opened.

Grimes got up and brushed himself off. This was not going according to plan. And where the hell was Crawford? Well, no matter. He had that immigrant pinko now. No more extensions, no more inspections, just CLOSED. Finis. Done with. He turned and pushed on one door, which flew back in his face as the shabby man rushed back out of the kitchen.

"Where the hell am I?" the man shouted, looking around wildly.

Grimes felt his nose gingerly. It didn't seem to be broken, but it was dripping blood onto his shirt and tie. He placed his folded handkerchief under it. He felt strangely calm in spite of all the shouting and confusion, bums and Indians and colored fry cooks and communist restaurant owners. Ed Crawford would be here any minute and he could wash his hands of this place forever.

Tomacheski and Duffy had followed the bum out of the kitchen and were trying to calm him down. The Indian was standing by Duffy's elbow looking back over his shoulder at

Grimes, who was looking at the Ladies' Room wall. Sweet
Jesus, it was happening again!

A churning nothingness was growing out of the wall, or
into it, shaping itself into a long ovoid that stretched and
grew as he watched, unable to speak or look away. Now
Tomacheski could see it too, and he was backing away in
torturous slow motion, grabbing Duffy by the arm. Their
mouths were moving, but all Grimes could hear was the
awful roaring. He realized he was moving toward the
hole—not walking, it seemed—just gliding across (above?)
the linoleum toward the Ladies' Room wall.

He put his hand out as he came up to it and it tingled like
before, but this time he found it a somewhat pleasant
sensation, and did not pull away. It engulfed his hand,
moved up his arm to his chest, and was all over him in an
instant. From somewhere far away, he felt his face form a
smile.

He was still smiling when he realized he was no longer in
the diner, but in a plain white room with no windows. He
was sitting on a white box on a white floor. The bum and the
Indian were seated on identical boxes, and their faces slowly
began to echo his confusion as they looked around at the
featureless room. A door he hadn't seen opened and a
woman stepped through. She was wearing fewer clothes
than a Pageant Pin-Up, and her hair was bright blue.

"Hello, Mr. Grimes. I hope we haven't startled you."

Grimes thought about it and decided he was definitely
startled. "Where's Tomacheski? Where am I? This can't be
the Ladies' Room." He looked around. Two other odd-
looking people were talking to the bum and the Indian, who
looked pretty startled, too.

The woman smiled. "No, Mr. Grimes, I'm afraid
you're . . . someplace else. This is a holding area, actually. Visually sterile, to minimize unfamiliarity. I'll change
it for you if you like."

A wall appeared, a desk, some bookshelves. The boxes
became chairs. They were alone. She was behind the desk in
a white jacket, a stethoscope peeking out of one pocket. Bad
choice. Doctors' offices always made him sick.

"It's only a temporary displacement, we hope. We seem to have a bug in the system."

"Bug?" Grimes' upper lip wrinkled involuntarily. "There's been a . . . glitch?"

He stared at her blankly.

"A fuck-up."

Grimes blanched.

"Technical difficulties beyond our control. At any rate, we'll have you back in A.D. 1956 very soon." She watched him as he absorbed this, then took a fountain pen out of her coat. "In the meantime, let's talk about Mr. Tomacheski. Give me your hand, please."

He held out his hand and she pushed up his sleeve and passed the pen across the inside of his arm. It didn't leave a mark, so maybe it wasn't a pen, but he began to feel better immediately. Calmer. He still didn't understand, but it didn't seem to matter as much. "What about Tomacheski?" he asked.

"Given your present course of action in A.D. 1956, it seems unlikely that he'll be able to continue doing business in that location."

Grimes shrugged. "I don't particularly want him to stay in business."

"I see. But we do. And we don't consider your wishes to be more important than our own in this matter." She looked around, indicated the paneled office with her hands. "This spot is quite simply the best natural spacetime nexus on this continent, and as long as we control it, we will have things the way we want them. We have decided that Tomacheski will remain in business until A.D. 1975, when he will retire peacefully to California." She looked him in the eye. "We have plans. Those plans require things to remain as they are at Tomacheski's. We won't allow any tampering."

Grimes tried to summon up indignation. "Nobody tells Morton Grimes how to do his job." He didn't sound very indignant, he realized, and he probably ought to be frightened, too, but he couldn't mange it, somehow. "Nobody."

"Wrong Mr. Grimes. We do." She swung her feet up onto the desk. "Of course there is an alternative." She smiled a thin smile not unlike his own. "We could always keep you here."

"You could what? What do you mean keep me? I'm a citizen. I have rights. I want to call my lawyer! Who the hell are you, anyway?" He suddenly remembered how to be frightened.

She leaned forward and stroked his arm again with the pen. Or whatever. "One point at a time, Mr. Grimes. To begin with, your rights are moot here. If by 'you' you mean me, I am the person currently giving you orders. Think of me as a doctor of sorts. If you mean all of us here, we are the party, clan, race—choose one or more as you wish—currently in charge of this locus. However powerful you may imagine us to be from what you have seen, you will almost certainly be underestimating us. We try not to be deliberately cruel to primitives, but we don't take shit from anybody. I hope that answers your questions. Believe me when I say that nothing can stop us from keeping you if we wish to do so."

Grimes nodded and shook a finger at her unsteadily. "You're talking time travel, here. I've seen 'Science Fiction Theater'; I know about these things. Well, then, what about my life? Won't it change something if I don't go back?"

She leaned back in the chair, hands in pockets. "Frankly, Mr. Grimes, you'd scarcely be missed. You never marry, never have children, never really affect another person's life in any significant way."

"You don't mean it. You can't keep me here." He crossed his arms in front of him, made an effort to frown, abandoned it.

"You don't know that, Mr. Grimes." She chuckled softly, shaking her head. "It's amusing, actually, when you see it from our point of view. You think you have a right to control other people's fate—Duffy, Tomacheski, the Indian—because you think you're naturally superior to them. That's bigotry. We control your fate because we actually *are* superior. That's simple fact."

The words stung. Grimes searched for a retort, but nothing came to him that he couldn't imagine her laughing off in that arrogant way, and then the moment for rebuttal passed, leaving him silent and powerless.

She watched him calmly for a moment, then cocked her head to one side as though listening to something he couldn't hear. "The malfunction has been repaired," she said, getting up from behind the desk. "The others will be waiting." The room dissolved to featureless white.

They were standing beside the Indian and the bum and two people even stranger-looking than his "doctor." The wall was going funny. A blinding whiter whiteness opened up in it—the sun on snow, with tall firs on a hill. The Indian shouldered his bags of Tomacheski's food and stepped through.

The hole closed, and opened again on an alley at night with a moon and streetlights shining on brick walls and wet pavement. There was a scent of rain and garbage. One of the people handed the bum a wad of genuine-looking currency and shook his hand. The bum gave Grimes a little wave and walked in.

"Your turn, Mr. Grimes," the doctor said, turning to him. "Which will it be? Return on our terms—or stay?"

He thought for a moment. How important was this immigrant diner-jockey in Morton Grimes' scheme of things? The world was going to hell anyway, and it wasn't going to get there any faster if one Russian hired one Negro to grill hamburgers. Maybe he shouldn't worry so much.

He had a choice, she said. He supposed he did, but he wouldn't have any problem making it. The world was changing a little faster than he would like, even in 1956, but even given that, it was a damn sight better than dirty-talking blue-haired women and disappearing doctors' offices and being treated like an invading bacillus. None of it seemed to be worth his time and trouble at this point.

"I can go back if I promise to leave Tomacheski alone?"

"You are not permitted to take any action that will endanger him or his business."

He supposed he could live with that. "Fine," he told her. "I'll go." He buttoned his shirtsleeve, straightened his tie and jacket. His hat must have blown off as he came through.

He ran fingers through his hair as the hole began to grow again.

"You should arrive within a minute or so of your departure. Have an adequate life, Mr. Grimes, and remember—we'll be watching."

The hole punched through to the diner, with an agitated Tomacheski and Duffy talking and gesturing to someone he couldn't see. Grimes looked back for a moment to see if he was really free to go.

"You'd better hurry, or you'll miss this one. Go on." She made a hurry along gesture to him, and he stepped forward onto his hat and into the arms of Ed Crawford.

"Mort! What the hell were you doing in the Ladies' Room? And where's that Indian you were raving about? You okay, Mort? You look terrible."

Grimes stepped back and turned around. The wall was a wall again. He picked up the hat and made a few useless attempts at straightening it, then put it on his head. He needed a drink, he decided—maybe two. He turned to Tomacheski, who was watching him expectantly. "My inspection is completed. Don't bother to see me out—I'll leave your A-placard on my way. Coming, Ed?"

Crawford looked confused, but turned to go.

"What about the Indian?" Tomacheski whispered, pointing at the wall.

"And the bum?" Duffy added.

Grimes stooped to pick up his portfolio from the hallway floor. Suddenly he felt incredibly tired. He didn't understand the present, and the future stunk. He looked from Duffy to Tomacheski and nodded slowly, more to himself than to either of them. "Home," he said, tucking the case under his arm and following Crawford out of the hallway. "They've gone home."

Straightening his shoulders, Grimes walked down the narrow length of shining linoleum, pulsing pink and green with neon light, and paused to flip the A-placard onto the counter before he opened the screen door and let it click shut behind him.

•   •   •

He was home too, he supposed, but he couldn't find much joy in it, not given what he knew. He turned and looked back at the little diner and the garish sign, and at Duffy and Tomacheski watching him from the doorway. He scowled at them; they smiled and waved.

"The world is going straight to hell," he told them . . . but not loud enough so that they'd hear.

He pulled his hat low against the sunlight, and walked away.

TIME'S ARROW

Jack McDevitt

Born in Philadelphia, Jack McDevitt now lives in Brunswick, Georgia with his family. He is a frequent contributor to Asimov's Science Fiction *and has also sold stories to* Analog. The *Magazine of Fantasy and Science Fiction, Full Spectrum, Universe, The Twilight Zone Magazine, Chess Life, and elsewhere. An ex-naval officer, ex-English teacher, and ex-customs inspector, he retired in 1995 and now works full time as a writer. His first novel,* The Hercules Text, *was a second place winner of the Philip K. Dick award. His next novel was the popular* A Talent for War. *His most recent books are a major new novel,* Ancient Shores, *and a collection of his short work,* Standard Candles. *Coming up is another new novel,* Eternity Road.*

Here he gives us an ingenious story that suggests that if you open a window into the turbulent and dangerous past, you sometimes might not like the view . . .

"It can't be done." I stared at him, and at the gunmetal ten-foot-high torus that dominated the room. "Time travel is prohibited."

He pushed a stack of printouts off a coffee table to make room for his Coors, and fell onto the sofa. It sagged and threatened to collapse under his bulk. "Gillie," he said, "you've got all those old Civil War flags and that drum from—ah—?"

"Fredericksburg."

"Yeah. And how many times have you been to the battlefields? Listen, we can go see the real thing. Fort Sumter. Bull Run. You name it." His easy, confident smile chilled me. "It is possible to reverse the arrow of time.

Tonight you and I will have dinner in the nineteenth century."

"Mac," I said, adopting a reasonable tone, "think about it a minute. If it could be done, someone will eventually learn how. If that ever happens, history would be littered with tourists. They'd be *everywhere*. They'd be on the *Santa Maria*, they'd be at Appomattox with Polaroids, they'd be waiting outside the tomb, for God's sake, on Easter morning."

He nodded. "I know. It *is* odd. I don't understand why there's no evidence."

I drew back thick curtains. Sunlight sliced through grimy windows. Across the empty street, I could see Harvey Keating, trying to get his lawnmower started. "In fact, if you were the father of time travel, they'd be out there now. Knocking down barricades—"

He nodded. "I hear what you're saying." He looked past me, and out toward the front of the house. A pickup cruised by. Keating's lawnmower kicked into life. "Still," he said quietly, "it works." He jabbed an index finger toward the torus, and then expanded his arms in a grand gesture that took in the entire room, computer banks, gauges, power cord tangles, rolltop desk. Everything. "It works," he repeated, even more softly. "I've tested it."

I blinked. "How? Are you saying you've been to the nineteenth century?"

His gray eyes lost focus. "I've been *somewhere*," he said. "I'm not sure where." He wiped the back of his hand across his mouth. "I finally realized the problem was in the stasis coils—"

"What happened, Mac?"

"Gillie, I landed in the middle of a riot."

"You're kidding."

"Yes. I damn near got trampled. There was a labor demonstration on the other side."

"On the other side?"

"Of the nexus." He gestured toward the torus. "At least that's what it looked like. People carrying signs, making speeches. Just as I crossed over, a bomb went off. In the back of the crowd somewhere. Cops waded in, swinging sticks. It was pretty grim. *But they had handlebar mustaches. And old-time uniforms.*" He took a deep breath. "We were outside somewhere. In the street." His eyes focused behind me. "Goddammit, Gillie, I've done it. I was *really* there."

"Where? Where *were* you?"

"I think it was the Haymarket Riot. I was on Jefferson Street, and that's where it happened. I spent the day at the library trying to pin it down."

"The Haymarket Riot? Why would you go there?"

"I was trying to get to the Scopes monkey trial." He shrugged. "I missed. But what difference does it make?" His eyes gleamed. "I've *done* it." He swept up a half-full beer can and heaved it across the room. "I have goddam done it!"

"Show me," I said.

He smiled. Genuine pleasure. "That's why you're here. How would you like to see *Our American Cousin*? On *the* night?"

I stared at him.

He handed me another Coors—it was mine that had gone for a ride—stepped over a snarl of power cables and octopus plugs, turned on a couple of the computers and opened a closet. Status lamps glowed, and columns of numbers appeared on monitors. "You'll need these," he said, tossing me some clothes. "We don't want to be conspicuous."

"I think I'd prefer to see him at Gettysburg."

"Oh." He looked annoyed. "I could arrange that, but I'd have to recalibrate. It would take a couple of days." The clothes were right out of *Gone With the Wind*. He produced a second set for himself.

"I don't think they'll fit," I said.

He nodded his satisfaction as if I hadn't spoken, and jabbed at a keyboard. A legend appeared on one of the monitors: **TEMPORAL INTERLOCK GREEN**. "The heart of the system," he said, indicating a black box with two alternately flashing red mode lamps. "It's the Transdimen-

sional Interface. The TDI." He placed his right hand gently
against its polished surface. "It coordinates power applica-
tions with field angles—"

I let him talk, understanding none of it. I was an old
friend of McHugh's, which was why I was there. But I was
no physicist. Not that you had to be, to understand that the
past is irrevocable. While he rambled on, I climbed reluctantly into the clothes he'd provided.

The twin lamps blinked at a furious rate, slowed, changed
to amber, and came gradually to a steady green.

"The energy field will be established along the nexus.
We'll make our transition about a mile and a half outside
D.C., at nine in the morning, local time. Should allow us to
travel to the theater at our leisure."

His fingers danced across the keyboard. Relays clicked,
and somewhere in the walls power began to build. A splinter
of white light ignited in the center of the torus. It brightened,
lengthened, rotated. "Don't look at it," McHugh said. I
turned away.

The floor trembled. Windows rattled, a few index cards
fluttered off a shelf, a row of black binders fell one by one
out of a bookcase. "Any moment now, Gillie," he said. The
general clatter intensified until I thought the building would
come down on us. It ended in a loud electrical bang and a
burst of sudden sunlight. Ozone flooded the room. Time
broke off. Stopped. McHugh held one arm high, shielding
his eyes. A final binder tottered and crashed. Then a blast of
wind knocked me off my feet and across the coffee table. I
went down in a hurricane of printouts, pencils, clips, and
beer cans, grabbed a table leg, and held on. Magnetic disks
and plastic plates whipped through the room. A chair fell
over and began to move toward the torus. Windows ex-
ploded; the curtains flapped wildly.

A rectangular piece of clear sky, a cloud-flecked hole,
filled the torus. Everything not bolted down, books, paper
plates, card files, monitors, a Rolodex, you name it, was
being sucked toward it, and blown through. McHugh almost
went too when the console to which he was clinging broke
loose.

He bounced past, terrified, and seized the sofa. The console crunched through the hole, sailed out among the clouds. Mac's lower half went next. He screamed.

The sky was full of clothes and printouts and magazines and index cards.

I maneuvered my table closer until I could reach him. He held out a hand, but I ignored it and wrapped my arms around his shoulders. His eyes were wide with terror. The paper storm continued: where the hell was it all coming from? A computer broke loose and went out.

Like the console, it slid across the sky. I watched it, and, impossibly, my senses rotated, the way they do when you're sitting under one of those giant cinema screens, and I realized I was looking straight down. I could see forest down there, and a river. And green and gold squares of cultivated land.

Something with feathers flapped through a window, blurred across the room and was flung out among the clouds.

The river flowed past farmhouses, past orchards, past a town.

The land was unbroken by highways or automobile traffic. But down through the clouds a half-built obelisk gleamed in full sunlight.

"Gillie—" He let go of me long enough to clap me on the back. "That's the Washington Monument."

"Mac," I howled. "What the hell's going on?"

"We're *here*, goddammit. *Now* what do you say?" He laughed and his eyes watered and the table lurched a few inches. Matter of time.

Do something. Close the goddam hole. An octopus socket lay nearby. Cut the power, that was it. But when I picked it up, McHugh's state of alarm soared. He stabbed a frantic finger at his legs. I'd pulled him back somewhat, but everything below his knees was still thrust out into space.

Okay: try something else. The coffee table was too wide to go through the hole. But if I could keep it sideways, I might be able to wedge it against the torus. Block off the hole. Not all of it, but enough.

I changed my position, got behind the table. And pushed. McHugh saw what I was doing, and nodded encouragement. Yes. His lips formed the word. Yes, yes. I held on as long as I could, fearful that the table would twist in the gale, that I would lose it, and then follow it. "Get your legs out of the way," I screamed. "I need room."

He shook his head. Can't do it. But I didn't need to tell him that I no longer controlled events, that the table was moving under its own power, and that he should do it or his legs were going south. He made another effort, and wrenched himself clear just as the furniture and I arrived at the nexus. The table jammed tight against the sides of the torus.

It shut off *some* of the drag. Not much, but some. More important, it gave McHugh a place to put his feet. He was now reeling in the octopus plug himself, and began methodically, angrily, disconnecting everything. Across the room, a radio came on. Then, abruptly, the hurricane died.

"You were right," I said in the sudden silence. "We were about a mile and a half from D.C."

"Ready?" He stood by the TDI. It was almost two weeks after the first attempt.

"Should we wear seatbelts?"

He grinned. Very much the man in charge. "You can have your little joke. But I've made some adjustments on the transition phase. I think I can promise we'll be at ground level this time." The twin mode lamps on the TDI went to green.

"Same destination?"

"Of course." He hovered over the Macintosh which would initiate the sequence. "Ready?"

I nodded, positioning myself near the table.

He touched the keyboard, and the tiny star reappeared. I turned away as it brightened. We got the electrical effects again, and the ozone. And the sudden, intoxicating bite of salt air. The hole was back.

It was night on the other side of the torus. A lovely evening, composed of a broad dark sea, blazing constellations, and a lighthouse. A quarter moon lay on the surface. Surf boomed, and a line of white water approached.

I felt spray.

"Goddam." McHugh froze.

The ocean surged in. Black water crashed against the furniture, boiled around the walls, smashed the windows. And shorted the lights.

The hole collapsed.

"Here we go." He wiped his jaw with the back of his hand. Sweat stood out on his forehead.

"Okay."

"This time we'll get it right." There was no smile now.

Everything was bolted down and well off the floor. The room had been cleared of all furniture and nonessentials. I wondered whether we hadn't been lucky. What would have happened if the hole had opened in the depths of the ocean? Or far beneath the surface in a stratum crushed under ten thousand feet of rock? "Mac," I said, "maybe we should forget it."

He shook his head vigorously. "Don't be ridiculous."

"I mean it. I get the feeling somebody's trying to tell us something."

McHugh pulled on his waistcoat and bent over a display. "System's fully charged. We're all set, Gillie. You want to do the honors?"

Reluctantly, I walked over to the TDI, looked at him, looked at the torus. Looked at the keyboard. It was a new computer.

"Okay," he said, trying to look casual, but bracing himself all the same. "Any time."

I did it, and the process started again.

This time, we found summer. Green meadows stretched toward a nearby line of wooded hills. Goldenrod, thistles, and black-eyed susans covered the fields. Afternoon invaded the room, and, with a thump, the air conditioner kicked in.

"At last," said McHugh, standing before the torus, gazing through it. "1865," he breathed. For a long time, he didn't move. Then: "Now, listen, Gillie: the nexus will close five minutes after we pass through. But it will open again for five minutes every twelve hours until we come back to shut it down. Okay? Make sure you remember where we are. In case you have to find your own way back."

Without another word, he stepped through. His image flickered momentarily, as if in a heat wave. On the other side, he raised a fist in silent triumph, and gazed at his surroundings. "Come on, Gillie. Come on over." He produced a bottle and two glasses, filled them, and held one toward me.

I hesitated.

"It's okay," he said.

I gathered my courage, and stepped through the time device. I will admit I was now convinced. Maybe it was that the notion of time travel was no more absurd than the presence of a broad field in one's living room. In any case, I strolled from the carpet onto dry grass. The air was thick with the drowsy buzz of insects and the heat of the sun. I took the glass. The bright liquid within sparkled. "To you, Mac," I said.

McHugh loosened his tie. "To the Creator," he said, "who has given us a universe with such marvelous possibilities."

The afternoon smelled vaguely of sulfur. I took my coat off. We stood on a broad field enclosed by rising forest. A dark haze hung over the valley. In the distance, I could make out a town. It looked small. Hot and dusty. Several clusters of farm buildings were distributed at the foot of the ridges, guarded by low stone walls and fences constructed of posts and rails. A wagon waited in one of the farmyards. But they all stood strangely empty. No farmers. No cows. No horses or dogs. A dirt road, also fenced, wandered through the center of the valley.

I fell in beside McHugh and we angled off toward the road. "Where the hell is everybody?" I asked.

He ignored the question. "Do you notice the farmhouses have no TV antennas?"

"I notice," I said. "On the other hand, it must be July or August." I mopped my brow. "Certainly not April."

He nodded, but showed no sign of disappointment. He was happy to have arrived somewhere. *Anywhere*, if it turned out to be Lincoln's America. "I agree. We've missed again. But what the hell—"

Nothing moved anywhere in the valley. The sun was hot in my eyes, and I knew the landscape.

I knew the ridges, the farms, the town. "Mac," I said, "where are the birds?" The sky was empty. Behind us, the torus hovered, McHugh's computer-laden back room vivid against the rolling hills and forest. "Maybe we should go back."

He responded by removing his jacket. "You go back if you want to, Gillie." His eyes gleamed, and he looked happier than I'd ever seen him. He fished his watch out of his pocket, glanced at it, looked at the sun, which was on our left, and shrugged. "Let's make it three o'clock," he said, setting the timepiece and winding it. He dropped it back into the pocket and folded the coat over his arm.

Near the town, a flag fluttered from a stone wall. We were too far away to count the number of stars in the blue field, but it *was* the national colors. I was squinting at it, when I heard the breath catch in McHugh's throat. He was peering over my shoulder, back toward the torus, toward the line of hills behind it.

"What's wrong?" I asked. His workroom still floated peacefully in the afternoon.

"The woods," he said. "Behind the nexus."

Yes: among the trees, something was moving.

As I watched, the sun struck metal, and the forest came alive with men in gray uniforms. They remained within the shelter of the trees, but I could see them moving, kneeling just beyond the sunlight, others coming in behind. Forming up.

My God. "What's going on?" asked McHugh. "Where are we?"

A bugle call split the afternoon.

And they came out in oiled precision, bayonets gleaming among battle flags. Drums rolled. Columns wheeled smartly into line and started quickstep toward us.

Behind them, on the hilltops, guns roared. Puffs of smoke appeared on the opposite ridge. And I got a good look at the standards: "Son of a bitch, Mac," I said. "It's the 24th Virginia."

I watched them come. They seemed unaware of the torus, which I suspected was invisible from the rear. Their lines were perfectly dressed, officers with drawn swords on horseback. There were thousands of them, literally parading out into that open field as far as I could see.

"Over there," I said. "The 7th Virginia. And up the line will be the 11th. Jesus." I was overwhelmed by the majesty of it. "You're right, Mac. We're *here*. Son of a bitch—"

"Gillie," he said, "we're *where?* What the hell's going on?"

A long orchestrated crescendo shook the top of the opposite ridge. "Down," I screamed, throwing myself on my belly and covering my head.

The ground erupted. Earth and rocks flew. Holes were blown in the ranks of the advancing men. Others hurried to fill up the spaces. "This is *Kemper's* Brigade," I said. He was staring at me, not comprehending I was surveying the ridges and road. The fences and stone walls. The farms. The town. "You've been dumped on again, Mac." I was getting to my feet. "We've got to get away from here."

The cannonade was deafening. Thunder rolled down from both slopes. The troops came on. Silent. Walking into the fire because their generals didn't understand yet that the war had changed.

McHugh was trying to restrain me. "Stay down," he said. "We'll wait it out."

"No," I shrieked. "Not this one. We've got to get back before the hole closes."

"You're crazy. You'll get killed."

"We won't survive out here." I was shaking my head violently. "You know what that is back there? It's Seminary Ridge."

McHugh was close to my ear, but he had to shout anyway. "So what?"

"Pickett's Charge," I said. "We're in the middle of Pickett's Charge."

We got back moments before a cannonball roared through the workroom, blew three walls apart, collapsed the front porch, and nailed Harvey Keating's Toyota, which was parked in his driveway.

The equipment was in ruins. Again.

Nevertheless, McHugh was exultant. "You see?" he said. "It *is* possible."

And I trembled. I trembled because I knew that, for a few minutes on the third day of the battle, I had actually been at Gettysburg.

And I trembled for another reason. "Mac," I said. "You've made four attempts now. All four have been disasters."

"But we're *learning*," he said. "We're getting better. You have to expect problems. But we *know* how to *travel*."

"That's what scares me." I looked around the smoking ruins. "What are the odds against *accidentally* arriving at the exact time and place of a major event?"

He shrugged. "Slim, I would think."

"You've done it twice."

I knew he wouldn't quit, though. He bought more equipment, and went back to work. "Making improvements," he said. A few weeks later he was ready to try again, and issued another invitation. I told him no thanks. I could see he was disappointed in me.

But hell, I can take a hint.

So I wasn't too surprised when his newspapers started piling up. I waited a couple of days and broke in.

The house was empty.

In the back room, I found his equipment intact. Except for the TDI: a stone-tipped feathered arrow jutted from its polished black metal. It had penetrated right between the mode lamps.

ANNIVERSARY PROJECT

Joe Haldeman

We never really know what the future holds in store for us, in spite of all the money people spend on psychic hot lines and Tarot card readings. And, as the sly and ironic story that follows demonstrates, perhaps that's just as well . . .

Born in Oklahoma City, Oklahoma, Joe Haldeman took a B.S. degree in physics and astronomy from the University of Maryland and did postgraduate work in mathematics and computer science. But his plans for a career in science were cut short by the U.S. Army, which sent him to Vietnam in 1968 as a combat engineer. Seriously wounded in action, Haldeman returned home in 1969 and began to write. He sold his first story to Galaxy in 1969, and by 1976 had garnered both the Nebula Award and the Hugo Award for his famous novel, The Forever War, one of the landmark books of the 1970s. He won another Hugo Award in 1977 for his story "Tricentennial," and then the Rhysling Award in 1983 for the best science fiction poem of the year. (Although usually thought of primarily as a "hard-science" writer, Haldeman is, in fact, also an accomplished poet and has sold poetry to most of the major professional markets in the genre.) He won both the Nebula and the Hugo Award in 1991 for the novella version of "The Hemingway Hoax." His story "None So Blind" won the Hugo Award in 1995. His other books include a mainstream novel, War Year, the SF novels Mindbridge, All My Sins Remembered, There Is No Darkness (written with his brother, SF writer Jack C. Haldeman II) Worlds, Worlds Apart, Worlds Enough and Time, Buying Time, and The Hemingway Hoax, the "techno-thriller" Tools of the Trade, the collections Infinite Dreams, Dealing in Futures, and Vietnam and Other Alien Worlds, and, as editor, the anthologies Study War No More, Cosmic Laughter, and Nebula Award Stories Seventeen. His most recent books are a major new mainstream novel, 1969, and a new collection, None So Blind. Haldeman lives part of the year in

*Boston, where he teaches writing at the Massachusetts
Institute of Technology, and the rest in Florida, where he and
his wife, Gay, make their home.*

H*is name is* Three-phasing and he is bald and wrinkled,
slightly over one meter tall, large-eyed, toothless and all
bones and skin, sagging pale skin shot through with
traceries of delicate blue and red. He is considered very
beautiful but most of his beauty is in his hands and is due to
his extreme youth. He is over two hundred years old and is
learning how to talk. He has become reasonably fluent in
sixty-three languages, all dead ones, and has only ten to go.

The book he is reading is a facsimile of an early edition
of Goethe's *Faust*. The nervous angular Fraktur letters
goose-step across pages of paper-thin platinum.

The *Faust* had been printed electrolytically and, with
several thousand similarly worthwhile books, sealed in an
argon-filled chamber and carefully lost, in 2012 A.D.; a very
wealthy man's legacy to the distant future.

In 2012 A.D., Polaris had been the pole star. Men
eventually got to Polaris and built a small city on a frosty
planet there. By that time, they weren't dating by prophets'
births any more, but it would have been around 4900 A.D.
The pole star by then, because of procession of the
equinoxes, was a dim thing once called Gamma Cephei. The
celestial pole kept reeling around, past Deneb and Vega and
through barren patches of sky around Hercules and Draco;
a patient clock but not the slowest one of use, and when it
came back to the region of Polaris, then 26,000 years had
passed and men had come back from the stars, and the
book-filled chamber had shifted 130 meters on the floor of
the Pacific, had rolled onto the shallow trench, and eventually was buried in an underwater landslide.

The thirty-seventh time this slow clock ticked, men had
moved the Pacific, not because they had to, and had found
the chamber, opened it up, identified the books and carefully

sealed them up again. Some things by then were more important to men than the accumulation of knowledge: in half of one more circle of the poles would come the millionth anniversary of the written word. They could wait a few millennia.

As the anniversary, as nearly as they could reckon it, approached, they caused to be born two individuals: Nine-hover (nominally female) and Three-phasing (nominally male). Three-phasing was born to learn how to read and speak. He was the first human being to study these skills in more than a quarter of a million years.

Three-phasing has read the first half of *Faust* forwards and, for amusement and exercise, is reading the second half backwards. He is singing as he reads, lisping.

"Fain' Looee w'mun . . . wif all'r die-mun ringf . . ." He has not put in his teeth because they make his gums hurt.

Because he is a child of two hundred, he is polite when his father interrupts his reading and singing. His father's "voice" is an arrangement of logic and aesthetic that appears in Three-phasing's mind. The flavor is lost by translating into words:

"Three-phasing my son-ly atavism of tooth and vocal cord," sarcastically in the reverent mode, "Couldst tear thyself from objects of manifest symbol, and visit to share/help/learn, me?"

"?" He responds, meaning, "with/with/of what?"

Withholding mode: "Concerning thee: past, future."

He shuts the book without marking his place. It would never occur to him to mark his place, since he remembers perfectly the page he stops on, as well as every word preceding, as well as every event, no matter how trivial, that he has observed from the precise age of one year. In this respect, at least, he is normal.

He thinks the proper coordinates as he steps over the mover-transom, through a microsecond of black, and onto his father's mover-transom, about four thousand kilometers away on a straight line through the crust and mantle of the earth.

Ritual mode: "As ever, father." The symbol he uses for

"father" is purposefully wrong, chiding. Crude biological connotation.

His father looks cadaverous and has in fact been dead twice. In the infant's small-talk mode he asks "From crude babblings of what sort have I torn your interest?"

"The tale called *Faust*, of a man so named, never satisfied with {symbol for slow but continuous accretion} of his knowledge and power; written in the language of Prussia."

"Also depended-ing on this strange word of immediacy, your Prussian language?"

"As most, yes. The word of 'to be': *sein*. Very important illusion in this and related languages/cultures; that events happen at the 'time' of perception, infinitesimal midpoint between past and future."

"Convenient illusion but retarding."

"As we discussed 129 years ago, yes." Three-phasing is impatient to get back to his reading, but adds:

"Obvious that to-be-ness $\begin{cases} \text{same order of illusion as three-dimensionality of external world.} \\ \text{thrust upon observer by geometric limitation of synaptic degrees of freedom.} \end{cases}$"

"You always stick up for them."

"I have great regard for what they accomplished with limited faculties and so short lives." Stop beatin' around the bush, Dad. *Tempis fugit*, eight to the bar. Did Mr. Handy Moves-dat-man-around-by-her-apron-strings, 20th-century American poet, intend cultural translation of *Lysistrata?* If so, inept. African were-beast legendry, yes.

Withholding mode (coy): "Your father stood with Nine-hover all morning."

"," broadcasts Three-phasing: well?

"The machine functions, perhaps inadequately."

The young polyglot tries to radiate calm patience.

"Details I perceive you want; the idea yet excites you. You can never have satisfaction with your knowledge, either. What happened-s to the man in your Prussian book?"

"He lived-s one hundred years and died-s knowing that a man can never achieve true happiness, despite the appearance of success."

"For an infant, a reasonable perception."

Respectful chiding mode: "One hundred years makes-ed Faust a very old man, for a Dawn man."

"As I stand," same mode, less respect, "yet an infant." They trade silent symbols of laughter.

After a polite tenth-second interval, Three-phasing uses the light interrogation mode: "The machine of Nine-hover . . . ?"

"It begins to work but so far not perfectly." This is not news.

Mild impatience: "As before, then, it brings back only rocks and earth and water and plants?"

"Negative, beloved atavism." Offhand: "This morning she caught two animals that look as man may once have looked.

"!" Strong impatience, "I go?"

"." His father ends the conversation just two seconds after it began.

Three-phasing stops off to pick up his teeth, then goes directly to Nine-hover.

A quick exchange of greeting-symbols and Nine-hover presents her prizes. "Thinking I have two different species," she stands: uncertainty, query.

Three-phasing is amused. "Negative, time-caster. The male and female took very dissimilar forms in the Dawn times." He touches one of them. "The round organs, here, served-ing to feed infants, in the female."

The female screams.

"She manipulates spoken symbols now," observes Nine-hover.

Before the woman has finished her startled yelp, Three-phasing explains: "Not manipulating concrete symbols; rather, she communicates in a way called 'non-verbal,' the use of such communication predating even speech." Slipping into the pedantic mode: "My reading indicates that such a loud noise occurs either

$$\left\{\begin{array}{l}\text{-following a stimu-}\\\text{lus under conditions of}\end{array}\right.$$

$\left.\begin{array}{l}\text{that produces pain}\\\text{extreme agitation}\end{array}\right\{$ since she seems not in pain, then she must fear me or you or both of us.

"Or the machine," Nine-hover adds.

Symbol for continuing. "We have no symbol for it but in Dawn days most humans observed 'xenophobia,' reacting to the strange with fear instead of delight. We stand as strange to them as they do to us, thus they register fear. In their era this attitude encouraged-s survival.

"Our silence must seem strange to them, as well as our appearance and the speed with which we move. I will attempt to speak to them, so they will know they need not fear us."

Bob and Sarah Graham were having a desperately good time. It was September of 1951 and the papers were full of news about the brilliant landing of U.S. Marines at Inchon. Bob was a Marine private with two days left of the thirty days' leave they had given him, between boot camp and disembarkation for Korea. Sarah had been Mrs. Graham for three weeks.

Sarah poured some more bourbon into her Coke. She wiped the sand off her thumb and stoppered the Coke bottle, then shook it gently. "What if you just don't show up?" she said softly.

Bob was staring out over the ocean and part of what Sarah said was lost in the crash of breakers rolling in. "What if I what?"

"Don't show up." She took a swig and offered the bottle.

"Just stay here with me. With us." Sarah was sure she was pregnant. It was too early to tell, of course; her calendar was off but there could be other reasons.

He gave the Coke back to her and sipped directly from the bourbon bottle. "I suppose they'd go on without me. And I'd still be in jail when they came back."

"Not if—"

"Honey, don't even talk like that. It's a just cause."

She picked up a small shell and threw it toward the water.

"Besides, you read the *Examiner* yesterday."

"I'm cold. Let's go up." She stood and stretched and delicately brushed sand away. Bob admired her long naked dancer's body. He shook out the blanket and draped it over her shoulders.

"It'll be over by the time I get there. We'll push those bastards—"

"Let's not talk about Korea. Let's not talk."

He put his arm around her and they started walking back toward the cabin. Halfway there, she stopped and enfolded the blanket around both of them, drawing him toward her. He always closed his eyes when they kissed, but she always kept hers open. She saw it: the air turning luminous, the seascape fading to be replaced by bare metal walls. The sand turns hard under her feet.

At her sharp intake of breath, Bob opens his eyes. He sees a grotesque dwarf, eyes and skull too large, body small and wrinkled. They stare at one another for a fraction of a second. Then the dwarf spins around and speeds across the room to what looks like a black square painted on the floor. When he gets there, he disappears.

"What the hell?" Bob says in a hoarse whisper.

Sarah turns around just a bit too late to catch a glimpse of Three-phasing's father. She does see Nine-hover before Bob does. The nominally-female time-caster is a flurry of movement, sitting at the console of her time net, clicking switches and adjusting various dials. All of the motions are unnecessary, as is the console. It was built at Three-phasing's suggestion, since humans from the era into which they could cast would feel more comfortable in the presence of a machine that looked like a machine. The actual time net was roughly the size and shape of an asparagus stalk, was controlled completely by thought, and had no moving parts. It does not exist any more, but can still be used, once understood. Nine-hover has been trained from birth for this special understanding.

Sarah nudges Bob and points to Nine-hover. She can't find her voice; Bob stares open-mouthed.

In a few seconds, Three-phasing appears. He looks at Nine-hover for a moment, then scurries over to the Dawn couple and reaches up to touch Sarah on the left nipple. His body temperature is considerably higher than hers, and the unexpected warm moistness, as much as the suddenness of the motion, makes her jump back and squeal.

Three-phasing correctly classified both Dawn people as Caucasian, and so assumes that they speak some Indo-European language.

"*GuttenTagsprechesieDeutsch?*" he says in rapid soprano.

"Huh?" Bob says.

"*Guten-Tag-sprechen-sie-Deutsch?*" Three-phasing clears his throat and drops his voice down to the alto he uses to sing about the St. Louis woman. "*Guten Tag,*" he says, counting to a hundred between each word. "*Sprechen sie Deutsch?*"

"That's Kraut," says Bob, having grown up on jingoistic comic books. "Don't tell me you're a—"

Three-phasing analyzes the first five words and knows that Bob is an American from the period 1935–1955. "Yes, yes—and no, no—to wit, how very very clever of you to have identified this phrase as having come from the language of Prussia, Germany as you say; but I am, no, not a German person; at least, I no more belong to the German nationality than I do to any other, but I suppose that is not too clear and perhaps I should fully elucidate the particulars of your own situation at this, as you say, 'time,' and 'place.'"

The last English-language author Three-phasing studied was Henry James.

"Huh?" Bob says again.

"Ah. I should simplify." He thinks for a half-second, and drops his voice down another third. "Yeah, simple. Listen, Mac. First thing I gotta know's whatcher name. Watcher broad's name."

"Well . . . I'm Bob Graham. This is my wife, Sarah Graham."

"Pleasta meetcha, Bob. Likewise, Sarah. Call me, uh . . ." The only twentieth-century language in which Three-phasing's name makes sense is propositional calculus. "George. George Boole."

"I 'poligize for bumpin' into ya, Sarah. That broad in the corner, she don't know what a tit is, so I was just usin' one of yours. Uh, lack of immediate culchural perspective, I shoulda knowed better."

Sarah feels a little dizzy, shakes her head slowly. "That's all right. I know you didn't mean anything by it."

"I'm dreaming," Bob says. "Shouldn't have—"

"No you aren't," says Three-phasing, adjusting his diction again. "You're in the future. Almost a million years. Pardon me." He scurries to the mover-transom, is gone for a second, reappears with a bedsheet, which he hands to Bob. "I'm sorry, we don't wear clothing. This is the best I can do, for now." The bedsheet is too small for Bob to wear the way Sarah is using the blanket. He folds it over and tucks it around his waist, in a kilt. "Why us?" he asks.

"You were taken at random. We've been time casting"— he checks with Nine-hover—"for twenty-two years, and have never before caught a human being. Let alone two. You must have been in close contact with one another when you intersected the time-caster beam. I assume you were copulating."

"What-ing?" Bob says.

"No, we weren't!" Sarah says indignantly.

"Ah, quite so." Three-phasing doesn't pursue the topic. He knows the humans of this culture were reticent about their sexual activity. But from their literature he knows they spent most of their "time" thinking about, arranging for, enjoying and recovering from a variety of sexual contacts.

"Then that must be a time machine over there," Bob says, indicating the fake console.

"In a sense, yes." Three-phasing decides to be partly honest. "But the actual machine no longer exists. People did a lot of time-traveling about a quarter of a million years ago. Shuffled history around. Changed it back. The fact that the machine once existed, well, that enables us to use it, if you see what I mean."

"Uh, no. I don't." Not with synapses limited to three degrees of freedom.

"Well, never mind. It's not really important." He senses the next question. "You will be going back . . . I don't know exactly when. It depends on a lot of things. You see, time is like a rubber band." No, it isn't. "Or a spring." No, it isn't. "At any rate, within a few days, weeks at most, you will leave this present and return to the moment you were experiencing when the time-caster beam picked you up."

"I've read stories like that," Sarah says. "Will we remember the future, after we go back?"

"Probably not," he says charitably. Not until your brains evolve. "But you can do us a great service."

Bob shrugs. "Sure, long as we're here. Anyhow, you did us a favor." He puts his arm around Sarah. "I've gotta leave Sarah in a couple of days; don't know for how long. So you're giving us more time together."

"Whether we remember it or not," Sarah says.

"Good, fine. Come with me." They follow Three-phasing to the mover-transom, where he takes their hands and transports them to his home. It is as unadorned as the time-caster room, except for bookshelves along one wall, and a low podium upon which the volume of *Faust* rests. All of the books are bound identically, in shiny metal with flat black letters along the spines.

Bob looks around. "Don't you people ever sit down?"

"Oh," Three-phasing says. "Thoughtless of me." With his mind he shifts the room from utility mood to comfort mood. Intricate tapestries now hang on the walls; soft cushions that look like silk are strewn around in pleasant disorder. Chiming music, not quite discordant, hovers at the edge of audibility, and there is a faint odor of something like jasmine. The metal floor has become a kind of soft leather, and the room has somehow lost its corners.

"How did that happen?" Sarah asks.

"I don't know." Three-phasing tries to copy Bob's shrug, but only manages a spasmodic jerk. "Can't remember not being able to do it."

Bob drops into a cushion and experimentally pushes at the floor with a finger. "What is it you want us to do?"

Trying to move slowly, Three-phasing lowers himself into a cushion and gestures at a nearby one, for Sarah. "It's very simple, really. Your being here is most of it.

"We're celebrating the millionth anniversary of the written word." How to phrase it? "Everyone is interested in this anniversary, but . . . nobody reads any more."

Bob nods sympathetically. "Never have time for it myself."

"Yes, uh . . . you *do* know how to read, though?"

"He knows," Sarah says. "He's just lazy."

"Well, yeah." Bob shifts uncomfortably in the cushion. "Sarah's the one you want. I kind of, uh, prefer to listen to the radio."

"I read all the time," Sarah says with a little pride. "Mostly mysteries. But sometimes I read good books, too."

"Good, good." It was indeed fortunate to have found this pair, Three-phasing realizes. They had used the metal of the ancient books to "tune" the time-caster, so potential subjects were limited to those living some eighty years before and after 2012 A.D. Internal evidence in the books indicated that most of the Earth's population was illiterate during this period.

"Allow me to explain. Any one of us can learn how to read. But to us it is like a code; an unnatural way of communicating. Because we are all natural telepaths. We can reach each other's minds from the age of one year."

"Golly!" Sarah says. "Read minds?" And Three-pushing sees in her mind a fuzzy kind of longing, much of which is love for Bob and frustration that she knows him only imperfectly. He dips into Bob's mind and finds things she is better off not knowing.

"That's right. So what we want is for you to read some of these books, and allow us to go into your minds while you're doing it. This way we will be able to recapture an experience that has been lost to the race for over a half-million years."

"I don't know," Bob says slowly. "Will we have time for anything else? I mean, the world must be pretty strange. Like to see some of it."

"Of course; sure. But the rest of the world is pretty much like my place here. Nobody goes outside any more. There isn't any air." He doesn't want to tell them how the air was lost, which might disturb them, but they seem to accept that as part of distant future.

"Uh, George." Sarah is blushing. "We'd also like, uh, some time to ourselves. Without anybody . . . inside our minds."

"Yes, I understand perfectly. You will have your own room, and plenty of time to yourselves." Three-phasing neglects to say that there is no such thing as privacy in a telepathic society.

But sex is another thing they don't have any more. They're almost as curious about that as they are about books.

So the kindly men of the future gave Bob and Sarah Graham plenty of time to themselves: Bob and Sarah reciprocated. Through the Dawn couple's eyes and brains, humanity shared again the visions of Fielding and Melville and Dickens and Shakespeare and almost a dozen others. And as for the 98% more, that they didn't have time to read or that were in foreign languages—Three-phasing got the hang of it and would spend several millennia entertaining those who were amused by this central illusion of literature: that there could be order, that there could be beginnings and endings and logical workings-out in between; that you could count on the third act or the last chapter to tie things up. They knew how profound an illusion this was because each of them knew every other living human with an intimacy and accuracy far superior to that which even Shakespeare could bring to the study of even himself. And as for Sarah and as for Bob:

Anxiety can throw a person's ovaries way off schedule. On that beach in California, Sarah was no more pregnant than Bob was. But up there in the future, some somatic tension finally built up to the breaking point, and an egg went sliding down the left Fallopian tube, to be met by a wiggling intruder approximately halfway; together they were the first manifestation of organism that nine months later, or a million years earlier, would be christened Douglas MacArthur Graham.

This made a problem for time, or Time, which is neither like a rubber band nor like a spring; nor even like a river nor a carrier wave—but which, like all of these things, can be deformed by certain stresses. For instance, two people going into the future and three coming back on the same time-casting beam.

In an earlier age, when time travel was more common, time-casters would have made sure that the baby, or at least its aborted embryo, would stay in the future when the mother returned to her present. Or they could arrange for the mother to stay in the future. But these subtleties had long been forgotten when Nine-hover relearned the dead art. So Sarah went back to her present with a hitch-hiker, an interloper, firmly imbedded in the lining of her womb. And its dim sense of life set up a kind of eddy in the flow of time, that Sarah had to share.

The mathematical explanation is subtle, and can't be comprehended by those of us who synapse with fewer than four degrees of freedom. But the end effect is clear: Sarah had to experience all of her own life backwards, all the way back to that embrace on the beach. Some highlights were:

In 1992, slowly dying of cancer, in a mental hospital.

In 1979, seeing Bob finally succeed in suicide on the American Plan, not quite finishing his 9,527th bottle of liquor.

In 1970, having her only son returned in a sealed casket from a country she'd never heard of.

In the 1960's, helplessly watching her son become more and more neurotic because of something that no one could name.

In 1953, Bob coming home with one foot, the other having been lost to frostbite; never having fired a shot in anger.

In 1952, the agonizing breech presentation.

Like her son, Sarah would remember no details of the backward voyage through her life. But the scars of it would haunt her forever.

They were kissing on the beach.

Sarah dropped the blanket and made a little noise. She started crying and slapped Bob as hard as she could, then ran on alone, up to the cabin.

Bob watched her progress up the hill with mixed feelings. He took a healthy slug from the bourbon bottle, to give him an excuse to wipe his own eyes.

He could go sit on the beach and finish the bottle; let her get over it by herself. Or he could go comfort her.

He tossed the bottle away, the gesture immediately making him feel stupid, and followed her. Later that night she apologized, saying she didn't know what had gotten into her.

THE SECRET PLACE

Richard McKenna

The late Richard McKenna was probably best known in his lifetime as author of the fat and thoughtful bestselling mainstream novel The Sand Pebbles—*later made into a big-budget but inferior (to the book) screen spectacular starring Steve McQueen. During his short career, before his tragically early death in 1964, he also wrote a handful of powerful and elegant short science fiction stories that stand among the best work of the first half of the 1960s. The roster of them, alas, is short: the poignant and powerful "Casey Agonistes," the strange and wonderful novella "Fiddler's Green," "The Night of Hoggy Darn," "Mine Own Ways," "Hunter, Come Home," "Bramble Bush," and the story that follows, "The Secret Place," for which he won a posthumous Nebula Award. Many of these stories question the nature of reality and investigate our flawed and prejudiced perceptions of it with a depth and complexity rivaled elsewhere at that time only by the work of Philip K. Dick. All them reveal the sure touch of a master craftsman, and it is intriguing—if, of course, pointless—to wonder what kind of work McKenna would be turning out now, if fate had spared him. Almost all of McKenna's short fiction was collected in* Casey Agonistes and Other Science Fiction and Fantasy Stories. *A collection of his essays,* New Eyes For Old, *was published after his death.*

In the compassionate story that follows, he shows us that sometimes it matters less what you see than whose eyes you see it through . . .

This morning my son asked me what I did in the war. He's fifteen and I don't know why he never asked me before. I don't know why I never anticipated the question.

He was just leaving for camp, and I was able to put him off by saying I did government work. He'll be two weeks at camp. As long as the counselors keep pressure on him, he'll do well enough at group activities. The moment they relax it, he'll be off studying an ant colony or reading one of his books. He's on astronomy now. The moment he comes home, he'll ask me again just what I did in the war, and I'll have to tell him.

But I don't understand just what I did in the war. Sometimes I think my group fought a death fight with a local myth and only Colonel Lewis realized it. I don't know who won. All I know is that war demands of some men risks more obscure and ignoble than death in battle. I know it did of me.

It began in 1931, when a local boy was found dead in the desert near Barker, Oregon. He had with him a sack of gold ore and one thumb-sized crystal of uranium oxide. The crystal ended as a curiosity in a Salt Lake City assay office until, in 1942, it became of strangely great importance. Army agents traced its probable origin to a hundred-square-mile area near Barker. Dr. Lewis was called to duty as a reserve colonel and ordered to find the vein. But the whole area was overlain by thousands of feet of Miocene lava flows and of course it was geological insanity to look there for a pegmatite vein. The area had no drainage pattern and had never been glaciated. Dr. Lewis protested that the crystal could have gotten there only by prior human agency.

It did him no good. He was told he's not to reason why. People very high up would not be placated until much money and scientific effort had been spent in a search. The army sent him young geology graduates, including me, and demanded progress reports. For the sake of morale, in a kind of frustrated desperation, Dr. Lewis decided to make the project a model textbook exercise in mapping the number and thickness of the basalt beds over the search area all the way down to the prevolcanic Miocene surface. That would at least be a useful addition to Columbia Plateau lithology. It would also be proof positive that no uranium ore existed there, so it was not really cheating.

That Oregon countryside was a dreary place. The search area was flat, featureless country with black lava outcropping everywhere through scanty gray soil in which sagebrush grew hardly knee high. It was hot and dry in summer and dismal with thin snow in winter. Winds howled across it at all seasons. Barker was about a hundred wooden houses on dusty streets, and some hay farms along a canal. All the young people were away at war or war jobs, and the old people seemed to resent us. There were twenty of us, apart from the contract drill crews who lived in their own trailer camps, and we were gown against town, in a way. We slept and ate at Colthorpe House, a block down the street from our headquarters. We had our own "gown" table there, and we might as well have been men from Mars.

I enjoyed it, just the same. Dr. Lewis treated us like students, with lectures and quizzes and assigned reading. He was a fine teacher and a brilliant scientist, and we loved him. He gave us all a turn at each phase of the work. I started on surface mapping and then worked with the drill crews, who were taking cores through the basalt and into the granite thousands of feet beneath. Then I worked on taking gravimetric and seismic readings. We had fine team spirit and we all knew we were getting priceless training in field geophysics. I decided privately that after the war I would take my doctorate in geophysics. Under Dr. Lewis, of course.

In early summer of 1944 the field phase ended. The contract drillers left. We packed tons of well logs and many boxes of gravimetric data sheets and seismic tapes for a move to Dr. Lewis's Midwestern university. There we would get more months of valuable training while we worked our data into a set of structure contour maps. We were all excited and talked a lot about being with girls again and going to parties. Then the army said part of the staff had to continue the field search. For technical compliance, Dr. Lewis decided to leave one man, and he chose me.

It hit me hard. It was like being flunked out unfairly. I thought he was heartlessly brusque about it.

"Take a jeep run through the area with a Geiger once a day," he said. "Then sit in the office and answer the phone."

"What if the army calls when I'm away?" I asked sullenly.

"Hire a secretary," he said. "You've an allowance for that."

So off they went and left me, with the title of field chief and only myself to boss. I felt betrayed to the hostile town. I decided I hated Colonel Lewis and wished I could get revenge. A few days later old Dave Gentry told me how.

He was a lean, leathery old man with a white mustache and I sat next to him in my new place at the "town" table. Those were grim meals. I heard remarks about healthy young men skulking out of uniform and wasting tax money. One night I slammed my fork into my half-emptied plate and stood up.

"The army sent me here and the army keeps me here," I told the dozen old men and women at the table. "I'd like to go overseas and cut Japanese throats for you kind hearts and gentle people, I really would! Why don't you all write your Congressman?"

I stamped outside and stood at one end of the veranda, boiling. Old Dave followed me out.

"Hold your horses, son," he said. "They hate the government, not you. But government's like the weather, and you're a man they can get aholt of."

"With their teeth," I said bitterly.

"They got reasons," Dave said. "Lost mines ain't supposed to be found the way you people are going at it. Besides that, the Crazy Kid mine belongs to us here in Barker."

He was past seventy and he looked after horses in the local feedyard. He wore a shabby, open vest over faded suspenders and gray flannel shirts and nobody would ever have looked for wisdom in that old man. But it was there.

"This is big, new, lonesome country and it's hard on people," he said. "Every town's got a story about a lost mine or a lost gold cache. Only kids go looking for it. It's enough for most folks just to know it's there. It helps 'em to stand the country."

"I see," I said. Something stirred in the back of my mind.

"Barker never got its lost mine until thirteen years ago," Dave said. "Folks just naturally can't stand to see you people find it this way, by main force and so soon after."

"We know there isn't any mine," I said. "We're just proving it isn't there."

"If you could prove that, it'd be worse yet," he said. "Only you can't. We all saw and handled that ore. It was quartz, just rotten with gold in wires and flakes. The boy went on foot from his house to get it. The lode's got to be right close by out there."

He waved toward our search area. The air above it was luminous with twilight and I felt a curious surge of interest. Colonel Lewis had always discouraged us from speculating on that story. If one of us brought it up, I was usually the one who led the hooting and we all suggested he go over the search area with a dowsing rod. It was an article of faith with us that the vein did not exist. But now I was all alone and my own field boss.

We each put up one foot on the veranda rail and rested our arms on our knees. Dave bit off a chew of tobacco and told me about Owen Price.

"He was always a crazy kid and I guess he read every book in town," Dave said. "He had a curious heart, that boy."

I'm no folklorist, but even I could see how myth elements were already creeping into the story. For one thing, Dave insisted the boy's shirt was torn off and he had lacerations on his back.

"Like a cougar clawed him," Dave said. "Only they ain't never been cougars in that desert. We backtracked that boy till his trail crossed itself so many times it was no use, but we never found one cougar track."

I could discount that stuff, of course, but still the story gripped me. Maybe it was Dave's slow, sure voice; perhaps the queer twilight; possibly my own wounded pride. I thought of how great lava upwellings sometimes tear loose and carry along huge masses of the country rock. Maybe such an erratic mass lay out there, perhaps only a few hundred feet across and so missed by our drill cores, but rotten with uranium. If I could find it, I would make a fool of Colonel Lewis. I would discredit the whole science of geology. I, Duard Campbell, the despised and rejected one, could do that. The front of my mind shouted that it was nonsense, but something far back in my mind began composing a devastating letter to Colonel Lewis and comfort flowed into me.

"There's some say the boy's youngest sister could tell where he found it, if she wanted," Dave said. "She used to go into that desert with him a lot. She took on pretty wild when it happened and then was struck dumb, but I hear she talks again now." He shook his head. "Poor little Helen. She promised to be a pretty girl."

"Where dose she live?" I asked.

"With her mother in Salem," Dave said. "She went to business school and I hear she works for a lawyer there."

Mrs. Price was a flinty old woman who seemed to control her daughter absolutely. She agreed Helen would be my secretary as soon as I told her the salary. I got Helen's security clearance with one phone call; she had already been investigated as part of tracing that uranium crystal. Mrs. Price arranged for Helen to stay with a family she knew in Barker, to protect her reputation. It was in no danger. I meant to make love to her, if I had to, to charm her out of her secret, if she had one, but I would not harm her. I knew perfectly well that I was only playing a game called "The Revenge of Duard Campbell." I knew I would not find any uranium.

Helen was a plain little girl and was made of frightened ice. She wore low-heeled shoes and cotton stockings and plain dresses with white cuffs and collars. Her one good feature was her flawless fair skin against which her peaked, black Welsh eyebrows and smoky blue eyes gave her an elfin look at times. She liked to sit neatly tucked into herself, feet together, elbows in, eyes cast down, voice hardly audible, as smoothly self-contained as an egg. The desk I gave her faced mine and she sat like that across from me and did the busy work I gave her and I could not get through to her at all.

I tried joking and I tried polite little gifts and attentions, and I tried being sad and needing sympathy. She listened and worked and stayed as far away as the moon. It was only after two weeks and by pure accident that I found the key to her.

I was trying the sympathy gambit. I said it was not so bad, being exiled from friends and family, but what I could not stand was the dreary sameness of that search area. Every spot was like every other spot and there was no single, recognizable *place* in the whole expanse. It sparked something in her and she roused up at me.

"It's full of just wonderful places," she said.

"Come out with me in the jeep and show me one," I challenged.

She was reluctant, but I hustled her along regardless. I guided the jeep between outcrops, jouncing and lurching. I had our map photographed on my mind and I knew where we were every minute, but only by map coordinates. The desert had our marks on it: well sites, seismic blast holes, wooden stakes, cans, bottles and papers blowing in that everlasting wind, and it was all dismally the same anyway.

"Tell me when we pass a 'place' and I'll stop," I said.

"It's all places," she said. "Right there's a place."

I stopped the jeep and looked at her in surprise. Her voice was strong and throaty. She opened her eyes wide and smiled; I had never seen her look like that.

"What's special, that makes it a place?" I asked.

She did not answer. She got out and walked a few steps. Her whole posture was changed. She almost danced along. I followed and touched her shoulder.

"Tell me what's special," I said.

She faced around and stared right past me. She had a new grace and vitality and she was a very pretty girl.

"It's where all the dogs are," she said.

"Dogs?"

I looked around at the scrubby sagebrush and thin soil

and ugly black rock and back at Helen. Something was wrong.

"Big, stupid dogs that go in herds and eat grass," she said. She kept turning and gazing. "Big cats chase the dogs and eat them. The dogs scream and scream. Can't you hear them?"

"That's crazy!" I said. "What's the matter with you?"

I might as well have slugged her. She crumpled instantly back into herself and I could hardly hear her answer.

"I'm sorry. My brother and I used to play out fairy tales here. All this was a kind of fairyland to us." Tears formed in her eyes. "I haven't been here since . . . I forget myself. I'm sorry."

I had to swear I needed to dictate "field notes" to force Helen into that desert again. She sat stiffly with pad and pencil in the jeep while I put on my act with the Geiger and rattled off jargon. Her lips were pale and compressed and I could see her fighting against the spell the desert had for her, and I could see her slowly losing.

She finally broke down into that strange mood and I took good care not to break it. It was weird but wonderful, and I got a lot of data. I made her go out for "field notes" every morning and each time it was easier to break her down. Back in the office she always froze again and I marveled at how two such different persons could inhabit the same body. I called her two phases "Office Helen" and "Desert Helen."

I often talked with old Dave on the veranda after dinner. One night he cautioned me.

"Folks here think Helen ain't been right in the head since her brother died," he said. "They're worrying about you and her."

"I feel like a big brother to her," I said. "I'd never hurt her, Dave. If we find the lode, I'll stake the best claim for her."

He shook his head. I wished I could explain to him how it was only a harmless game I was playing and no one would ever find gold out there. Yet, as a game, it fascinated me.

Desert Helen charmed me when, helplessly, she had to

uncover her secret life. She was a little girl in a woman's body. Her voice became strong and breathless with excitement and she touched me with the same wonder that turned her own face vivid and elfin. She ran laughing through the black rocks and scrubby sagebrush and momentarily she made them beautiful. She would pull me along by the hand and sometimes we ran as much as a mile away from the jeep. She treated me as if I were a blind or foolish child.

"No, no, Duard, that's a cliff!" she would say, pulling me back.

She would go first, so I could find the stepping stones across streams. I played up. She pointed out woods and streams and cliffs and castles. There were shaggy horses with claws, golden birds, camels, witches, elephants and many other creatures. I pretended to see them all, and it made her trust me. She talked and acted out the fairy tales she had once played with Owen. Sometimes he was enchanted and sometimes she, and the one had to dare the evil magic of a witch or giant to rescue the other. Sometimes I was Duard and other times I almost thought I was Owen.

Helen and I crept into sleeping castles, and we hid with pounding hearts while the giant grumbled in search of us and we fled, hand in hand, before his wrath.

Well, I had her now. I played Helen's game, but I never lost sight of my own. Every night I sketched in on my map whatever I had learned that day of the fairyland topography. Its geomorphology was remarkably consistent.

When we played, I often hinted about the giant's treasure. Helen never denied it existed, but she seemed troubled and evasive about it. She would put her finger to her lips and look at me with solemn, round eyes.

"You only take the things nobody cares about," she would say. "If you take the gold or jewels, it brings you terrible bad luck."

"I got a charm against bad luck and I'll let you have it too," I said once. "It's the biggest, strongest charm in the whole world."

"No. It all turns into trash. It turns into goat beans and dead snakes and things," she said crossly. "Owen told me. It's a rule, in fairyland."

Another time we talked about it as we sat in a gloomy ravine near a waterfall. We had to keep our voices low or we would wake up the giant. The waterfall was really the giant snoring and it was also the wind that blew forever across that desert.

"Doesn't Owen ever take anything?" I asked.

I had learned by then that I must always speak of Owen in the present tense.

"Sometimes he has to," she said. "Once right here the witch had me enchanted into an ugly toad. Owen put a flower on my head and that made me be Helen again."

"A really truly flower? That you could take home with you?"

"A red and yellow flower bigger than my two hands," she said. "I tried to take it home, but all the petals came off."

"Does Owen ever take anything home?"

"Rocks, sometimes," she said. "We keep them in a secret nest in the shed. We think they might be magic eggs."

I stood up. "Come and show me."

She shook her head vigorously and drew back. "I don't want to go home," she said. "Not ever."

She squirmed and pouted, but I pulled her to her feet.

"Please, Helen, for me," I said. "Just for one little minute."

I pulled her back to the jeep and we drove to the old Price place. I had never seen her look at it when we passed it and she did not look now. She was freezing fast back into Office Helen. But she led me around the sagging old house with its broken windows and into a tumbledown shed. She scratched away some straw in one corner, and there were the rocks. I did not realize how excited I was until disappointment hit me like a blow in the stomach.

They were worthless waterworn pebbles of quartz and rosy granite. The only thing special about them was that they could never have originated on that basalt desert.

•   •   •

After a few weeks we dropped the pretense of field notes and simply went into the desert to play. I had Helen's fairyland almost completely mapped. It seemed to be a recent fault block mountain with a river parallel to its base and a gently sloping plain across the river. The scarp face was wooded and cut by deep ravines and it had castles perched on its truncated spurs. I kept checking Helen on it and never found her inconsistent. Several times when she was in doubt I was able to tell her where she was, and that let me even more deeply into her secret life. One morning I discovered just how deeply.

She was sitting on a log in the forest and plaiting a little basket out of fern fronds. I stood beside her. She looked up at me and smiled.

"What shall we play today, Owen?" she asked.

I had not expected that, and I was proud of how quickly I rose to it. I capered and bounded away and then back to her and crouched at her feet.

"Little sister, little sister, I'm enchanted," I said. "Only you in all the world can uncharm me."

"I'll uncharm you," she said, in that little girl voice. "What are you, brother?"

"A big, black dog," I said. "A wicked giant named Lewis Rawbones keeps me chained up behind his castle while he takes all the other dogs out hunting."

She smoothed her gray skirt over her knees. Her mouth dropped.

"You're lonesome and you howl all day and you howl all night," she said. "Poor doggie."

I threw back my head and howled.

"He's a terrible, wicked giant and he's got all kinds of terrible magic," I said. "You mustn't be afraid, little sister. As soon as you uncharm me I'll be a handsome prince and I'll cut off his head."

"I'm not afraid." Her eyes sparkled. "I'm not afraid of fire or snakes or pins or needles or anything."

"I'll take you away to my kingdom and we'll live happily ever afterward. You'll be the most beautiful queen in the world and everybody will love you."

I wagged my tail and laid my head on her knees. She stroked my silky head and pulled my long black ears.

"Everybody will love me." She was very serious now. "Will magic water uncharm you, poor old doggie?"

"You have to touch my forehead with a piece of the giant's treasure," I said. "That's the only onliest way to uncharm me."

I felt her shrink away from me. She stood up, her face suddenly crumpled with grief and anger.

"You're not Owen, you're just a man! Owen's enchanted and I'm enchanted too and nobody will ever uncharm us!"

She ran away from me and she was already Office Helen by the time she reached the jeep.

After that day she refused flatly to go into the desert with me. It looked as if my game was played out. But I gambled that Desert Helen could still hear me, underneath somewhere, and I tried a new strategy. The office was an upstairs room over the old dance hall and, I suppose, in frontier days skirmishing had gone on there between men and women. I doubt anything went on as strange as my new game with Helen.

I always had paced and talked while Helen worked. Now I began mixing common-sense talk with fairyland talk and I kept coming back to the wicked giant, Lewis Rawbones. Office Helen tried not to pay attention, but now and then I caught Desert Helen peeping at me out of her eyes. I spoke of my blighted career as a geologist and how it would be restored to me if I found the lode. I mused on how I would live and work in exotic places and how I would need a wife to keep house for me and help with my paper work. It disturbed Office Helen. She made typing mistakes and dropped things. I kept it up for days, trying for just the right mixture of fact and fantasy, and it was hard on Office Helen.

One night old Dave warned me again.

"Helen's looking peaked, and there's talk around. Miz Fowler says Helen don't sleep and she cries at night and she won't tell Miz Fowler what's wrong. You don't happen to know what's bothering her, do you?"

"I only talk business stuff to her," I said. "Maybe she's homesick. I'll ask her if she wants a vacation." I did not like the way Dave looked at me. "I haven't hurt her. I don't mean her any harm, Dave," I said.

"People get killed for what they do, not for what they mean," he said. "Son, there's men in this here town would kill you quick as a coyote, if you hurt Helen Price."

I worked on Helen all the next day and in the afternoon I hit just the right note and I broke her defenses. I was not prepared for the way it worked out. I had just said, "All life is a kind of playing. If you think about it right, everything we do is a game." She poised her pencil and looked straight at me, as she had never done in that office, and I felt my heart speed up.

"You taught me how to play, Helen. I was so serious that I didn't know how to play."

"Owen taught me to play. He had magic. My sisters couldn't play anything but dolls and rich husbands and I hated them."

Her eyes opened wide and her lips trembled and she was almost Desert Helen right there in the office.

"There's magic and enchantment in regular life, if you look at it right," I said. "Don't you think so, Helen?"

"I know it!" she said. She turned pale and dropped her pencil. "Owen was enchanted into having a wife and three daughters and he was just a boy. But he was the only man we had and all of them but me hated him because we were so poor." She began to tremble and her voice went flat. "He couldn't stand it. He took the treasure and it killed him." Tears ran down her cheeks. "I tried to think he was only enchanted into play-dead and if I didn't speak or laugh for seven years, I'd uncharm him."

She dropped her head on her hands. I was alarmed. I came over and put my hand on her shoulder.

"I did speak." Her shoulders heaved with sobs. "They made me speak, and now Owen won't ever come back."

I bent and put my arm across her shoulders.

"Don't cry, Helen. He'll come back," I said. "There are other magics to bring him back."

I hardly knew what I was saying. I was afraid of what I had done, and I wanted to comfort her. She jumped up and threw off my arm.

"I can't stand it! I'm going home!"

She ran out into the hall and down the stairs and from the window I saw her run down the street, still crying. All of a sudden my game seemed cruel and stupid to me and right that moment I stopped it. I tore up my map of fairyland and my letters to Colonel Lewis and I wondered how in the world I could ever have done all that.

After dinner that night old Dave motioned me out to one end of the veranda. His face looked carved out of wood.

"I don't know what happened in your office today, and for your sake I better not find out. But you send Helen back to her mother on the morning stage, you hear me?"

"All right, if she wants to go," I said. "I can't just fire her."

"I'm speaking for the boys. You better put her on that morning stage, or we'll be around to talk to you."

"All right, I will, Dave."

I wanted to tell him how the game was stopped now and how I wanted a chance to make things up with Helen, but I thought I had better not. Dave's voice was flat and savage with contempt and, old as he was, he frightened me.

Helen did not come to work in the morning. At nine o'clock I went out myself for the mail. I brought a large mailing tube and some letters back to the office. The first letter I opened was from Dr. Lewis, and almost like magic it solved all my problems.

On the basis of his preliminary structure contour maps Dr. Lewis had gotten permission to close out the field phase. Copies of the maps were in the mailing tube, for my information. I was to hold an inventory and be ready to turn everything over to an army quartermaster team coming in a few days. There was still a great mass of data to be worked up in refining the map. I was to join the group again and I would have a chance at the lab work after all.

I felt pretty good. I paced and whistled and snapped my fingers. I wished Helen would come, to help on the inventory. Then I opened the tube and looked idly at the maps. There were a lot of them, featureless bed after bed of basalt, like layers of a cake ten miles across. But when I came to the bottom map, of the prevolcanic Miocene landscape, the hair on my neck stood up.

I had made that map myself. It was Helen's fairytale. The topography was point by point the same.

I clenched my fists and stopped breathing. Then it hit me a second time, and the skin crawled up my back.

The game was real. I couldn't end it. All the time the game had been playing me. It was still playing me.

I ran out and down the street and overtook old Dave hurrying toward the feedyard. He had a holstered gun on each hip.

"Dave, I've got to find Helen," I said.

"Somebody seen her hiking into the desert just at day-light," he said. "I'm on my way for a horse." He did not slow his stride. "You better get out of there in your stinkwagon. If you don't find her before we do, you better just keep on going, son."

I ran back and got the jeep and roared it out across the scrubby sagebrush. I hit rocks and I do not know why I did not break something. I knew where to go and feared what I would find there. I knew I loved Helen Price more than my own life and I knew I had driven her to her death.

I saw her far off, running and dodging. I headed the jeep to intercept her and I shouted, but she neither saw me nor heard me. I stopped and jumped out and ran after her and the world darkened. Helen was all I could see, and I could not catch up with her.

"Wait for me, little sister!" I screamed after her. "I love you, Helen! Wait for me!"

She stopped and crouched and I almost ran over her. I knelt and put my arms around her and then it was on us.

They say in an earthquake, when the direction of up and down tilts and wobbles, people feel a fear that drives them mad if they can not forget it afterward. This was worse. Up and down and here and there and now and then all rushed together. The wind roared through the rock beneath us and the air thickened crushingly above our heads. I know we clung to each other, and were there for each other while nothing else was and that is all I know, until we were in the jeep and I was guiding it back toward town as headlong as I had come.

Then the world had shape again under a bright sun. I saw a knot of horsemen on the horizon. They were heading for where Owen had been found. That boy had run a long way, alone and hurt and burdened.

I got Helen up to the office. She sat at her desk with her head down on her hands and she quivered violently. I kept my arm around her.

"It was only a storm inside our two heads, Helen," I said, over and over. "Something black blew away out of us. The game is finished and we're free and I love you."

Over and over I said that, for my sake as well as hers. I meant and believed it. I said she was my wife and we would marry and go a thousand miles away from that desert to raise our children. She quieted to a trembling, but she would not speak. Then I heard hoofbeats and the creak of leather in the street below and then I heard slow footsteps on the stairs.

Old Dave stood in the doorway. His two guns looked as natural on him as hands and feet. He looked at Helen, bowed over the desk, and then at me, standing beside her.

"Come on down, son. The boys want to talk to you," he said.

I followed him into the hall and stopped.

"She isn't hurt," I said. "The lode is really out there, Dave, but nobody is ever going to find it."

"Tell that to the boys."

"We're closing out the project in a few more days," I said. "I'm going to marry Helen and take her away with me."

"Come down or we'll drag you down!" he said harshly. "We'll send Helen back to her mother."

I was afraid. I did not know what to do.

"No, you won't send me back to my mother!"

It was Helen beside me in the hall. She was Desert Helen, but grown up and wonderful. She was pale, pretty, aware and sure of herself.

"I'm going with Duard," she said. "Nobody in the world is ever going to send me around like a package again."

Dave rubbed his jaw and squinted his eyes at her.

"I love her, Dave," I said. "I'll take care of her all my life."

I put my left arm around her and she nestled against me. The tautness went out of old Dave and he smiled. He kept his eyes on Helen.

"Little Helen Price," he said, wonderingly. "Who ever would've thought it?" He reached out and shook us both gently. "Bless you youngsters," he said, and blinked his eyes. "I'll tell the boys it's all right."

He turned and went slowly down the stairs. Helen and I looked at each other, and I think she saw a new face too.

That was sixteen years ago. I am a professor myself now, graying a bit at the temples. I am as positivistic a scientist as you will find anywhere in the Mississippi drainage basin. When I tell a seminary student "That assertion is operationally meaningless," I can make it sound downright obscene. The students blush and hate me, but it is for their own good. Science is the only safe game, and it's safe only if it is kept pure. I work hard at that, I have yet to meet the student I can not handle.

My son is another matter. We named him Owen Lewis, and he has Helen's eyes and hair and complexion. He learned to read on the modern sane and sterile children's books. We haven't a fairy tale in the house—but I have a science library. And Owen makes fairy tales out of science. He is taking the measure of space and time now, with Jeans and Eddington. He cannot possibly understand a tenth of what he reads, in the way I understand it. But he understands all of it in some other way privately his own.

Not long ago he said to me, "You know, Dad, it isn't only space that's expanding. Time's expanding too, and that's what makes us keep getting farther away from when we used to be."

And I have to tell him just what I did in the war. I know I found manhood and a wife. The how and why of it I think and hope I am incapable of fully understanding. But Owen has, through Helen, that strangely curious heart. I'm afraid. I'm afraid he will understand.

THE PRICE OF ORANGES

Nancy Kress

Here's a funny, bittersweet, and deeply moving study of friendship, faith, love . . . and some very hard choices.

Born in Buffalo, New York, Nancy Kress now lives in Brockport, New York. She began selling her elegant and incisive stories in the mid seventies and has since become a frequent contributor to Asimov's Science Fiction, The Magazine of Fantasy and Science Fiction, Omni, *and elsewhere. Her books include the novels* The Prince of Morning Bells, The Golden Grove, The White Pipes, An Alien Light, *and* Brain Rose, *the collection* Trinity And Other Stories, *the novel version of her Hugo and Nebula-winning story,* Beggars in Spain, *and a sequel,* Beggars and Choosers. *Her most recent books include a new collection,* The Aliens of Earth, *and a new novel,* Oaths & Miracles. *She has also won a Nebula Award for her story "Out Of All Them Bright Stars."*

"**I**'m worried about my granddaughter," Henry Kramer said, passing half of his sandwich to Manny Feldman. Manny took it eagerly. The sandwich was huge, thick slices of beef and horseradish between fresh slabs of crusty bread. Pigeons watched the park bench hopefully.

"Jackie. The granddaughter who writes books," Manny said. Harry watched to see that Manny ate. You couldn't trust Manny to eat enough; he stayed too skinny. At least in Harry's opinion. Manny, Jackie——the world, Harry sometimes thought, had all grown too skinny when he somehow hadn't been looking. Skimpy. Stretch-feeling. Harry nodded to see horseradish spurt in a satisfying stream down Manny's scraggly beard.

"Jackie. Yes," Harry said.

"So what's wrong with her? She's sick?" Manny eyed Harry's strudel, cherry with real yeast bread. Harry passed it to him. "Harry, the whole thing? I couldn't."

"Take it, take it, I don't want it. You should eat. No, she's not sick. She's miserable." When Manny, his mouth full of strudel, didn't answer, Harry put a hand on Manny's arm. "*Miserable*."

Manny swallowed hastily. "How do you know? You saw her this week?"

"No. Next Tuesday. She's bringing me a book by a friend of hers. I know from this." He drew a magazine from an inner pocket of his coat. The coat was thick tweed, almost new, with wooden buttons. On the cover of the glossy magazine a woman smiled contemptuously. A woman with hollow, starved-looking cheeks who obviously didn't get enough to eat either.

"That's not a book," Manny pointed out.

"So she writes stories, too. Listen to this. Just listen. 'I stood in my backyard, surrounded by the false bright toxin-fed green, and realized that the earth was dead. What else could it be, since we humans swarmed upon it like maggots on carrion, growing our hectic gleaming molds, leaving our slime trails across the senseless surface?' Does that sound like a happy woman?"

"Hoo boy," Manny said.

"It's all like that. 'Don't read my things, Popsy,' she says. 'You're not in the audience for my things.' Then she smiles without ever once showing her teeth." Harry flung both arms wide. "Who else should be in the audience but her own grandfather?"

Manny swallowed the last of the strudel. Pigeons fluttered angrily. "She never shows her teeth when she smiles? Never?"

"Never."

"Hoo boy," Manny said. Did you want all of that orange?"

"No, I bought it for you, to take home. But did you finish that whole half a sandwich already?"

"I thought I'd take it home," Manny said humbly. He

showed Harry the tip of the sandwich, wrapped in the thick brown butcher paper, protruding from the pocket of his old coat.

Harry nodded approvingly. "Good, good. Take the orange, too. I bought it for you."

Manny took the orange. Three teenagers carrying huge shrieking radios sauntered past. Manny started to put his hands over his ears, received a look of dangerous contempt from the teenager with green hair, and put his hands on his lap. The kid tossed an empty beer bottle onto the pavement before their feet. It shattered. Harry scowled fiercely but Manny stared straight ahead. When the cacophony had passed, Manny said, "Thank you for the orange. Fruit, it costs so much this time of year."

Harry still scowled. "Not in 1937."

"Don't start that again, Harry."

Harry said sadly, "Why won't you ever believe me? Could I afford to bring all this food if I got it at 1988 prices? Could I afford this coat? Have you seen buttons like this in 1988, on a new coat? Have you seen sandwiches wrapped in that kind of paper since we were young? Have you? Why won't you believe me?"

Manny slowly peeled his orange. The rind was pale, and the orange had seeds. "Harry. Don't start."

"But why won't you just come to my room and *see*?"

Manny sectioned the orange. "Your room. A cheap furnished room in a Social Security hotel. Why should I go? I know what will be there. What will be there is the same thing in my room. A bed, a chair, a table, a hot plate, some cans of food. Better I should meet you here in the park, get at least a little fresh air." He looked at Harry meekly, the orange clutched in one hand. "Don't misunderstand. It's not from a lack of friendship I say this. You're good to me, you're the best friend I have. You bring me things from a great deli, you talk to me, you share with me the family I don't have. It's enough, Harry. It's *more* than enough. I don't need to see where you live like I live."

Harry gave it up. There were moods, times, when it was

just impossible to budge Manny. He dug in, and in he stayed. "Eat your orange."

"It's a good orange. So tell me more about Jackie."

"Jackie." Harry shook his head. Two kids on bikes tore along the path. One of them swerved towards Manny and snatched the orange from his hand. "Aw riggghhhttt!"

Harry scowled after the child. It had been a girl. Manny just wiped the orange juice off his fingers onto the knee of his pants. "Is everything she writes so depressing?"

"Everything," Harry said. "Listen to this one." He drew out another magazine, smaller, bound in rough paper with a stylized linen drawing of a woman's private parts on the cover. On the cover! Harry held the magazine with one palm spread wide over the drawing, which made it difficult to keep the pages open while he read. " 'She looked at her mother in the only way possible: with contempt, contempt for all the betrayals and compromises that had been her mother's life, for the sad soft lines of defeat around her mother's mouth, for the bright artificial dress too young for her wasted years, for even the leather handbag, Gucci of course, filled with blood money for having sold her life to a man who had long since ceased to want it.' "

"Hoo boy," Manny said. "About a *mother* she wrote that?"

"About everybody. All the time."

"And where *is* Barbara?"

"Reno again. Another divorce." How many had that been? After two, did anybody count? Harry didn't count. He imagined Barbara's life as a large roulette wheel like the ones on TV, little silver men bouncing in and out of red and black pockets. Why didn't she get dizzy?

Manny said slowly, "I always thought there was a lot of love in her."

"A lot of that she's got," Harry said dryly.

"Not Barbara—Jackie. A lot of . . . I don't know. Sweetness. Under the way she is."

"The way she is," Harry said gloomily. "Prickly. A cactus. But you're right, Manny, I know what you mean.

She just needs someone to soften her up. Love her back, maybe. Although *I* love her."

The two old men looked at each other. Manny said, "Harry. . . ."

"I know, I know. I'm only a grandfather, my love doesn't count, I'm just there. Like air. 'You're wonderful, Popsy,' she says, and still no teeth when she smiles. But you know, Manny—you are right!" Harry jumped up from the bench. "You are! What she needs is a young man to love her!"

Manny looked alarmed. "I didn't say—"

"I don't know why I didn't think of it before!"

"Harry—"

"And her stories, too! Full of ugly murders, ugly places, unhappy endings. What she needs is something to show her that writing could be about sweetness, too."

Manny was staring at him hard. Harry felt a rush of affection. That Manny should have the answer! Skinny wonderful Manny!

Manny said slowly, "Jackie said to me, 'I write about reality.' That's what she said, Harry."

"So there's no sweetness in reality? Put sweetness in her life, her writing will go sweet. She *needs* this, Manny. A really nice fellow!"

Two men in jogging suits ran past. One of their Reeboks came down on a shard of beer bottle. "Every fucking time!" he screamed, bending over to inspect his shoe. "Fucking park!"

"Well, what do you expect?" the other drawled, looking at Manny and Harry. "Although you'd think that if we could clean up Lake Erie. . . ."

"Fucking derelicts!" the other snarled. They jogged away.

"Of course," Harry said, "it might not be easy to find the sort of guy to convince Jackie."

"Harry, I think you should maybe think—"

"Not here," Harry said suddenly. "Not here. *There*. In 1937."

"*Harry*. . . ."

"Yeah," Harry said, nodding several times. Excitement

filled him like light, like electricity. What an idea! "It was different then."

Manny said nothing. When he stood up, the sleeve of his coat exposed the number tattooed on his wrist. He said quietly, "It was no paradise in 1937 either, Harry."

Harry seized Manny's hand. "I'm going to do it, Manny. Find someone for her there. Bring him here."

Manny sighed. "Tomorrow at the chess club, Harry? At one o'clock? It's Tuesday."

"I'll tell you then how I'm coming with this."

"Fine, Harry. Fine. All my wishes go with you. You know that."

Harry stood up too, still holding Manny's hand. A middle-aged man staggered to the bench and slumped onto it. The smell of whiskey rose from him in waves. He eyed Manny and Harry with scorn. "Fucking fags."

"Good night, Harry."

"Manny—if you'd only come . . . money goes so much farther there. . . ."

"Tomorrow at one. At the chess club."

Harry watched his friend walk away. Manny's foot dragged a little; the knee must be bothering him again. Harry wished Manny would see a doctor. Maybe a doctor would know why Manny stayed so skinny.

Harry walked back to his hotel. In the lobby, old men slumped in upholstery thin from wear, burned from cigarettes, shiny in the seat from long sitting. Sitting and sitting, Harry thought—life measured by the seat of the pants. And now it was getting dark. No one would go out from here until the next daylight. Harry shook his head.

The elevator wasn't working again. He climbed the stairs to the third floor. Halfway there, he stopped, felt in his pocket, counted five quarters, six dimes, two nickels, and eight pennies. He returned to the lobby. "Could I have two dollar bills for this change, please? Maybe old bills?"

The clerk looked at him suspiciously. "Your rent paid up?"

"Certainly," Harry said. The woman grudgingly gave him the money.

"Thank you. You look very lovely today, Mrs. Raduski." Mrs. Raduski snorted.

In his room, Harry looked for his hat. He finally found it under his bed—how had it gotten under his bed? He dusted it off and put it on. It had cost him $3.25. He opened the closet door, parted the clothes hanging from their metal pole—like Moses parting the sea, he always thought, a Moses come again—and stepped to the back of the closet, remembering with his body rather than his mind the sharp little twist to the right just past the far gray sleeve of his good wool suit.

He stepped out into the bare corner of a warehouse. Cobwebs brushed his hat; he had stepped a little too far right. Harry crossed the empty concrete space to where the lumber stacks started, and threaded his way through them. The lumber, too, was covered with cobwebs, not much building going on. On his way out the warehouse door, Harry passed the night watchman coming on duty.

"Quiet all day, Harry?"

"As a church, Rudy," Harry said. Rudy laughed. He laughed a lot. He was also indisposed to question very much. The first time he had seen Harry coming out of the warehouse in a bemused daze, he must have assumed that Harry had been hired to work there. Peering at Rudy's round, vacant face, Harry realized that he must hold this job because he was someone's uncle, someone's cousin, someone's something. Harry had felt a small glow of approval; families should take care of their own. He had told Rudy that he had lost his key and asked him for another.

Outside it was late afternoon. Harry began walking. Eventually there were people walking past him, beside him, across the street from him. Everybody wore hats. The women wore bits of velvet or wool with dotted veils across their noses and long, graceful dresses in small prints. The men wore fedoras with suits as baggy as Harry's. When he reached the park there were children, girls in long black

tights and hard shoes, boys in buttoned shirts. Everyone
looked like it was Sunday morning.

Pushcarts and shops lined the sidewalks. Harry bought a
pair of socks, thick gray wool, for 89 cents. When the man
took his dollar, Harry held his breath: each first time made
a little pip in his stomach. But no one ever looked at the
dates of old bills. He bought two oranges for five cents each,
and then, thinking of Manny, bought a third. At a candystore
he bought *G-8 And His Battle Aces* for fifteen cents. At
The Collector's Cozy in the other time they would gladly
give him thirty dollars for it. Finally, he bought a cherry
Coke for a nickel and headed towards the park.

"Oh, excuse me," said a young man who bumped into
Harry on the sidewalk. "I'm sorry!" Harry looked at him
hard: but, no. Too young. Jackie was twenty-eight.

Some children ran past, making for the movie theater.
Spencer Tracy in *Captains Courageous*. Harry sat down on
a green-painted wooden bench under a pair of magnificent
Dutch elms. On the bench lay a news-magazine. Harry
glanced at it to see when in September this was: the 28th.
The cover pictured a young blond Nazi soldier standing at
stiff salute. Harry thought again of Manny, frowned, and
turned the magazine cover down.

For the next hour, people walked past. Harry studied them
carefully. When it got too dark to see, he walked back to the
warehouse, on the way buying an apple kuchen at a bakery
with a curtain behind the counter looped back to reveal a man
in his shirt sleeves eating a plate of stew at a table bathed in
soft yellow lamplight. The kuchen cost thirty-two cents.

At the warehouse, Harry let himself in with his key,
slipped past Rudy nodding over *Paris Nights*, and walked to
his cobwebby corner. He emerged from his third-floor closet
into his room. Beyond the window, sirens wailed and would
not stop.

"So how's it going?" Manny asked. He dripped kuchen
crumbs on the chessboard; Harry brushed them away.
Manny had him down a knight.

"It's going to take time to find somebody that's right,"

Harry said. "I'd like to have someone by next Tuesday when I meet Jackie for dinner, but I don't know. It's not easy. There are requirements. He has to be young enough to be attractive, but old enough to understand Jackie. He has to be sweet-natured enough to do her some good but strong enough not to panic at jumping over fifty-two years. Somebody educated. An educated man—he might be more curious than upset by my closet. Don't you think?"

"Better watch your queen," Manny said, moving his rook. "So how are you going to find him?"

"It takes time," Harry said. "I'm working on it."

Manny shook his head. "You have to get somebody here, you have to convince him he *is* here, you have to keep him from turning right around and running back in time through your shirts. . . . I don't know, Harry. I don't know. I've been thinking. This thing is not simple. What if you did something wrong? Took somebody important out of 1937?"

"I won't pick anybody important."

"What if you make a mistake and brought your own grandfather? And something happened to him here?"

"My grandfather was already dead in 1937."

"What if you brought me? I'm already here."

"You didn't live here in 1937."

"What if you brought *you*?"

"I didn't live here either."

"What if you. . . ."

"Manny." Harry said, "I'm not bringing somebody important. I'm not bringing somebody we know. I'm not bringing somebody for permanent. I'm just bringing a nice guy for Jackie to meet, go dancing, see a different kind of nature. A different view of what's possible. An innocence. I'm sure there are fellows here that would do it, but I don't know any, and I don't know how to bring any to her. From there I know. Is this so complicated? Is this so unpredictable?"

"Yes," Manny said. He had on his stubborn look again. How could somebody so skimpy look so stubborn? Harry sighed and moved his lone knight.

"I brought you some whole socks."

"Thank you. That knight, it's not going to help you much."

"Lectures. That's what there was there that there isn't here. Everybody went to lectures. No TV, movies cost money, they went to free lectures."

"I remember," Manny said. "I was a young man myself. Harry, this thing is not simple."

"Yes, it is," Harry said stubbornly.

"1937 was not simple."

"It will work, Manny."

"Check," Manny said.

That evening, Harry went back. This time it was the afternoon of September 16. On newsstands the *New York Times* announced that President Roosevelt and John L. Lewis had talked pleasantly at the White House. Cigarettes cost thirteen cents a pack. Women wore cotton stockings and clunky, high-heeled shoes. Schrafft's best chocolates were sixty cents a pound. Small boys addressed Harry as "sir."

He attended six lectures in two days. A Madame Trefania lectured on theosophy to a hall full of badly-dressed women with thin, pursed lips. A union organizer roused an audience to a pitch that made Harry leave after the first thirty minutes. A skinny, nervous missionary showed slides of religious outposts in China. An archaeologist back from a Mexican dig gave a dry, impatient talk about temples to an audience of three people. A New Deal Democrat spoke passionately about aiding the poor, but afterwards addressed all the women present as "Sister." Finally, just when Harry was starting to feel discouraged, he found it.

A museum offered a piece of lectures on "Science of Today—and Tomorrow." Harry heard a slim young man with a reddish beard speak with idealistic passion about travel to the moon, the planets, the stars. It seemed to Harry that compared to stars, 1989 might seem reasonably close. The young man had warm hazel eyes and a sense of humor. When he spoke about life in a space ship, he mentioned in passing that women would be freed from much domestic drudgery they now endured. Throughout the lecture, he smoked, lighting cigarettes with a masculine squinting of eyes and cupping of hands. He said that imagination was the human quality that would most help people adjust to the future. His shoes were polished.

But most of all, Harry thought, he had a *glow*. A fine golden Boy Scout glow that made Harry think of old covers for the *Saturday Evening Post*. Which here cost five cents.

After the lecture, Harry stayed in his chair in the front row, outwaiting even the girl with bright red lipstick who lingered around the lecturer, this Robert Gernshon. From time to time, Gernshon glanced over at Harry with quizzical interest. Finally the girl, red lips pouting, sashayed out of the hall.

"Hello," Harry said. "I'm Harry Kramer. I enjoyed your talk. I have something to show you that you would be very interested in."

The hazel eyes turned away. "Oh, no, no," Harry said. "Something *scientific*. Here, look at this." He handed Gernshon a filtered Vantage Light.

"How long it is," Grenshon said. "What's this made of?"

"The filter? It's made of . . . a new filter material. Tastes moldier and cuts down on the nicotine. Much better for you. Look at this." He gave Gernshon a styrofoam cup from McDonald's. "It's made of a new material, too. Very cheap. Disposable."

Gernshon fingered the cup. "Who are you?" he said quietly.

"A scientist. I'm interested in the science of tomorrow, too. Like you. I'd like to invite you to see my laboratory, which is in my home."

"In your home?"

"Yes. In a small way. Just dabbling you know." Harry could feel himself getting rattled; the young hazel eyes stared at him so steadily. *Jackie*, he thought. Dead earths. Maggots and carrion. Contempt for mothers. What would Gernshon say? When would Gernshon say *anything*?

"Thank you," Gernshon finally said. "When would be convenient?"

"Now?" Harry said. He tried to remember what time of day it was now. All he could picture was lecture halls.

Gernshon came. It was nine-thirty in the evening of Friday, September 17. Harry walked Gernshon through the streets, trying to talk animatedly to distract. He said that he himself was very interested in travel to the stars. He said it had always been his dream to stand on another planet and take in great gulps of completely unpolluted air. He said his great heroes were those biologists who made that twisty model of DNA. He said science had been his life. Gernshon walked more and more silently.

"Of course," Harry said hastily, "like most scientists, I'm mostly familiar with my own field. You know how it is."

"What is your field, Dr. Kramer?" Gernshon asked quietly.

"Electricity," Harry said, and hit him on the back of the head with a solid brass candlestick from the pocket of his coat. The candlestick had cost him three dollars at a pawn shop.

They had walked past the stores and pushcarts to a point where the locked business offices and warehouses began. There were no passers-by, no muggers, no street dealers, no Guardian Angels, no punk gangs. Only him, hitting an unarmed man with a candlestick. He was no better than the punks. But what else could he do? What else could he *do*? Nothing but hit him softly, so softly that Grenshon was struggling again almost before Harry got his hands and feet tied, well before he got on the blindfold and gag. "I'm sorry, I'm sorry," he kept saying to Gernshon. Gernshon did not look as if the apology made any difference. Harry dragged him into the warehouse.

Rudy was asleep over *Spicy Stories*. Breathing very hard, Harry pulled the young man—not more than 150 pounds, it was good Harry had looked for slim—to the far corner, through the gate, and into his closet.

"Listen," he said urgently to Grenshon after removing the gag. "Listen. I can call the Medicare Emergency Hotline. If your head feels broken. Are you feeling faint? Do you think you maybe might go into shock?"

Gernshon lay on Harry's rug, glaring at him, saying nothing.

"Listen, I know this is maybe a little startling to you. But I'm not a pervert, not a cop, not anything but a grandfather with a problem. My granddaughter. I need your help to solve it, but I won't take much of your time. You're now somewhere besides where you gave your lecture. A pretty long ways away. But you don't have to stay here long, I promise. Just two weeks, tops, and I'll send you back. I promise, on my mother's grave. And I'll make it worth your while. I promise."

"Untie me."

"Yes. Of course. Right away. Only you have to not attack me, because I'm the only one who can get you back from here." He had a sudden inspiration. "I'm like a foreign consul. You've maybe traveled abroad?"

Gernshon looked around the dingy room. "Untie me."

"I will. In two minutes. Five, tops. I just want to explain a little first."

"Where am I?"

"1989."

Gernshon said nothing. Harry explained brokenly, talking as fast as he could, saying he could move from 1989 to September, 1937 when he wanted to, but he could take Gernshon back too, no problem. He said he made the trip often, it was perfectly safe. He pointed out how much farther a small Social Security check, no pension, could go at 1937 prices. He mentioned Manny's strudel. Only lightly did he touch on the problem of Jackie, figuring there would be a better time to share difficulties, and his closet he didn't mention at all. It was hard to keep his eyes averted from the closet door. He did mention how bitter people could be in 1989, how lost, how weary from expecting so much that nothing was a delight, nothing a sweet surprise. He was just working up to a tirade on innocence when Gernshon said again, in a different tone, "Untie me."

"Of course," Harry said quickly, "I don't expect you to believe me. Why should you think you're in 1989? Go, see for yourself. Look at that light, it's still early morning. Just be careful out there, is all." He untied Gernshon and stood with his eyes squeezed shut, waiting.

When nothing hit him, Harry opened his eyes. Gernshon was at the door. "Wait!" Harry cried. "You'll need more money!" He dug into his pocket and pulled out a twenty-dollar bill, carefully saved for this, and all the change he had.

Gernshon examined the coins carefully, then looked up at Harry. He said nothing. He opened the door and Harry, still trembling, sat down in his chair to wait.

Gernshon came back three hours later, pale and sweating. "My God!"

"I know just what you mean," Harry said. "A zoo out there. Have a drink."

Gernshon took the mixture Harry had ready in his toothbrush glass and gulped it down. He caught sight of the bottle, which Harry had left on the dresser: Seagram's V.O., with the cluttered, tiny-print label. He threw the glass across the room and covered his face with his hands.

"I'm sorry," Harry said apologetically. "But then it cost only $3.37 the fifth."

Gernshon didn't move.

"I'm really sorry," Harry said. He raised both hands, palms up, and dropped them helplessly. "Would you . . . would you maybe like an orange?"

Gernshon recovered faster than Harry had dared hoped. Within an hour he was sitting in Harry's worn chair, asking questions about the space shuttle; within two hours taking notes; within three become again the intelligent and captivating young man of the lecture hall. Harry, answering as much as he could as patiently as he could, was impressed by the boy's resilience. It couldn't have been easy. What if he, Harry, suddenly had to skip fifty-two more years? What if he found himself in 2041? Harry shuddered.

"Do you know that a movie now costs six dollars?"

Gernshon blinked. "We were talking about the moon landing."

"Not any more, we're not. I want to ask *you* some

questions, Robert. Do you think the earth is dead, with people sliming all over it like on carrion? Is this a thought that crosses your mind?"

"I . . . no."

Harry nodded. "Good, good. Do you look at your mother with contempt?"

"Of course not. Harry—"

"No, it's my turn. Do you think a woman who marries a man, and maybe the marriage doesn't work out perfect, whose does, but they raise at least one healthy child—say a daughter—that that woman's life has been a defeat and a failure?"

"No. I—"

"What would you think if you saw a drawing of a woman's private parts on the cover of a magazine?"

Gernshon blushed. He looked as if the blush annoyed him, but also as if he couldn't help it.

"Better and better," Harry said. "Now, think carefully on this next one—take your time—no hurry. Does reality seem to you to have sweetness in it as well as ugliness? Take your time."

Gernshon peered at him. Harry realized they had talked right through lunch. "But not all the time in the world, Robert."

"Yes," Gernshon said. "I think reality has more sweetness than ugliness. And more strangers than anything else. Very much more." He looked suddenly dazed. "I'm sorry, I just—all this has happened so—"

"Put your head between your knees," Harry suggested. "There—better now? Good. There's someone I want you to meet."

Manny sat in the park, on their late-afternoon bench. When he saw them coming, his face settled into long sorrowful ridges. "Harry. Where have you been for two days? I was worried, I went to your hotel—"

"Manny," Harry said, "this is Robert."

"So I see," Manny said. He didn't hold out his hand.

"*Him*," Harry said.

"Harry. Oh, Harry."

"How do you do, sir," Gernshon said. He held out his hand. "I'm afraid I didn't get your full name. I'm Robert Gernshon."

Manny looked at him—at the outstretched hand, the baggy suit with wide tie, the deferential smile, the golden Baden-Powell glow. Manny's lips mouthed a silent word: *sir?*

"I have a lot to tell you," Harry said.

"You can tell all of us, then," Manny said. "Here comes Jackie now."

Harry looked up. Across the park a woman in jeans strode purposefully towards them. "Manny! It's only Monday!"

"I called her to come," Manny said. "You've been gone from your room two days, Harry, nobody at your hotel could say where—"

"But *Manny*," Harry said, while Gernshon looked, frowning, from one to the other and Jackie spotted them and waved.

She had lost more weight, Harry saw. Only two weeks, yet her cheeks had hollowed out and new, tiny lines touched her eyes. Skinny lines. They filled him with sadness. Jackie wore a blue tee-shirt that said LIFE IS A BITCH—THEN YOU DIE. She carried a magazine and a small can of mace disguised as hair spray.

"Popsy! You're here! Manny said—"

"Manny was wrong," Harry said. "Jackie, sweetheart, you look—it's good to see you. Jackie, I'd like you to meet somebody, darling. This is Robert. My friend. My friend Robert. Jackie Snyder."

"Hi," Jackie said. She gave Harry a hug, and then Manny one. Harry saw Gernshon gazing at her very tight jeans.

"Robert's a . . . a scientist," Harry said.

It was the wrong thing to say; Harry knew the moment he said it that it was the wrong thing. Science—all science—was, for some reason not completely clear to him, a touchy subject with Jackie. She tossed her long hair back from her eyes. "Oh, yeah? Not *chemical*, I hope?"

"I'm not actually a scientist," Gernshon said winningly.

"Just a dabbler. I popularize new scientific concepts, write about them to make them intelligible."

"Like what?" Jackie said.

Gernshon opened his mouth, closed it again. A boy suddenly flashed past on a skateboard, holding a boom box. Metallica blasted the air. Overhead, a jet droned. Gernshon smiled weakly. "It's hard to explain."

"I'm capable of understanding," Jackie said coldly. "Women *can* understand science, you know."

"Jackie, sweetheart," Harry said, "what have you got there? Is that your new book?"

"No." Jackie said. "this is one I said I'd bring you, by my friend. It's brilliant. It's about a man whose business partner betrays him by selling out to organized crime and framing the man. In jail he meets a guy who has founded his own religion, the House of Divine Despair, and when they both get out they start a new business, Suicide Incorporated, that helps people kill themselves for a fee. The whole thing is just a brilliant denunciation of contemporary America."

Gernshon made a small sound.

"It's a comedy," Jackie added.

"It sounds . . . it sounds a little depressing," Gernshon said.

Jackie looked at him. Very distinctly, she said, "It's reality."

Harry saw Gernshon glance around the park. A man nodded on a bench, his hands slack on his knees. Newspapers and McDonald's wrappers stirred fitfully in the dirt. A trash container had been knocked over. From beside a scrawny tree enclosed shoulder-height by black wrought iron, a child watched them with old eyes.

"I brought you something else, too, Popsy," Jackie said. Harry hoped that Gernshon noticed how much gentler her voice was when she spoke to her grandfather. "A scarf. See, it's llama wool. Very warm."

Gernshon said, "My mother has a scarf like that. No, I guess hers is some kind of fur."

Jackie's face changed. "What kind?"

"I—I'm not sure."

"Not an endangered species, I hope."

"No. Not that. I'm sure not . . . that."

Jackie stared at him a moment longer. The child who had been watching strolled towards them. Harry saw Gernshon look at the boy with relief. About eleven years old, he wore a perfectly tailored suit and Italian shoes. Manny shifted to put himself between the boy and Gernshon. "Jackie, darling, it's so good to see you. . . ."

The boy brushed by Gernshon on the other side. He never looked up, and his voice stayed boyish and low, almost a whisper. "Crack. . . ."

"Step on one and you break your mother's back," Gernshon said brightly. He smiled at Harry, a special conspiratorial smile to suggest that children, at least, didn't change in fifty years. The boy's head jerked up to look at Gernshon.

"You talking about my mama?"

Jackie groaned. "No," she said to the kid. "He doesn't mean anything. Beat it."

"I don't forget," the boy said. He backed away slowly.

Gernshon said, frowning, "I'm sorry. I'm not sure exactly what all that was, but I'm sorry."

"Are you for real?" Jackie said angrily. "What the fucking hell *was* all that? Don't you realize this park is the only place Manny and my grandfather can get some fresh air?"

"I didn't—"

"That punk runner meant it when he said he won't forget!"

"I don't like your tone," Gernshon said. "Or your language."

"My language!" The corners of Jackie's mouth tightened. Manny looked at Harry and put his hands over his face. The boy, twenty feet away, suddenly let out a noise like a strangled animal, so piercing all four of them spun around. Two burly teenagers were running towards him. The child's face crumpled; he looked suddenly much younger. He sprang away, stumbled, made the noise again, and hurled himself, all animal terror, towards the street behind the park bench.

"No!" Gernshon shouted. Harry turned towards the shout but Gernshon already wasn't there. Harry saw the twelve-wheeler bearing down, heard Jackie's scream, saw Gernshon's wiry body barrel into the boy's. The truck shrieked past, its air brakes deafening.

Gernshon and the boy rose in the street on the other side. Car horns blared. The boy bawled, "Leggo my suit! You tore my suit!" A red light flashed and a squad car pulled up. The two burly teenagers melted away, and then the boy somehow vanished as well.

"Never find him," the disgruntled cop told them over the clipboard on which he had written nothing. "Probably just as well." He went away.

"Are you hurt?" Manny said. It was the first time he had spoken. His face was ashen. Harry put a hand across his shoulders.

"No," Gernshon said. He gave Manny his sweet smile. "Just a little dirty."

"That took *guts*," Jackie said. She was staring at Gernshon with a frown between her eyebrows. "Why did you do it?"

"Pardon?"

"Why? I mean, given what that kid is, given—oh, all of it—" she gestured around the park, a helpless little wave of her strong young hands that tore at Harry's heart. "Why bother?"

Gernshon said gently, "What the kid is, is a kid."

Manny looked skeptical. Harry moved to stand in front of Manny's expression before anyone wanted to discuss it. "Listen, I've got a wonderful idea, you two seem to have so much to talk about, about . . . bothering, and . . . everything. Why don't you have dinner together, on me? My treat." He pulled another twenty dollar bill from his pocket. Behind him he could feel Manny start.

"Oh, I couldn't," Gernshon said, at the same moment that Jackie said warningly, "Popsy. . . ."

Harry put his palms on both sides of her face. "Please. Do

this for me, Jackie. Without the questions, without the female protests. Just this once. For me."

Jackie was silent a long moment before she grimaced, nodded, and turned with half-humorous appeal to Gernshon.

Gernshon cleared his throat. "Well, actually, it would probably be better if all four of us came. I'm embarrassed to say that prices are higher in this city than in . . . that is, I'm not able to . . . but if we went somewhere less expensive, the Automat maybe, I'm sure all four of us could eat together."

"No, no," Harry said. "We already ate." Manny looked at him.

Jackie began, offended, "I certainly don't want—just what do you think is going on here, buddy? This is just to please my grandfather. Are you afraid I might try to jump your bones?"

Harry saw Gernshon's quick, involuntary glance at Jackie's tight jeans. He saw, too, that Gernshon fiercely regretted the glance the instant he had made it. He saw that Manny saw, and that Jackie saw, and that Gernshon saw that they saw. Manny made a small noise. Jackie's face began to turn so black that Harry was astounded when Gernshon cut her off with a dignity no one had expected.

"No, of course not," he said quietly. "But *I* would prefer all of us to have dinner together for quite another reason. My wife is very dear to me, Miss Snyder, and I wouldn't do anything that might make her feel uncomfortable. That's probably irrational, but that's the way it is."

Harry stood arrested, his mouth open. Manny started to shake with what Harry thought savagely had better not be laughter. And Jackie, after staring at Gernshon a long while, broke into the most spontaneous smile Harry had seen from her in months.

"Hey," she said softly. "That's nice. That's really, genuinely, fucking nice."

The weather turned abruptly colder. Snow threatened but didn't fall. Each afternoon Harry and Manny took a quick walk in the park and then went inside, to the chess club or a coffee shop or the bus station or the library, where there was a table deep in the stacks on which they could eat lunch without detection. Harry brought Manny a poor boy with mayo, sixty-three cents, and a pair of imported wool gloves, one dollar on pre-season sale.

"So where are they today?" Manny asked on Saturday, removing the gloves to peek at the inside of the poor boy. He sniffed appreciatively. "Horseradish. You remembered, Harry."

"The museum, I think," Harry said miserably.

"What museum?"

"How should I know? He says, 'The museum today, Harry,' and he's gone by eight o'clock in the morning, no more details than that."

Manny stopped chewing. "What museum opens at eight o'clock in the morning?"

Harry put down his sandwich, pastrami on rye, thirty-nine cents. He had lost weight the past week.

"Probably," Manny said hastily, "they just talk. You know, like young people do, just talk. . . ."

Harry eyed him balefully. "You mean like you and Leah did when you were young and left completely alone."

"You better talk to him soon, Harry. No, to her." He seemed to reconsider Jackie. "No, to *him*."

"Talk isn't going to do it," Harry said. He looked pale and determined. "Gernshon has to be sent back."

"Be sent?"

"He's *married*, Manny! I wanted to help Jackie, show her life can hold some sweetness, not be all struggle. What kind of sweetness is she going to find if she falls in love with a married man? You know how that goes! Jackie—" Harry groaned. How had all this happened? He had intended only the best for Jackie. Why didn't that count more? "He has to go back, Manny."

"How?" Manny said practically. "You can't hit him again, Harry. You were just lucky last time that you didn't hurt him. You don't want that on your conscience. And if you show him your, uh . . . your—"

"My closet. Manny, if you'd only come see, for a dollar you could get—"

"—then he could just come back any time he wants. So how?"

A sudden noise startled them both. Someone was coming through the stacks. "Librarians!" Manny hissed. Both of them frantically swept the sandwiches, beer (fifteen cents), and strudel into shopping bags. Manny, panicking, threw in the wool gloves. Harry swept the table free of crumbs. When the intruder rounded the nearest bookshelf, Harry was bent over *Making Paper Flowers* and Manny over *Porcelain of the Yung Cheng Dynasty*. It was Robert Gernshon.

The young man dropped into a chair. His face was ashen. In one hand he clutched a sheaf of paper, the handwriting on the last one trailing off into shaky squiggles.

After a moment of silence, Manny said diplomatically, "So where are you coming from, Robert?"

"Where's Jackie?" Harry demanded.

"Jackie?" Gernshon said. His voice was thick; Harry realized with a sudden shock that he had been crying. "I haven't seen her for a few days."

"A few *days*?" Harry said.

"No. I've been . . . I've been. . . ."

Manny sat up straighter. He looked intently at Gernshon over *Porcelain of the Yung Cheng Dynasty* and then put the book down. He moved to the chair next to Gernshon's and gently took the papers form his hand. Gernshon leaned over the table and buried his head in his arms.

"I'm so awfully sorry, I'm being such a baby. . . ." His shoulders trembled. Manny separated the papers and spread them out on the library table. Among the hand-copied notes were two slim books, one bound between black covers and the other a pamphlet. *A Memoir of Auschwitz. Countdown to Hiroshima.*

For a long moment nobody spoke. Then Harry said, to no one in particular, "I thought he was going to science museums."

Manny laid his arm, almost casually, across Gernshon's shoulders. "So now you'll know not to be at either place.

More people should have only known." Harry didn't recognize the expression on his friend's face, nor the voice with which Manny said to Harry, "You're right. He has to go back."

"But Jackie. . . ."

"Can do without this 'sweetness,'" Manny said harshly. "So what's so terrible in her life anyway that she needs so much help? Is she dying? Is she poor? Is she ugly? Is anyone knocking on her door in the middle of the night? Let Jackie find her own sweetness. She'll survive."

Harry made a helpless gesture. Manny's stubborn face, carved wood under the harsh fluorescent light, did not change. "Even *him* . . . Manny, the things he knows now—"

"You should have thought of that earlier."

Gernshon looked up. "Don't, I—I'm sorry. It's just coming across it, I never thought human beings—"

"No," Manny said. "But they can. You been here, every day, at the library, reading it all?"

"Yes. That and museums. I saw you two come in earlier. I've been reading, I wanted to *know*—"

"So now you know," Manny said in that same surprisingly casual, tough voice. "You'll survive, too."

Harry said, "Does Jackie know what's going on? Why you've been doing all this . . . learning?"

"No."

"And you—what will you do with what you now know?"

Harry held his breath. What if Gernshon just refused to go back? Gernshon said slowly, "At first, I wanted to not return. At all. How can I watch it, World War II and the camps—I have *relatives* in Poland. And then later the bomb and Korea and the gulags and Vietnam and Cambodia and the terrorists and AIDS—"

"Didn't miss anything," Harry muttered.

"—and not to be able to *do* anything, not be able to even hope, knowing that everything to come is already set into history—how could I watch all that without any hope that it isn't really as bad as it seems to be at the moment?"

"It all depends what you look at," Manny said, but Gernshon didn't seem to hear him.

"But neither can I stay, there's Susan and we're hoping for a baby . . . I need to think."

"No, you don't," Harry said. "You need to go *back*. This is all my mistake. I'm sorry. You need to go back, Gernshon."

"Lebanon," Gernshon said. "D.D.T. The Cultural Revolution. Nicaragua. Deforestation. Iran—"

"Penicillin," Manny said suddenly. His beard quivered. "Civil rights. Mahatma Gandhi. Polio vaccines. Washing machines." Harry stared at him, shocked. Could Manny once have worked in a hand laundry?

"Or," Manny said, more quietly, "Hitler. Auschwitz. Hoovervilles. The Dust Bowl. What you *look* at, Robert."

"I don't know," Gernshon said. "I need to think. There's so much . . . and then there's that girl."

Harry stiffened. "Jackie?"

"No, no. Someone else she and I met a few days ago, at a coffee shop. She just walked in. I couldn't believe it. I looked at her and just went into shock—and maybe she did too, for all I know. The girl looked exactly like me. And she *felt* like—I don't know. It's hard to explain. She felt like *me*. I said hello but I didn't tell her my name, I didn't dare." His voice fell to a whisper. "I think she's my granddaughter."

"Hoo boy," Manny said.

Gernshon stood. He made a move to gather up his papers and booklets, stopped, left them there. Harry stood, too, so abruptly that Gernshon shot him a sudden, hard look across the library table. "Going to hit me again, Harry? Going to kill me?"

"Us?" Manny said. "Us, Robert?" His tone was gentle.

"In a way, you already have. I'm not who I was, certainly."

Manny shrugged. "So be somebody better."

"Damn it, I don't think you understand—"

"I don't think *you* do, Reuven, boychik. This is the way it *is*. That's all. Whatever you had back there, you have still. Tell me, in all that reading, did you find anything about yourself, anything personal? Are you in the history books, in the library papers?"

"The Office of Public Documents takes two weeks to do

a search for birth and death certificates," Gernshon said, a
little sulkily.

"So you lost nothing, because you really *know* nothing,"
Manny said. "Only history. History is cheap. Everybody
gets some. You can have all the history you want. It's what
you make of it that counts."

Gernshon didn't nod agreement. He looked a long time at
Manny, and something moved behind the unhappy hazel
eyes, something that made Harry finally let out a breath he
didn't know he'd been holding. It suddenly seemed that
Gernshon was the one that was old. And he *was*—with the
fifty-two years he'd gained since last week, he was older
than Harry had been in the 1937 of *Captains Courageous*
and wide-brimmed fedoras and clean city parks. But that
was a good time, the one that Gernshon was going back to,
the one Harry himself would choose, if it weren't for Jackie
and Manny . . . still, he couldn't watch as Gernshon
walked out of the book stacks, parting the musty air as
heavily as if it were water.

Gernshon paused. Over his shoulder he said, "I'll go
back. Tonight. I will."

After he left, Harry said, "This is my fault."

"Yes," Manny agreed.

"Will you come to my room when he goes? To . . . to
help?"

"Yes, Harry."

Somehow, that only made it worse.

Gernshon agreed to a blindfold. Harry led him through the
closet, the warehouse, the street. Neither of them seemed
very good at this; they stumbled into each other, hesitated,
tripped over nothing. In the warehouse Gernshon nearly
walked into a pile of lumber, and in the sharp jerk Harry
gave Gernshon's arm to deflect him, something twisted and
gave way in Harry's back. He waited, bent over, behind a
corner of a building while Gernshon removed his blindfold,
blinked in the morning light, and walked slowly away.

Despite his back, Harry found that he couldn't return
right away. Why not? He just couldn't. He waited until

Gernshon had a large head start and then hobbled towards the park. A carousel turned, playing bright organ music: September 24. Two children he had never noticed before stood just beyond the carousel, watching it with hungry, hopeless eyes. Flowers grew in immaculate flower beds. A black man walked by, his eyes fixed on the sidewalk, his head bent. Two small girls jumping rope were watched by a smiling woman in a blue-and-white uniform. On the sidewalk, just beyond the carousel, someone had chalked a swastika. The black man shuffled over it. A Lincoln Zephyr V-12 drove by, $1090. There was no way it would fit through a closet.

When Harry returned, Manny was curled up on the white chenille bedspread that Harry had bought for $3.29, fast asleep.

"What did I accomplish, Manny? What?" Harry said bitterly. The day had dawned glorious and warm, unexpected Indian summer. Trees in the park showed bare branches against a bright blue sky. Manny wore an old red sweater, Harry a flannel workshirt. Harry shifted gingerly, grimacing, on his bench. Sunday strollers dropped ice cream wrappers, cigarettes, newspapers. Diet Pepsi cans, used tissues, popcorn. Pigeons quarreled and children shrieked.

"Jackie's going to be just as hard as ever—and why not?" Harry continued. "She finally meets a nice fellow, he never calls her again. Me, I leave a young man miserable on a sidewalk. Before I leave him, I ruin his life. While I leave him, I ruin my back. *After* I leave him, I sit here guilty. There's no answer, Manny."

Manny didn't answer. He squinted down the curving path.

"I don't know, Manny. I just don't know."

Manny said suddenly, "Here comes Jackie."

Harry looked up. He squinted, blinked, tried to jump up. His back made sharp protest. He stayed where he was, and his eyes grew wide.

"Popsy!" Jackie cried. "I've been looking for you!"

She looked radiant. All the lines were gone from around her eyes, all the sharpness from her face. Her very collar bones, Harry thought dazedly, looked softer. Happiness haloed her like light. She held the hand of a slim, red-haired woman with strong features and direct hazel eyes.

"This is Ann," Jackie said. "I've been looking for you, Popsy, because . . . well, because I need to tell you something." She slid onto the bench next to Harry, on the other side from Manny, and put one arm around Harry's shoulders. The other hand kept a close grip on Ann, who smiled encouragement. Manny stared at Ann as at a ghost.

"You see, Popsy, for a while now I've been struggling with something, something really important. I know I've been snappy and difficult, but it hasn't been—everybody needs somebody to love, you've often told me that, and I know how happy you and Grammy were all those years. And I thought there would never be anything like that for me, and certain people were making everything all so hard. But now . . . well, now there's Ann. And I wanted you to know that."

Jackie's arm tightened. Her eyes pleaded. Ann watched Harry closely. He felt as if he were drowning.

"I know this must come as a shock to you," Jackie went on, "but I also know you've always wanted me to be happy. So I hope you'll come to love her the way I do."

Harry stared at the red-haired woman. He knew what was being asked of him, but he didn't believe in it, it wasn't real, in the same way weather going on in other countries wasn't really real. Hurricanes. Drought. Sunshine. When what you were looking at was a cold drizzle.

"I think that of all the people I've ever known, Ann is the most together. The most compassionate. And the most moral."

"Ummm," Harry said.

"Popsy?"

Jackie was looking right at him. The longer he was silent, the more her smile faded. It occurred to him that the smile had showed her teeth. They were very white, very even. Also very sharp.

"I . . . I . . . hello, Ann."

"Hello," Ann said.

"See, I told you he'd be great!" Jackie said to Ann. She

let go of Harry and jumped up from the bench, all energy and lightness. "You're wonderful, Popsy! You, too, Manny! Oh, Ann, this is Popsy's best friend, Manny Feldman. Manny, Ann Davies."

"Happy to meet you," Ann said. She had a low, rough voice and a sweet smile. Harry felt hurricanes, drought, sunshine.

Jackie said, "I know this is probably a little unexpected—"

Unexpected. "Well—" Harry said, and could say no more.

"It's just that it was time for me to come out of the closet."

Harry made a small noise. Manny managed to say, "So you live here, Ann?"

"Oh, yes. All my life. And my family, too, since forever."

"Has Jackie . . . has Jackie met any of them yet?"

"Not yet," Jackie said. "It might be a little . . . tricky, in the case of her parents." She smiled at Ann. "But we'll manage."

"I wish," Ann said to her, "that you could have met *my* grandfather. He would have been just as great as your Popsy here. He always was."

"Was?" Harry said faintly.

"He died a year ago. But he was just a wonderful man. Compassionate *and* intelligent."

"What . . . what did he do?"

"He taught history at the university. He was also active in lots of organizations—Amnesty International, the ACLU, things like that. During World War II he worked for the Jewish rescue league, getting people out of Germany."

Manny nodded. Harry watched Jackie's teeth.

"We'd like you both to come to dinner soon," Ann said. She smiled. "I'm a good cook."

Manny's eyes gleamed.

Jackie said, "I know this must be hard for you—" but Harry saw that she didn't really mean it. She didn't think it was hard. For her it was so real that it was natural weather, unexpected maybe, but not strange, not out of place, not out of time. In front of the bench, sunlight striped the pavement like bars.

Suddenly Jackie said, "Oh, Popsy, did I tell you that it was your friend Robert who introduced us? Did I tell you that already?"

"Yes, sweetheart," Harry said. "You did."

"He's kind of a nerd, but actually all right."

After Jackie and Ann left, the two old men sat silent for a long time. Finally Manny said diplomatically, "You want to get a snack, Harry?"

"She's happy, Manny."

"Yes. You want to get a snack, Harry?"

"She didn't even recognize him?"

"No. You want to get a snack?"

"Here, have this. I got it for you this morning." Harry held out an orange, a deep-colored navel with flawless rind: seedless, huge, guaranteed juicy, nurtured for flavor, perfect.

"Enjoy," Harry said. "It cost me ninety-two cents."

FULL CHICKEN RICHNESS

Avram Davidson

For many years, the late Avram Davidson was one of the most eloquent and individual voices in science fiction and fantasy, and there were few writers in any literary field who could match his wit, his erudition, or the stylish elegance of his prose. During his long career, Davidson won the Hugo, the Edgar, and the World Fantasy Awards, and his short work was assembled in landmark collections such as The Best of Avram Davidson, Or All the Seas With Oysters, The Redward Edward Papers, *and* Collected Fantasies. *His novels include the renowned* The Phoenix and the Mirror, Masters of the Maze, Rogue Dragon, Peregrine: Primus, Rork!, Clash of Star Kings, *and* Vergil In Averno. *His most recent books are a novel in collaboration with Grania Davis,* Marco Polo and the Sleeping Beauty, *the marvelous collection* The Adventures of Doctor Esterhazy *(one of the best collections of the decade), and a posthumously released collection of his erudite and witty essays,* Adventures in Unhistory. *Upcoming is a new and updated version of* The Best of Avram Davidson.*

All of Davidson's talents are displayed to good effect in the sly and witty story that follows, which features—among many other delights—what is probably the single silliest reason for time travel in the entire history of time-travel stories . . .

La Bunne Burger was said to have the best hamburger on The Street; the only trouble with that was that Fred Hopkins didn't care much for hamburger. However there were other factors to consider, such as these: other items on La Bunne's menu were probably just a bit better than comparable items composed elsewhere on The Street, they sold for just a bit

less than, etc. etc., and also Fred Hopkins found the company
just a bit more interesting than elsewhere, etc. What else? It
was nearer to his studio loft than any eating-place else. Any
place else save for a small place called The Old Moulmein
Pagoda, the proprietor of which appeared to speak very
fluent Cantonese for a Burman, and the Old Moulmein
Pagoda was not open until late afternoon. *Late* afternoon.

Late morning was more Fred's style.

He was likely to find there, at any given time of late
morning, a number of regulars, such as: well, there was
Tilly, formerly Ottilie, with red cheeks, her white hair
looking windblown even on windless days; Tilly had her
own little routine, which consisted of ordering coffee and
toast; with the toast came a small plastic container of jelly,
and this she spread on one of the slices of toast. That eaten,
she would hesitantly ask Rudolfo if she might have more
jelly . . . adding, that she would pay for it. Rudolfo would
hand her one or two or three more, she would tentatively
offer him a palm of pennies and nickels and he would
politely decline them. Fred was much moved by this little
drama, but after the twelfth and succedant repetitions it left
him motionless. (Once he was to encounter Tillie in a
disused doorway downtown standing next to a hat with
money while she played—and played beautifully—endless
Strauss waltzes on that rather un-Strauss-like-instrument,
the harmonica.)

Also unusually present in La Bunne Burger in the 40
minutes before the noon rush were Volodya and Carl. They
were a sort of twosome there; that is, they were certainly not
a twosome elsewhere. Carl was tall and had long blond hair
and a long blond beard and was already at his place along
the counter when Volodya walked in. Carl never said anything to Volodya, Volodya always said anything to Carl.
Volodya was wide and gnarly and had small pale eyes like
those of a malevolent pig. Among the things he called Carl
were *Pópa! Moskúey! Smaravátchnik!*—meaning (Fred
Hopkins found out by and by) Priest! Inhabitant of Moscow!
and One Who, For Immoral Purposes, Pretends to be a
Chimney Sweep! Fred by and by tried to dissuade Volodya

of this curious delusion; "He's a Minnesota Swede," Fred
explained. But Volodya would have none of it. *"He's A
Rahshian Artoducks priest!"* was his explosive come-
back—and he went on to denounce the last Czar of Russia
as having been in the pay of the freemasons. Carl always
said nothing, munched away on droplets of egg congealed
on his beard.

And there was, in La Bunne Burger, often, breaking fast
on a single sausage and a cup of tea, a little old oriental man,
dressed as though for the winters of Manchuria; once Fred
had, speaking slowly and clearly, asked him please to pass
the ketchup: "Say, I ain't deef," said the l.o.o.m., in tones
the purest American Gothic.

Fred himself was not in the least eccentric, he was an *artist*,
not even starving, though . . . being unfashionably represen-
tational . . . not really prospering, either. His agent said that
this last was his, Fred's, own fault. "Paint doctors' wives!" his
agent insisted. "If you would only paint portraits for doctors'
wives, I could get you lots of commissions. Old buildings," the
agent said, disdainfully. "Old buildings, old buildings." But the
muse kisseth where she listeth and if anything is not on the list,
too bad: Fred had nothing against doctor's wives; merely, he
preferred to paint pictures of old buildings. Now and then he
drove around looking for old buildings he hadn't painted
pictures of and he photographed them and put the photos up by
his canvas to help when he painted at home: this of course
caused him to be regarded with scorn by purists who painted
only from the model or the imagination; why either should be
less or more scornable, they disdained to say.

Whom else was F. Hopkins likely to see in La Bunne
Burger over his late breakfast or his brunch? Proprietors of
nearby businesses, for example, he was likely to see there;
mamma no longer brought pappa's dinner wrapped in a
towel to keep hot. Abelardo was sometimes there. Also Fred
might see tourists or new emigrés or visiting entrepreneurs
of alien status, come to taste the exotic tuna fish sandwich
on toast, the picturesque macaroni and cheese, the curious
cold turkey, and, of course, often, often, often the native La
Bunne De Luxe Special . . . said to be the best hamburger

on The Street. Abelardo had long looked familiar; Abelardo had in fact looked familiar from the first. Abelardo always came in from the kitchen and Abelardo always went back out through the kitchen, and yet Abelardo did not work in the kitchen. Evidently Abelardo delivered. Something.

Once, carrying a plate of . . . something . . . odd and fragrant, Rudolfo rested it a moment on the counter near Fred while he gathered cutlery; in response to Fred's look of curiosity and approbation, at once said, "Not on the menu. Only I give some to Abelardo, because our family come from the same country;" off he went.

Later: "You're not from Mexico, Rudolfo."

"No. South America." Rudolfo departs with glasses.

Later: "Which country in South America you from, Rudolfo?"

"Depend who you ask." Exit, Rudolfo, for napkins.

Fred Hopkins, idly observing paint on two of his own fingers, idly wondered that—a disputed boundary being clearly involved—Rudolfo was not out leading marches and demonstrations, or (*at least!*) with drippy brushes slapping up graffiti exhorting the reader to *Remember the 12th of January . . . the 3rd of April . . . the 24th of October* . . . and so on through the existing political calendar of Ibero-America . . . Clearly, Rudolfo was a anachronism. Perhaps he secretly served some fallen sovereign; a pseudo-crypto-Emperor of Brazil. Perhaps.

Though probably not likely.

One day, the hour being later than usual and the counter crowded, Fred's eyes wandered around in search of a seat; met those of Abelardo who, worldlessly, invited him to sit in the empty place at the two-person table. Which Fred did. And, so doing, realized why the man had always seemed familiar. Now, suppose you are a foreigner living in a small city or medium town in Latin America, as Fred Hopkins had once been, and it doesn't really matter which city or town or even which country . . . doesn't really matter for *this* purpose . . . and you are going slightly out of your *mind* trying to get your electricity (*la luz*) turned on and eventually you notice that there are a few large stones never moved

from the side of a certain street and gradually notice that
there is often the same man sitting on one of the boulders
and that this man wears very dusty clothes which do not
match and a hat rather odd for the locale (say, a beret) and
that he also wears glasses and that the lens of one is opaque
or dark and that this man often gives a small wave of his
hand to return the greetings of passersby but otherwise he
merely sits and looks. You at length have occasion to ask
him something, say, At what hour does the Municipal
Palace open? And not only does the man politely inform
you, he politely engages you in conversation and before
long he is giving you a fascinating discourse on an aspect of
history, religion, economics, or folklore, an aspect of which
you had been completely ignorant. Subsequent enquiry
discloses that the man is, say, a Don Eliseo, who had
attended the National University for nine years but took no
degree, that he is an *idiosyncratico*, and comes from a
family *muy honorado*—so much *honorado*, in fact, that
merely having been observed in polite discourse with him
results in your electricity being *connectido muy pronto*. You
have many discourses with Don Eliseo and eventually he
shows you his project, temporarily in abeyance, to perfect
the best tortilla making-and-baking machine in the world:
there is some minor problem, such as the difficulty of
scraping every third tortilla off the ceiling, but any day now
Don Eliseo will get this licked; and, in the meanwhile and
forever after, his house is your house.

This was why Abelardo had seemed familiar from the
start, and if Abelardo was not Eliseo's brother than he was
certainly his nephew or his cousin . . . in the spirit,
anyway.

Out of a polite desire that Fred Hopkins not be bored
while waiting to be served, Abelardo discussed various things
with him—that is, for the most part, Abelardo discussed.
Fred listened. La Bunne Burger was very busy.

"Now, the real weakness of the Jesuits in Paraguay,"
Abelardo explained.

"Now, in western South America," said Abelardo, "North
American corporations are disliked far less for their vices

than for their virtues. Bribery, favoritism, we can understand these things, we live with them. But an absolute insistence that one must arrive in one's office day after day at one invariable hour and that frequent prolonged telephone conversations from one's office to one's home and family is unfavored, this is against our conception of personal and domestic usement," Abelardo explained.

He assured Fred Hopkins that the Regent Isabella's greatest error, "though she made several," was in having married a Frenchman. "The Frankish temperament is not the Latin temperament," Abelardo declared.

Fred's food eventually arrived; Abelardo informed him that although individual enterprise and planned economy were all very well in their own ways, "one ignores the law of supply and demand at peril. I have been often in businesses, so I know, you see," said Abelardo.

Abelardo did not indeed wear eyeglasses with one dark or opaque lens, but one of his eyes was artificial. He had gold in his smile—that is, in his teeth—and his white coverall was much washed but never much ironed. By and by, with polite words and thanks for the pleasure of Fred's company, Abelardo vanished into the kitchen; when Fred strolled up for his bill, he was informed it had already been paid. This rather surprised Fred. So did the fact, conveyed to him by the clock, that the noon rush was over. Had *been* over.

"Abelardo seems like—Abelardo is a very nice guy."

Rudolfo's face, hands, and body made brief but persuasive signal that it went without saying that Abelardo was indeed a very nice guy. "But I don't know how he stays in business," said Rudolfo, picking up a pile of dishes and walking them off to the kitchen.

Fred had no reason to remain to discuss this, as it was an unknown to him how anybody stayed in business. Merely he was well aware how week after week the price of paints and brushes and canvases went up, up, up, while the price of his artwork stayed the same, same, same. Well, his agent, though wrong, was right. No one to blame but himself; he could have stayed in advertising, he might be an account executive by now. Or—Walking along The Street, he felt a

wry smile accompany memory of another of Abelardo's
comments: "Advertisage is like courtship, always involve
some measure of deceit."

This made him quickstep a bit back to the studio to get in
some more painting, for—he felt—tonight might be a good
one for what one might call courtship; "exploitation," some
would doubtless call it: though why? If ladies ("women!")
did not like to come back to his loft studio and see his
painting, why did they do so? And if they did not genuinely
desire to remain for a while of varying length, who could
make them? Did any one of them really desire to admire his
art, was there no pretense on the part of any of them? Why
was *he* not the exploited one? You women are all alike, you
only have one thing on your mind, all you think of is your
own pleasure . . . Oh well. Hell. Back to work.—It was
true that you could not sleep with an old building, but then
they never argued with you, either. And as for "some
measure of deceit," boy did that work both ways! Two
weeks before, he'd come upon a harmonious and almost
untouched, though tiny, commercial block in an area in
between the factories and the farms, as yet undestroyed by
the people curiously called "developers"; he'd taken lots of
color snaps of it from all angles, and he wanted to do at least
two large paintings, maybe two small ones as well. The
date, 1895, was up there in front. The front was false, but in
the harmony was truth.

A day that found him just a bit tired of the items staple in
breakfast found him ordering a cup of the soup du jour for
starters. "How you like the soup?"—Rudolfo.

Fred gave his head a silent shake. How. It had gone down
without exiting dismay. "Truthful with you. Had better, had
worse. Hm. What was it? Well, I was thinking of something
else. Uh—chicken vegetable with rice? Right? Right. Yours
or Campbell's?"

Neither.

"Half mine, half Abelardo's."

"I *beg* your pardon."

But Rudolfo had never heard the rude English story about
the pint of half-and-half, neither did Fred tell it to him.

Rudolfo said, "I make a stock with the bones after making chickens sandwiches and I mix it with this." He produced a large, a very large can, pushed it over to Fred. The label said. *FULL CHICKEN RICHNESS Chicken-Type Soup*.

"What-haht?" asked Fred, half-laughing. He read on. *Ingredients: Water, Other Poultry and Poultry Parts, Dehydrated Vegetables, Chickens and Chicken Parts, seasoning* . . . the list dribbled off into the usual list of chemicals. The label also said, *Canned for Restaurant and Institutional Usement.*

"Too big for a family," Rudolfo observed. "Well, not bad, I think, too. Help me keep the price down. Every little bit help, you know."

"Oh. Sure. No, not bad. But I wonder about that label," Rudolfo shrugged about that label. The Government, he said, wasn't going to worry about some little *chico* outfit way down from the outskirt of town. Fred chuckled at the bland non-identification of "Other Poultry"—Rudolfo said that turkey was still cheaper than chicken—"But I don't put it down, 'chicken soup,' I put it down, 'soup du jour'; anybody *ask*, I say, 'Oh, *you* know, chicken and rice and vegetable and, oh, stuff like that; *try* it, you don't like it I don't charge you.' Fair enough?—Yes," he expanded. "Abelardo, he is no businessman. He is a *filosofo*. His mind is always in the skies. I tell him, I could use more soup— twice, maybe even three times as many cans. What he cares. 'Ai! Supply and demand!' he says. Then he tells me about the old Dutch explorers, things like that—Hey! I ever tell you about the time he make his own automobile? (*"Abelar-*do did?") Sure! Abelardo did. He took a part from one car, a part from another, he takes parts not even from cars, *I* don't know what they from—"

Fred thought of Don Eliseo and the more perfect tortilla making-and-baking machine. "—well, it work! Finally! Yes! It start off, *vooom!* like a rocket! Sixty-three mile an hour! But oh boy when he try to slow it down! It stop! He start it again. Sixty-three mile an hour! No other rate of speed, well, what can you do with such a car? So he forget about it and he invent something else, who knows what;

then he got into the soup business.— Yes, sir! You ready to order?" Rudolfo moved on.

So did Fred. The paintings of the buildings 1895 were set aside for a while so that he could take a lot of pictures of a turn-of-the-century family home scheduled for destruction real soon. *This Site Will be Improved With a Modern Office Building*, what the hell did they mean by *Improved?* Alice came up and looked at the sketches of the family home, and at finished work. "I like them," she said. "I like *you*." She stayed. Everything fine. Then, one day, there was the other key on the table. On the note: *There is nothing wrong*, it said. *Just time to go now. Love.* No name. Fred sighed. Went on painting.

One morning late there was Abelardo in the Bunne. He nodded, smiled a small smile. By and by, some coffee down, Fred said, "Say, where do you buy your chickens?" Abelardo, ready to inform, though not yet ready to talk, took a card from his wallet.

> E. J. Binder Prime Poultry Farm
> also
> Game Birds Dressed To Order
> 1330 Valley Rd by the Big Oak

While Fred was still reading this, Abelardo passed him over another card, this one for the Full Chicken Richness Canned Soup Company. "You must visit me," he said. "Most time I am home."

Fred hadn't really cared where the chickens were bought, but now the devil entered into him. First he told Abelardo the story about the man who sold rabbit pie. Asked, wasn't there anyway maybe some horsemeat in the rabbit pie, said it was fifty-fifty: one rabbit, one horse. Abelardo reflected, then issued another small smile, a rather more painful one. Fred asked, "What about the turkey-meat in your chicken-type soup? I mean, uh, rather, the 'Other Poultry Parts?'"

Abelardo squinted. "Only the breast," he said. "The rest

are good enough.—For the *soup*, I mean. The rest, I sell to some mink ranchers."

"How's business?"

Abelardo shrugged. He looked a bit peaked. "Supply," he said. "Demand," he said. Then he sighed, stirred, rose. "You must visit me. Any time. Please," he said.

Abelardo wasn't there in the La Bunne Burger next late morning, but someone else was. Miles Marton, call him The Last of the Old-Time Land Agents, call him something less nice: there he was. "Been waiting," Miles Marton said. "Remember time I toll you bout ol stage-coach buildin? You never came. It comin down tomorrow. Ranch houses. Want to take its pitcher? Last chance, today. Make me a nice little paintin of it, price is right, I buy it. Bye now."

Down Fred went. Heartbreaking to think its weathered timbers, its mellowed red brick chimney and stone fireplace, were coming down; but Fred Hopkins was very glad he'd had the favor of a notice. Coming down, too, the huge trees with the guinea-fowl in them. *Lots* of photographs. Be a good painting. At least one. Driving back, lo! a sign saying **E.J. BINDER PRIME POULTRY FARM**; absolutely by a big oak. Still, Fred probably wouldn't have stopped if there hadn't been someone by the gate. Binder, maybe. Sure enough. Binder. "Say, do you know a South American named Abelardo?"

No problem. "Sure I do. Used to be a pretty good customer, too. Buy oh I forget how many chickens a week. Don't buy many nowdays. He send you here? Be glad to oblige you." Binder was an oldish man, highly sun-speckled.

"You supply his turkeys and turkey-parts, too?" The devil still inside Fred Hopkins.

Old Binder snorted, "'Turkeys,' no we don't handle turkeys, no sir, why chickens are enough trouble, cost of feeding going up, and—No, 'guinea-fowl,' no we never did. Just chickens and of course your cornish."

Still civil, E.J. Binder gave vague directions toward what he believed, he said, was the general location of Mr. Abelardo's place. Fred didn't find it right off, but he found it. As no one appeared in response to his calling and

honking, he got out and knocked. Nothing. *Pues*, "My house
is your house," okay: in he went through the first door. Well,
it wasn't a *large* cannery, but it was a *cannery*. Fred started
talking to himself; solitary artists often do. "Way I figure it,
Abelardo," he said, "is that you have been operating with
that 'small measure of deceit in advertising,' as you so aptly
put it. *I* think that in your own naive way you have believed
that so long as you called the product 'Chicken-Type Soup'
and included *some* chicken, well, it was all right. Okay, your
guilty secret is safe with me; where are you?" The place was
immaculate, except for. Except for a pile of . . . well . . .
shit . . . right in the middle of an aisle. It was as neat as a
pile of shit can be. Chicken-shits? Pigeon-poops? Turkey-
trots? *¿Quien sabe?*

At the end of the aisle was another door and behind that
door was a small apartment and in a large chair in the small
apartment sprawled Abelardo, dead drunk on mescal, *muzhik*-
grade vodka, and sneaky pete . . . according to the evidence. Alcoholism is not an especially Latin American trait?
Who said the poor guy was an alcoholic? Maybe this was
the first time he'd ever been stewed in his *life*. Maybe the
eternally perplexing matter of supply and demand had
finally unmanned him.

Maybe.

At the other end of that room was *another* door and
behind that other door was *another* room. And in that *other*
room was . . .

. . . something else. . . .

That other room was partly crammed with an insane
assortment of machinery and allied equipment, compared to
which Don Eliseo's more perfect make-and-bake tortilla
engine, with its affinities to the perpetual motion invention
of one's choice, was simplicity. The thing stood naked for
Fred's eyes, but his eyes told him very little: wires snaked
all around, that much he could say. There was a not-quite-
click, a large television screen flickered on. *No*. Whatever it
was at the room's end, sitting flush to the floor with a low,
chicken-wire fence around it, it was not a television, not
even if Abelardo had started from scratch as though there

had been no television before. The quality of the "image" was entirely different, for one thing; and the color, for another, was *wrong* . . . and wrong in the way that no TV color he had ever seen had been wrong. He reached to touch the screen, there *was* no "screen," it was as through his hand met a surface of unyielding gelatin. The non-screen, well, what the hell, *call* it a screen, was rather large, but not gigantically so. He was looking at a savannah somewhere, and among the trees were palms and he could not identify the others. A surf pounded not far off, but he could not hear it. There was no sound. He saw birds flying in and out of the trees. Looking back, he saw something else. A trail of broken bread through the room, right up to the, mmm, screen. A silent breeze now and then rifled grass, and something moved in the grass to one side. He stepped back, slightly. What the hell could it *mean?* Then the something which was in the grass to one side stepped, stiff-legged, into full view, and there was another odd, small sound as the thing—it was a bird—lurched through the screen and began to gobble bread. Hopkins watched, dry-mouthed. Crumb by crumb it ate. Then there was no more bread. It doddled up to the low fence, doddled back. It approached the screen, it brushed the screen, there was a Rube Goldberg series of motions in the external equipment, a sheet of chicken wire slid noisily down to the floor. The bird had been trapped.

Fred got down and peered into the past till his eyes and neck grew sore, but he could not see one more bird like it. He began to laugh and cry simultaneously. Then he stood up. "Inevitable," he croaked, throwing out his arms. "Inevitable! Demand exceeded supply!"

The bird looked up at him with imbecile, incurious eyes, and opened its incredible beak. "*Doh*-do," it said, halfway between a gobble and a coo. "*Doh*-do. *Doh*-do."

ANOTHER STORY

Ursula K. Le Guin

Ursula K. Le Guin is probably one of the best-known and most universally respected SF writers in the world today. Her famous novel The Left Hand of Darkness *may have been the most influential SF novel of its decade and shows every sign of becoming one of the enduring classics of the genre—even ignoring the rest of Le Guin's work, the impact of this one novel alone on future SF and future SF writers would be incalculably strong. (Her 1968 fantasy novel,* A Wizard of Earthsea, *would be almost as influential on future generations of High Fantasy writers.)* The Left Hand of Darkness *won both the Hugo and Nebula Awards, as did Le Guin's monumental novel* The Dispossessed *a few years later. Her novel,* Tehanu, *won her another Nebula in 1990, and she has also won three other Hugo Awards and a Nebula Award for her short fiction, as well as the National Book Award for Children's Literature for her novel,* The Farthest Shore, *part of her acclaimed Earthsea trilogy. Her other novels include* Planet of Exile, The Lathe of Heaven, City of Illusions, Rocannon's World, The Beginning Place, A Wizard of Earthsea, The Tombs of Atuan, Tehanu, Searoad, *and the controversial multimedia novel,* Always Coming Home. *She has had six collections:* The Wind's Twelve Quarters, Orsinian Tales, The Compass Rose, Buffalo Gals and Other Animal Presences, A Fisherman of the Inland Sea, *and her most recent book,* Four Ways to Forgiveness.*

Here she returns to the star-spanning, Hainish-settled interstellar community known as the Ekumen, the same fictional universe that provided the background for her most famous novels, for a strange, powerful, and somberly lyrical study of how sometimes even the longest and most difficult journeys serve only to bring you back to where you started from . . .

To the Stabiles *of the Ekumen on Hain, and to Gvonesh, Director of the Churten Field Laboratories at Ve Port:*

From Tiokunan'n Hideo, Farmholder of the Second Sedoretu of Udan, Derdan'nad, Oket, on O.

I shall make my report as if I told a story, this having been the tradition for some time now. You may, however, wonder why a farmer on the planet O is reporting to you as if he were a Mobile of the Ekumen. My story will explain that. But it does not explain itself. Story is our only boat for sailing on the river of time, but in the great rapids and the winding shallows, no boat is safe.

So: once upon a time when I was twenty-one years old I left my home and came on the NAFAL ship *Terraces of Darranda* to study at the Ekumenical Schools on Hain.

The distance between Hain and my home world is just over four lightyears, and there has been traffic between O and the Hainish system for twenty centuries. Even before the Nearly As Fast As Light drive, when ships spent a hundred years of planetary time instead of four to make the crossing, there were people who would give up their old life to come to a new world. Sometimes they returned; not often. There were tales of such sad returns to a world that had forgotten the voyager. I knew also from my mother a very old story called "The Fisherman of the Inland Sea," which came from her home world, Terra. The life of a ki'O child is full of stories, but of all I heard told by her and my othermother and my fathers and grandparents and uncles and aunts and teachers, that one was my favorite. Perhaps I liked it so well because my mother told it with deep feeling, though very plainly, and always in the same words (and I would not let her change the words if she ever tried to).

The story tells of a poor fisherman, Urashima, who went out daily in his boat alone on the quiet sea that lay between his home island and the mainland. He was a beautiful young man with long, black hair, and the daughter of the king of the sea saw him as he leaned over the side of the boat and she gazed up to see the floating shadow cross the wide circle of the sky.

Rising from the waves, she begged him to come to her palace under the sea with him. At first he refused, saying, "My children wait for me at home." But how could he resist the sea-king's daughter? "One night," he said. She drew him down with her under the water, and they spent a night of love in her green palace, served by strange undersea beings. Urashima came to love her dearly, and maybe he stayed more than one night only. But at last he said, "My dear, I must go. My children wait for me at home."

"If you go, you go forever," she said.

"I will come back," he promised.

She shook her head. She grieved, but did not plead with him. "Take this with you," she said, giving him a little box, wonderfully carved, and sealed shut. "Do not open it, Urashima."

So he went up onto the land, and ran up the shore to his village, to his house: but the garden was a wilderness, the windows were blank, the roof had fallen in. People came and went among the familiar houses of the village, but he did not know a single face. "Where are my children?" he cried. An old woman stopped and spoke to him: "What is your trouble, young stranger?"

"I am Urashima, of this village, but I see no one here I know!"

"Urashima!" the woman said—and my mother would look far away, and her voice as she said the name made me shiver, tears starting to my eyes—"Urashima! My grandfather told me a fisherman named Urashima was lost at sea, in the time of his grandfather's grandfather. There has been no one of that family alive for a hundred years."

So Urashima went back down to the shore; and there he opened the box, the gift of the sea-king's daughter. A little white smoke came out of it and drifted away on the sea wind. In that moment Urashima's black hair turned white, and he grew old, old, old; and he lay down on the sand and died.

Once, I remember, a traveling teacher asked my mother about the fable, as he called it. She smiled and said, "In the Annals of the Emperors of my nation of Terra it is recorded that a young man named Urashima, of the Yosa district, went away in the year 477, and came back to his village in the year 825, but soon departed again. And I have heard that the box was kept in a shrine for many centuries." Then they talked about something else.

My mother, Isako, would not tell the story as often as I demanded it. "That one is so sad," she would say, and tell instead about Grandmother and the rice dumpling that rolled away, or the painted cat who came alive and killed the demon rats, or the peach boy who floated down the river. My sister and my germanes, and older people, too, listened to her tales as closely as I did. They were new stories on O, and a new story is always a treasure. The painted-cat story was the general favorite, especially when my mother would take out her brush and the block of strange, black, dry ink from Terra, and sketch the animals—cat, rat—that none of us had ever seen: the wonderful cat with arched back and brave round eyes, the fanged and skulking rats, "pointed at both ends" as my sister said. But I waited always, through all other stories, for her to catch my eye, look away, smile a little and sigh, and begin, "Long, long ago, on the shore of the Inland Sea there lived a fisherman. . . ."

Did I know then what that story meant to her? That it was her story? That if she were to return to her village, her world, all the people she had known would have been dead for centuries?

Certainly I knew that she "came from another world," but what that meant to me as a five, or seven, or ten-year-old, is hard for me now to imagine, impossible to remember. I knew that she was a Terran and had lived on Hain; that was something to be proud of. I knew that she had come to O as a Mobile of the Ekumen (more pride, vague and grandiose) and that "your father and I fell in love at the Festival of Plays in Sudiran." I knew also that arranging the marriage had been a tricky business. Getting permission to resign her duties had not been difficult—the Ekumen is used to Mobiles going native. But as a foreigner, Isako did not belong to a ki'O moiety, and that was only the first problem. I heard all about it from my othermother, Tubdu, an endless source of family history, anecdote, and scandal. "You know," Tubdu told me when I was eleven or twelve, her eyes shining and her irrepressible, slightly wheezing, almost silent laugh beginning to shake her from the inside out— "you know, she didn't even know women got married? Where she came from, she said, women don't marry."

I could and did correct Tubdu: "Only in her part of it. She told me there's lots of parts of it where they do." I felt obscurely defensive of my mother, though Tubdu spoke without a shadow of malice or contempt; she adored Isako. She had fallen in love with her "the moment I saw her—that black hair! that mouth!"—and simply found it endearingly funny that such a woman could have expected to marry only a man.

"I understand," Tubdu hastened to assure me. "I know—on Terra it's different, their fertility was damaged, they have to think about marrying for children. And they marry in twos, too. Oh, poor Isako! How strange it must have seemed to her! I remember how she looked at me—" And off she went again into what we children called The Great Giggle, her joyous, silent, seismic laughter.

To those unfamiliar with our customs I should explain that on O, a world with a low, stable human population and an ancient climax technology, certain social arrangements are almost universal. The dispersed village, an association of farms, rather than the city or state, is the basic social unit. The population consists of two halves or moieties. A child is born into its mother's moiety, so that all ki'O (except the mountain folk of Ennik) belong either to the Morning People, whose time is from midnight to noon, or the Evening People, whose time is from noon to midnight. The sacred origins and functions of the moieties are recalled in the Discussions and the Plays and in the services at every farm shrine. The original social function of the moiety was probably to structure exogamy into marriage and so discourage inbreeding in isolated farmholds, since one can have sex with or marry only a person of the other moiety. The rule is severely reinforced. Transgressions, which of course occur, are met with shame, contempt, and ostracism.

One's identity as a Morning or an Evening Person is as deeply and intimately part of oneself as one's gender, and has quite as much to do with one's sexual life.

A ki'O marriage, called a sedoretu, consists of a Morning woman and man and an Evening woman and man; the heterosexual pairs are called Morning and Evening according to the woman's moiety; the homosexual pairs are called Day—the two women—and Night—the two men.

So rigidly structured a marriage, where each of four people must be sexually compatible with two of the others while never having sex with the fourth—clearly this takes some arranging. Making sedoretu is a major occupation of my people. Experimenting is encouraged; foursomes form and dissolve, couples "try on" other couples, mixing and matching. Brokers, traditionally elderly widowers, go about among the farmholds of the dispersed villages, arranging meetings, setting up field-dances, serving as universal confidants. Many marriages begin as a love match of one couple, either homosexual or heterosexual, to which another pair or two separate people become attached. Many marriages are brokered or arranged by the village elders from beginning to end. To listen to the old people under the village great tree making a sedoretu is like watching a master game of chess or tidhe. "If that Evening boy at Erdup were to meet young Tobo during the flour-processing at Gad'd. . . ." "Isn't Hodin'n of the Oto Morning a programmer? They could use a programmer at Erdup. . . ." The dowry a prospective bride or groom can offer is their skill, or their home farm. Otherwise undesired people may be chosen and honored for the knowledge or the property they bring to a marriage. The farmhold, in turn, wants its new members to be agreeable and useful. There is no end to the making of marriages on O. I should say that all in all they give as much satisfaction as any other arrangement to the participants, and a good deal more to the marriage-makers.

Of course many people never marry. Scholars, wandering Discussers, itinerant artists and experts, and specialists in the Centers seldom want to fit themselves into the massive permanence of a farmhold sedoretu. Many people attach

themselves to a brother's or sister's marriage as aunt or
uncle, a position with limited, clearly defined responsibilities; they can have sex with either or both spouses of the
other moiety, thus sometimes increasing the sedoretu from
four to seven or eight. Children of that relationship are
called cousins. The children of one mother are brothers or
sisters to one another; the children of the Morning and the
children of the Evening are germanes. Brothers, sisters, and
first cousins may not marry, but germanes may. In some less
conservative parts of O germane marriages are looked at
askance, but they are common and respected in my region.

My father was a Morning man of Udan Farmhold of
Derdan'nad Village in the hill region of the Northwest
Watershed of the Saduun River, on Oket, the smallest of the
six continents of O. The village comprises seventy-seven
farmholds, in a deeply rolling, stream-cut region of fields
and forests on the watershed of the Oro, a tributary of the
wide Saduun. It is fertile, pleasant country, with views west
to the Coast Range and south to the great floodplains of the
Saduun and the gleam of the sea beyond. The Oro is a wide,
lively, noisy river full of fish and children. I spent my
childhood in or on or by the Oro, which runs through Udan
so near the house that you can hear its voice all night, the
rush and hiss of the water and the deep drumbeats of rocks
rolled in its current. It is shallow and quite dangerous. We
all learned to swim very young in a quiet bay dug out as a
swimming pool, and later to handle rowboats and kayaks in
the swift current full of rocks and rapids. Fishing was one of
the children's responsibilities. I liked to spear the fat,
beady-eyed, blue ochid; I would stand heroic on a slippery
boulder in midstream, the long spear poised to strike. I was
good at it. But my germane Isidri, while I was prancing
about with my spear, would slip into the water and catch six
or seven ochid with her bare hands. She could catch eels and
even the darting ei. I never could do it. "You just sort of
move with the water and get transparent," she said. She
could stay under water longer than any of us, so long you
were sure she had drowned. "She's too bad to drown," her

mother, Tubdu, proclaimed. "You can't drown really bad people. They always bob up again."

Tubdu, the Morning wife, had two children with her husband Kap: Isidri, a year older than me, and Suudi, three years younger. Children of the Morning, they were my germanes, as was Cousin Had'd, Tubdu's son with Kap's brother Uncle Tobo. On the Evening side there were two children, myself and my younger sister. She was named Koneko, an old name in Oket, which has also a meaning in my mother's Terran language: "kitten," the young of the wonderful animal "cat" with the round back and the round eyes. Koneko, four years younger than me, was indeed round and silky like a baby animal, but her eyes were like my mother's, long, with lids that went up towards the temple, like the soft sheaths of flowers before they open. She staggered around after me, calling, "Deo! Deo! Wait!" — while I ran after fleet, fearless, ever-vanishing Isidri, calling, "Sidi! Sidi! Wait!"

When we were older, Isidri and I were inseparable companions, while Suudi, Koneko, and Cousin Had'd made a trinity, usually coated with mud, splotched with scabs, and in some kind of trouble — gates left open so the yamas got into the crops, hay spoiled by being jumped on, fruit stolen, battles with the children from Drehe Farmhold. "Bad, bad," Tubdu would say. "None of 'em will ever drown!" And she would shake with her silent laughter.

My father Dohedri was a hardworking man, handsome, silent, and aloof. I think his insistence on bringing a foreigner into the tight-woven fabric of village and farm life, conservative and suspicious and full of old knots and tangles of passions and jealousies, had added anxiety to a temperament already serious. Other ki'O had married foreigners, of course, but almost always in a "foreign marriage," a pairing; and such couples usually lived in one of the Centers, where all kinds of untraditional arrangements were common, even (so the village gossips hissed under the great tree) incestuous couplings between two Morning people! Two Evening people! — Or such pairs would leave O to live on Hain, or would cut all ties to all homes and become Mobiles on the NAFAL ships, only touching different worlds at different moments and then off again into an endless future with no past.

None of this would do for my father, a man rooted to the knees in the dirt of Udan Farmhold. He brought his beloved to his home, and persuaded the Evening People of Derdan'nad to take her into their moiety, in a ceremony so rare and ancient that a Caretaker had to come by ship and train from Noratan to perform it. Then he had persuaded Tubdu to join the sedoretu. As regards her Day marriage, this was no trouble at all, as soon as Tubdu met my mother; but it presented some difficulty as regards her Morning marriage. Kap and my father had been lovers for years; Kap was the obvious and willing candidate to complete the sedoretu; but Tubdu did not like him. Kap's long love for my father led him to woo Tubdu earnestly and well, and she was far too good-natured to hold out against the interlocking wishes of three people, plus her own lively desire for Isako. She always found Kap a boring husband, I think; but his younger brother, Uncle Tobo, was a bonus. And Tubdu's relation to my mother was infinitely tender, full of honor, of delicacy, of restraint. Once my mother spoke of it. "She knew how strange it all was to me," she said. "She knows how strange it all is."

"This world? Our ways?" I asked.

My mother shook her head very slightly. "Not so much that," she said in her quiet voice with the faint foreign accent. "But men and women, women and women, together love—it is always very strange. Nothing you know ever prepares you. Ever."

The saying is, "a marriage is made by Day," that is, the relationship of the two women makes or breaks it. Though my mother and father loved each other deeply, it was a love always on the edge of pain, never easy. I have no doubt that the radiant childhood we had in that household was founded on the unshakable joy and strength Isako and Tubdu found in each other.

So, then: twelve-year-old Isidri went off on the suntrain to school at Herhot, our district educational Center, and I

wept aloud, standing in the morning sunlight in the dust of
Derdan'nad Station. My friend, my playmate, my life was
gone. I was bereft, deserted, alone forever. Seeing her
mighty eleven-year-old elder brother weeping, Koneko set
up a howl too, tears rolling down her cheeks in dusty balls
like raindrops on a dirt road. She threw her arms about me,
roaring, "Hideo! She'll come back! She'll come back!"

I have never forgotten that. I can hear her hoarse little
voice, and feel her arms round me and the hot morning
sunlight on my neck.

By afternoon we were all swimming in the Oro, Koneko
and I and Suudi and Had'd. As their elder, I resolved on a
course of duty and stern virtue, and led the troop off to help
Second-Cousin Topi at the irrigation control station, until
she drove us away like a swarm of flies, saying, "Go help
somebody else and let me get some work done!" We went
and built a mud palace.

So, then: a year later, twelve-year-old Hideo and thirteen-
year-old Isidri went off on the suntrain to school, leaving
Koneko on the dusty siding, not in tears, but silent, the way
our mother was silent when she grieved.

I loved school. I know that the first days I was achingly
homesick, but I cannot recall that misery, buried under my
memories of the full, rich years at Herhot, and later at
Ran'n, the Advanced Education Center, where I studied
temporal physics and engineering.

Isidri finished the First Courses at Herhot, took a year of
Second in literature, hydrology, and oenology, and went
home to Udan Farmhold of Derdan'nad Village in the hill
region of the Northwest Watershed of the Saduun.

The three younger ones all came to school, took a year or
two of Second, and carried their learning home to Udan.
When she was fifteen or sixteen, Koneko talked of following me to Ran'n; but she was wanted at home because of her
excellence in the discipline we call "thick planning"—farm
management is the usual translation, but the words have no
hint of the complexity of factors involved in thick planning,
ecology, politics, profit, tradition, aesthetics, honor, and
spirit all functioning in an intensely practical and practically

invisible balance of preservation and renewal, like the homeostasis of a vigorous organism. Our "kitten" had the knack for it, and the Planners of Udan and Derdan'nad took her into their councils before she was twenty. But by then, I was gone.

Every winter of my school years I came back to the farm for the long holidays. The moment I was home I dropped school like a bookbag and became pure farmboy over-night—working, swimming, fishing, hiking, putting on Plays and farces in the barn, going to field-dances and house-dances all over the village, falling in and out of love with lovely boys and girls of the Morning from Derdan'nad and other villages.

In my last couple of years at Ran'n, my visits home changed mood. Instead of hiking off all over the country by day and going to a different dance every night, I often stayed home. Careful not to fall in love, I pulled away from my old, dear relationship with Sota of Drehe Farmhold, gradually letting it lapse, trying not to hurt him. I sat whole hours by the Oro, a fishing line in my hand, memorizing the run of the water in a certain place just outside the entrance to our old swimming-bay. There, as the water rises in clear strands racing towards two mossy, almost-submerged boul-ders, it surges and whirls in spirals, and while some of these spin away, grow faint, and disappear, one knots itself on a deep center, becoming a little whirlpool, which spins slowly downstream until, reaching the quick, bright race between the boulders, it loosens and unties itself, released into the body of the river, as another spiral is forming and knotting itself round a deep center upstream where the water rises in clear strands above the boulders. . . . Sometimes that winter the river rose right over the rocks and poured smooth, swollen with rain; but always it would drop, and the whirlpools would appear again.

In the winter evenings I talked with my sister and Suudi; serious, long talks by the fire. I watched my mother's beautiful hands work on the embroidery of new curtains for the wide windows of the dining room, which my father had sewn on the four-hundred-year-old sewing machine of

Udan. I worked with him on reprogramming the fertilizer systems for the east fields and the yama rotations, according to our thick-planning council's directives. Now and then he and I talked a little, never very much. In the evenings we had music; Cousin Had'd was a drummer, much in demand for dances, who could always gather a group. Or I would play Word-Thief with Tubdu, a game she adored and always lost at, because she was so intent to steal my words that she forgot to protect her own. "Got you, got you!" she would cry, and melt into the Great Giggle, seizing my letterblocks with her fat, tapering, brown fingers; and next move I would take all my letters back along with most of hers. "How did you see that?" she would ask, amazed, studying the scattered words. Sometimes my otherfather Kap played with us, methodical, a bit mechanical, with a small smile for both triumph and defeat.

Then I would go up to my room under the eaves, my room of dark wood walls and dark red curtains, the smell of rain coming in the window, the sound of rain on the tiles of the roof. I would lie there in the mild darkness and luxuriate in sorrow, in great, aching, sweet, youthful sorrow for this ancient home that I was going to leave, to lose forever, to sail away from on the dark river of time. For I knew, from my eighteenth birthday on, that I would leave Udan, leave O, and go out to the other worlds. It was my ambition. It was my destiny.

I have not said anything about Isidri, as I described those winter holidays. She was there. She played in the Plays, worked on the farm, went to the dances, sang the choruses, joined the hiking parties, swam in the river in the warm rain with the rest of us. My first winter home from Ran'n, as I swung off the train at Derdan'nad Station, she greeted me with a cry of delight and a great embrace, then broke away with a strange, startled laugh and stood back, a tall, dark, thin girl with an intent, watchful face. She was quite awkward with me that evening. I felt that it was because she had always seen me as a little boy, a child, and now, eighteen and a student at Ran'n, I was a man. I was complacent with Isidri, putting her at her ease, patronizing her. In the days that followed, she remained awkward, laughing inappropriately, never opening her heart to me in the kind of long talks we used to have, and even, I thought, avoiding me. My whole last tenday at home that year, Isidri spent visiting her father's relatives in Sabtodiu Village. I was offended that she had not put off her visit till I was gone.

The next year she was not awkward, but not intimate. She had become interested in religion, attending the shrine daily, studying the Discussions with the elders. She was kind, friendly, busy. I do not remember that she and I ever touched, that winter, until she kissed me goodbye. Among my people a kiss is not with the mouth; we lay our cheeks together for a moment, or for longer. Her kiss was as light as the touch of a leaf, lingering yet barely perceptible.

My third and last winter home, I told them I was leaving: going to Hain, and that from Hain I wanted to go on farther and forever.

How cruel we are to our parents! All I needed to say was that I was going to Hain. After her half-anguished, half-exultant cry of "I knew it!" my mother said in her usual soft voice, suggesting not stating, "After that, you might come back, for a while." I could have said, "Yes." That was all she asked. Yes, I might come back, for a while. With the impenetrable self-centeredness of youth, which mistakes itself for honesty, I refused to give her what she asked. I took from her the modest hope of seeing me after ten years, and gave her the desolation of believing that when I left she would never see me again. "If I qualify, I want to be a Mobile," I said. I had steeled myself to speak without palliations. I prided myself on my truthfulness. And all the time, though I didn't know it, nor did they, it was not the truth at all. The truth is rarely so simple, though not many truths are as complicated as mine turned out to be.

She took my brutality without the least complaint. She had left her own people, after all. She said that evening, "We can talk by ansible, sometimes, as long as you're on Hain." She said it as if reassuring me, not herself. I think she was remembering how she had said goodbye to her people and

boarded the ship on Terra, and when she landed a few
seeming hours later on Hain, her mother had been dead for
fifty years. She could have talked to Terra on the ansible;
but who was there for her to talk to? I did not know that
pain, but she did. She took comfort in knowing I would be
spared it, for a while.

Everything now was "for a while." Oh, the bitter sweetness of those days! How I enjoyed myself—standing,
again, poised on the slick boulder amidst the roaring water,
spear raised, the hero! How ready, how willing I was to
crush all that long, slow, deep, rich life of Udan in my hand
and toss it away!

Only for one moment was I told what I was doing, and
then so briefly that I could deny it.

I was down in the boat-house workshop, on the rainy,
warm afternoon of a day late in the last month of winter. The
constant, hissing thunder of the swollen river was the matrix
of my thoughts as I set a new thwart in the little red rowboat
we used to fish from, taking pleasure in the task, indulging
my anticipatory nostalgia to the full by imagining myself on
another planet a hundred years away, remembering this hour
in the boat-house, the smell of wood and water, the river's
incessant roar. A knock at the workshop door. Isidri looked
in. The thin, dark, watchful face, the long braid of dark hair,
not as black as mine, the intent, clear eyes. "Hideo," she
said, "I want to talk to you for a minute."

"Come on in!" I said, pretending ease and gladness,
though half aware that in fact I shrank from talking with
Isidri, that I was afraid of her—why?

She perched on the vise bench and watched me work in
silence for a little while. I began to say something common-
place, but she spoke: "Do you know why I've been staying
away from you?"

Liar, self-protective liar, I said, "Staying away from me?"

At that she sighed. She had hoped I would say I
understood, and spare her the rest. But I couldn't. I was
lying only in pretending that I hadn't noticed that she had
kept away from me. I truly had never, never until she told
me, imagined why.

"I found out I was in love with you, winter before last," she said. "I wasn't going to say anything about it because— well, you know. If you'd felt anything like that for me, you'd have known I did. But it wasn't both of us. So there was no good in it. But then, when you told us you're leaving. . . . At first I thought, all the more reason to say nothing. But then I thought, that wouldn't be fair. To me, partly. Love has a right to be spoken. And you have a right to know that somebody loves you. That somebody has loved you, could love you. We all need to know that. Maybe it's what we need most. So I wanted to tell you. And because I was afraid you thought I'd kept away from you because I didn't love you, or care about you, you know. It might have looked like that. But it wasn't that." She had slipped down off the table and was at the door.

"Sidi!" I said, her name breaking from me in a strange, hoarse cry, the name only, no words—I had no words. I had no feelings, no compassion, no more nostalgia, no more luxurious suffering. Shocked out of emotion, bewildered, blank, I stood there. Our eyes met. For four or five breaths we stood staring into each other's soul. Then Isidri looked away with a wincing desolate smile, and slipped out.

I did not follow her. I had nothing to say to her: literally. I felt that it would take me a month, a year, years, to find the words I needed to say to her. I had been so rich, so comfortably complete in myself and my ambition and my destiny, five minutes ago; and now I stood empty, silent, poor, looking at the world I had thrown away.

That ability to look at the truth lasted an hour or so. All my life since I have thought of it as "the hour in the boat-house." I sat on the high bench where Isidri had sat. The rain fell and river roared and the early night came on. When at last I moved, I turned on a light, and began to try to defend my purpose, my planned future, from the terrible plain reality. I began to build up a screen of emotions and evasions and versions; to look away from what Isidri had shown me; to look away from Isidri's eyes.

By the time I went up to the house for dinner I was in control of myself. By the time I went to bed I was master of my destiny again, sure of my decision, almost able to indulge myself in feeling sorry for Isidri—but not quite. Never did I dishonor her with that. I will say that much for myself. I had had the pity that is self-pity knocked out of me in the hour in the boat-house. When I parted from my family at the muddy little station in the village, a few days after, I wept, not luxuriously for them, but for myself, in honest, hopeless pain. It was too much for me to bear. I had had so little practice in pain! I said to my mother, "I will come back. When I finish the course—six years, maybe seven—I'll come back, I'll stay a while."

"If your way brings you," she whispered. She held me close to her, and then released me.

So, then: I have come to the time I chose to begin my story, when I was twenty-one and left my home on the ship *Terraces of Darranda* to study at the schools on Hain.

Of the journey itself I have no memory whatever. I think I remember entering the ship, yet no details come to mind, visual or kinetic; I cannot recollect being on the ship. My memory of leaving it is only of an overwhelming physical sensation, dizziness. I staggered and felt sick, and was so unsteady on my feet I had to be supported until I had taken several steps on the soil of Hain.

Troubled by this lapse of consciousness, I asked about it at the Ekumenical School. I was told that it is one of the many different ways in which travel at near lightspeed affects the mind. To most people it seems merely that a few hours pass in a kind of perceptual limbo; others have curious perceptions of space and time and event, which can be seriously disturbing; a few simply feel they have been asleep when they "wake up" on arrival. I did not even have that experience. I had no experience at all. I felt cheated. I wanted to have felt the voyage, to have known, in some way, the great interval of space: but as far as I was concerned, there was no interval. I was at the spaceport on O, and then I was at Ve Port, dizzy, bewildered, and at last, when I was able to believe that I was there, excited.

My studies and work during those years are of no interest

now. I will mention only one event, which may or may not
be on record in the ansible reception file at Fourth Beck
Tower, EY 21-11-93/1645. (The last time I checked, it was
on record in the ansible transmission file at Ran'n, ET date
30-11-93/1645. Urashima's coming and going was on record,
too, in the Annals of the Emperors.) 1645 was my first year
on Hain. Early in the term I was asked to come to the ansible
center, where they explained that they had received a
garbled screen-transmission, apparently from O, and hoped
I could help them reconstitute it. After a date nine days later
than the date of reception, it read:

> LES OKU N HIDE PROBLEM NETRU EMIT IT HURT DI IT
> MAY NOT BE SALV DEVIR

The words were gapped and fragmented. Some were standard Hainish, but *oku* and *netru* mean "north" and "sym-
metrical" in Sio, my native language. The ansible centers on
O had reported no record of the transmission, but the
Receivers thought the message might be from O because of
these two words and because the Hainish phrase "it may not
be salvageable" occurred in a transmission received almost
simultaneously from one of the Stabiles on O, concerning a
wave-damaged desalinization plant. "We call this a creased
message," the Receiver told me, when I confessed I could
make nothing of it and asked how often ansible messages
came through so garbled. "Not often, fortunately. We can't
be certain where or when they originated, or will originate.
They may be effects of a double field—interference phe-
nomena, perhaps. One of my colleagues here calls them
ghost messages."

Instantaneous transmission had always fascinated me,
and though I was then only a beginner in ansible principle,
I developed this fortuitous acquaintance with the Receivers
into a friendship with several of them. And I took all the
courses in ansible theory that were offered.

When I was in my final year in the school of temporal
physics, and considering going on to the Cetian Worlds for
further study—after my promised visit home, which seemed

sometimes a remote, irrelevant daydream and sometimes a yearning and yet fearful need—the first reports came over the ansible from Anarres of the new theory of transilience. Not only information, but matter, bodies, people might be transported from place to place without lapse of time. "Churten technology" was suddenly a reality, although a very strange reality, an implausible fact.

I was crazy to work on it. I was about to go promise my soul and body to the School if they would let me work on churten theory when they came and asked me if I'd consider postponing my training as a Mobile for a year or so to work on churten theory. Judiciously and graciously, I consented, I celebrated all over town that night. I remember showing all my friends how to dance the fen'n, and I remember setting off fireworks in the Great Plaza of the Schools, and I think I remember singing under the Director's windows, a little before dawn. I remember what I felt like next day, too; but it didn't keep me from dragging myself over to the Ti-Phy building to see where they were installing the Churten Field Laboratory.

Ansible transmission is of course enormously expensive, and I had only been able to talk to my family twice during my years on Hain; but my friends in the ansible center would occasionally "ride" a screen message for me on a transmission to O. I sent a message thus to Ran'n to be posted on to the First Sedoretu of Udan Farmhold of Derdan'nad Village of the hill district of the Northwest Watershed of the Saduun, Oket, on O, telling them that "although this research will delay my visit home, it may save me four years' travel." The flippant message revealed my guilty feeling; but we did really think then that we would have the technology within a few months.

The Field Laboratories were soon moved out to Ve Port, and I went with them. The joint work of the Cetian and Hainish churten research teams in those first three years was a succession of triumphs, postponements, promises, defeats, breakthroughs, setbacks, all happening so fast that anybody who took a week off was out of date. "Clarity hiding mystery," Gvonesh called it. Every time it all came clear it

all grew more mysterious. The theory was beautiful and
maddening. The experiments were exciting and inscrutable.
The technology worked best when it was most preposterous.
Four years went by in that laboratory like no time at all, as
they say.

I had now spent ten years on Hain and Ve, and was
thirty-one. On O, four years had passed while my NAFAL
ship passed a few minutes of dilated time going to Hain, and
four more would pass while I returned: so when I returned
I would have been gone eighteen of their years. My parents
were all still alive. It was high time for my promised visit
home.

But though churten research had hit a frustrating setback
in the Spring Snow Paradox, a problem the Cetians thought
might be insoluble, I couldn't stand the thought of being
eight years out of date when I got back to Hain. What if they
broke the paradox? It was bad enough knowing I must lose
four years going to O. Tentatively, not too hopefully, I
proposed to the Director that I carry some experimental
materials with me to O and set up a fixed double field
auxiliary to the ansible link between Ve Port and Ran'n.
Thus I could stay in touch with Ve, as Ve stayed in touch
with Urras and Anarres; and the fixed ansible link might be
preparatory to a churten link. I remember I said, "If you
break the paradox, we might eventually send some mice."

To my surprise my idea caught on; the temporal engineers
wanted a receiving field. Even our Director, who could be as
brilliantly inscrutable as churten theory itself, said it was a
good idea. "Mouses, bugs, gholes, who knows what we send
you?" she said.

So, then: when I was thirty-one years old I left Ve Port on
the NAFAL transport *Lady of Sorra* and returned to O. This
time I experienced the near-lightspeed flight the way most
people do, as an unnerving interlude in which one cannot
think consecutively, read a clockface, or follow a story.
Speech and movement become difficult or impossible.
Other people appear as unreal half-presences, inexplicably
there or not there. I did not hallucinate, but everything
seemed hallucination. It is like a high fever—confusing,

miserably boring, seeming endless, yet very difficult to recall once it is over, as if it were an episode outside one's life, encapsulated. I wonder now if its resemblance to the "churten experience" has yet been seriously investigated.

I went straight to Ran'n, where I was given rooms in the New Quadrangle, fancier than my old student room in the Shrine Quadrangle, and some nice lab space in Tower Hall to set up an experimental transilience field station. I got in touch with my family right away and talked to all my parents; my mother had been ill, but was fine now, she said. I told them I would be home as soon as I had got things going at Ran'n. Every tenday I called again and talked to them and said I'd be along very soon now. I was genuinely very busy, having to catch up the lost four years and to learn Gvonesh's solution to the Spring Snow Paradox. It was, fortunately, the only major advance in theory. Technology had advanced a good deal. I had to restrain myself, and to train my assistants almost from scratch. I had had an idea about an aspect of double-field theory that I wanted to work out before I left. Five months went by before I called them up and said at last, "I'll be there tomorrow." And when I did so, I realized that all along I had been afraid.

I don't know if I was afraid of seeing them after eighteen years, of the changes, the strangeness, or if it was myself I feared.

Eighteen years had made no difference at all to the hills beside the wide Saduun, the farmlands, the dusty little station in Derdan'nad, the old, old houses on the quiet streets. The village great tree was gone, but its replacement had a pretty wide spread of shade already. The aviary at Udan had been enlarged. The yama stared haughtily, timidly at me across the fence. A road-gate that I had hung on my last visit home was decrepit, needing its post re-set and new hinges, but the weeds that grew beside it were the same dusty, sweet-smelling summer weeds. The tiny dams of the irrigation runnels made their multiple, soft click and thump as they closed and opened. Everything was the same, itself. Timeless, Udan in its dream of work stood over the river that ran timeless in its dream of movement.

But the faces and bodies of the people waiting for me at the station in the hot sunlight were not the same. My mother, forty-seven when I left, was sixty-five, a beautiful and fragile elderly woman. Tubdu had lost weight; she looked shrunken and wistful. My father was still handsome and bore himself proudly, but his movements were slow and he scarcely spoke at all. My otherfather Kap, seventy now, was a precise, fidgety, little old man. They were still the First Sedoretu of Udan, but the vigor of the farmhold now lay in the Second and Third Sedoretu.

I knew of all the changes, of course, but being there among them was a different matter from hearing about them in letters and transmissions. The old house was much fuller than it had been when I lived there. The south wing had been reopened, and children ran in and out of its doors and across courtyards that in my childhood had been silent and ivied and mysterious.

My sister Koneko was now four years older than I instead of four years younger. She looked very like my early memory of my mother. As the train drew in to Derdan'nad Station, she had been the first of them I recognized, holding up a child of three or four and saying, "Look, look, it's your Uncle Hideo!"

The Second Sedoretu had been married for eleven years: Koneko and Isidri, sister-germanes, were the partners of the Day. Koneko's husband was my old friend Sota, a Morning man of Drehe Farmhold. Sota and I had loved each other dearly when we were adolescents, and I had been grieved to grieve him when I left. When I heard that he and Koneko were in love I had been very surprised, so self-centered am I, but at least I am not jealous: it pleased me very deeply. Isidri's husband, a man nearly twenty years older than herself, named Hedran, had been a travelling scholar of the Discussions. Udan had given him hospitality, and his visits had led to the marriage. He and Isidri had no children. Sota and Koneko had two Evening children, a boy of ten called Murmi, and Lasako, Little Isako, who was four.

The Third Sedoretu had been brought to Udan by Suudi, my brother-germane, who had married a woman from Aster

Village; their Morning pair also came from farmholds of Aster. There were six children in that sedoretu. A cousin whose sedoretu at Ekke had broken had also come to live at Udan with her two children; so the coming and going and dressing and undressing and washing and slamming and running and shouting and weeping and laughing and eating was prodigious. Tubdu would sit at work in the sunny kitchen courtyard and watch a wave of children pass. "Bad!" she would cry. "They'll never drown, not a one of 'em!" And she would shake with silent laughter that became a wheezing cough.

My mother, who had after all been a Mobile of the Ekumen, and had travelled from Terra to Hain and from Hain to O, was impatient to hear about my research. "What is it, this churtening? How does it work, what does it do? Is it an ansible for matter?"

"That's the idea," I said. "Transilience: instantaneous transference of being from one s-tc point to another."

"No interval?"

"No interval."

Isako frowned. "It sounds wrong," she said. "Explain."

I had forgotten how direct my soft-spoken mother could be; I had forgotten that she was an intellectual. I did my best to explain the incomprehensible.

"So," she said at last, "you don't really understand how it works."

"No. Nor even what it does. Except that—as a rule—when the field is in operation, the mice in Building One are instantaneously in Building Two, perfectly cheerful and unharmed. Inside their cage, if we remembered to keep their cage inside the initiating churten field. We used to forget. Loose mice everywhere."

"What's mice?" said a little Morning boy of the Third Sedoretu, who had stopped to listen to what sounded like a story.

"Ah," I said in a laugh, surprised. I had forgotten that at Udan mice were unknown, and rats were fanged, demon enemies of the Painted Cat. "Tiny, pretty, furry animals," I said, "that come from grandmother Isako's world. They are

friends of scientists. They have travelled all over the Known
Worlds."

"In tiny little spaceships?" the child said hopefully.

"In large ones, mostly," I said. He was satisfied, and went
away.

"Hideo," said my mother, in the terrifying way women
have of passing without interval from one subject to another
because they have them all present in their mind at once,
"you haven't found any kind of relationship?"

I shook my head, smiling.

"None at all?"

"A man from Alterra and I lived together for a couple of
years," I said. "It was a good friendship; but he's a Mobile
now. And . . . oh, you know . . . people here and there.
Just recently, at Ran'n, I've been with a very nice woman
from East Oket."

"I hoped, if you intend to be a Mobile, that you might
make a couple-marriage with another Mobile. It's easier, I
think," she said. Easier than what? I thought, and knew the
answer before I asked.

"Mother, I doubt now that I'll travel farther than Hain.
This churten business is too interesting. I want to be in on
it. And if we do learn to control the technology, you know,
then travel will be nothing. There'll be no need for the kind
of sacrifice you made. Things will be different. Unimagin-
ably different! You could go to Terra for an hour and come
back here: and only an hour would have passed."

She thought about that. "If you do it, then," she said,
speaking slowly, almost shaking with the intensity of com-
prehension, "you will . . . you will shrink the galaxy—
the universe?—to . . ." and she held up her left hand,
thumb and fingers all drawn together to a point.

I nodded. "A mile or a lightyear will be the same. There
will be no distance."

"It can't be right," she said after a while. "To have event
without interval. . . . Where is the dancing? Where is the
way? I don't think you'll be able to control it, Hideo." She
smiled. "But of course you must try."

And after that we talked about who was coming to the field dance at Drehe tomorrow.

I did not tell my mother that I had invited Tasi, the nice woman from East Oket, to come to Udan with me and that she refused, had, in fact, gently informed me that she thought this was a good time for us to part. Tasi was tall, with a braid of dark hair, not coarse, bright black like mine but soft, fine, dark, like the shadows in a forest. A typical ki'O woman, I thought. She had deflated my protestations of love skillfully and without shaming me. "I think you're in love with somebody, though," she said. "Somebody on Hain, maybe. Maybe the man from Alterra you told me about?" No, I said. No, I'd never been in love. I wasn't capable of an intense relationship, that was clear by now. I'd dreamed too long of travelling the galaxy with no attachments anywhere, and then worked too long in the churten lab, married to a damned theory that couldn't find its technology. No room for love, no time.

But why had I wanted to bring Tasi home with me?

Tall but no longer thin, a woman of forty, not a girl, not typical, not comparable, not like anyone anywhere, Isidri had greeted me quietly at the door of the house. Some farm emergency had kept her from coming to the village station to meet me. She was wearing an old smock and leggings like any fieldworker, and her hair, dark beginning to gray, was in a rough braid. As she stood in that wide doorway of polished wood she was Udan itself, the body and soul of that thirty-century-old farmhold, its continuity, its life. All my childhood was in her hands, and she held them out to me.

"Welcome home, Hideo," she said with a smile as radiant as the summer light on the river. As she brought me in, she said, "I cleared the kids out of your old room. I thought you'd like to be there—would you?" Again she smiled, and I felt her warmth, the solar generosity of a woman in the prime of life, married, settled, rich in her work and being. I had not needed Tasi as a defense. I had nothing to fear from Isidri. She felt no rancor, no embarrassment. She had loved me when she was young, another person. It would be altogether inappropriate for me to feel embarrassment, or shame, or anything but the old affectionate loyalty of the years when we played and worked and fished and dreamed together, children of Udan.

So, then: I settled down in my old room under the tiles. There were new curtains, rust and brown. I found a stray toy under the chair, in the closet, as if I as a child had left my playthings there and found them now. At fourteen, after my entry ceremony in the shrine, I had carved my name on the deep windowjamb among the tangled patterns of names and symbols that had been cut into it for centuries. I looked for it now. There had been some additions. Beside my careful, clear *Hideo*, surrounded by my ideogram, the cloud-flower, a younger child had hacked a straggling *Dohedri*, and nearby was carved a delicate three-roofs ideogram. The sense of being a bubble in Udan's river, a moment in the permanence of life in this house on this land on this quiet world, was almost crushing, denying my identity, and profoundly reassuring, confirming my identity. Those nights of my visit home I slept as I had not slept for years, lost, drowned in the waters of sleep and darkness, and woke to the summer mornings as if reborn, very hungry.

The children were still all under twelve, going to school at home. Isidri, who taught them literature and religion and was the school planner, invited me to tell them about Hain, about NAFAL travel, about temporal physics, whatever I pleased. Visitors to ki'O farmholds are always put to use. Evening-Uncle Hideo became rather a favorite among the children, always good for hitching up the yama-cart or taking them fishing in the big boat, which they couldn't yet handle, or telling a story about his magic mice who could be in two places at the same time. I asked them if Evening Grandmother Isako had told them about the Painted Cat who came alive and killed the demon rats—"And his mouf was all BLUGGY in the morning!" shouted Lasako, her eyes shining. But they didn't know the tale of Urashima.

"Why haven't you told them 'The Fisherman of the Inland Sea?'" I asked my mother.

She smiled and said, "Oh, that was your story. You always wanted it."

I saw Isidri's eyes on us, clear and tranquil, yet watchful still.

I knew my mother had had repair and healing to her heart a year before, and I asked Isidri later, as we supervised some work the older children were doing, "Has Isako recovered, do you think?"

"She seems wonderfully well since you came. I don't know. It's damage from her childhood, from the poisons in the Terran biosphere; they say her immune system is easily depressed. She was very patient about being ill. Almost too patient."

"And Tubdu—does she need new lungs?"

"Probably. All four of them are getting older, and stubborner. . . . But you look at Isako for me. See if you see what I mean."

I tried to observe my mother. After a few days I reported back that she seemed energetic and decisive, even imperative, and that I hadn't seen much of the patient endurance that worried Isidri. She laughed.

"Isako told me once," she said, "that a mother is connected to her child by a very fine, thin cord, like the umbilical cord, that can stretch lightyears without any difficulty. I asked her if it was painful, and she said, 'Oh, no, it's just there, you know, it stretches and stretches and never breaks.' It seems to me it must be painful. But I don't know. I have no child, and I've never been more than two days' travel from my mothers." She smiled and said in her soft, deep voice, "I think I love Isako more than anyone, more even than my mother, more even than Koneko. . . ."

Then she had to show one of Suudi's children how to reprogram the timer on the irrigation control. She was the hydrologist for the village and the oenologist for the farm. Her life was thickplanned, very rich in necessary work and wide relationships, a serene and steady succession of days, seasons, years. She swam in life as she had swum in the river, like a fish, at home. She had borne no child, but all the children of the farmhold were hers. She and Koneko were as deeply attached as their mothers had been. Her relation with her rather fragile, scholarly husband seemed peaceful and

respectful. I thought his Night marriage with my old friend
Sota might be the stronger sexual link; but Isidri clearly
admired and depended on his intellectual and spiritual
guidance. I thought his teaching a bit dry and disputatious;
but what did I know about religion? I had not given worship
for years, and felt strange, out of place, even in the home
shrine. I felt strange, out of place, in my home. I did not
acknowledge it to myself.

I was conscious of the month as pleasant, uneventful,
even a little boring. My emotions were mild and dull. The
wild nostalgia, the romantic sense of standing on the brink
of my destiny, all that was gone with the Hideo of twenty-
one. Though now the youngest of my generation, I was a
grown man, knowing his way, content with his work, past
emotional self-indulgence. I wrote a little poem for the
house album about the peacefulness of following a chosen
course. When I had to go, I embraced and kissed everyone,
dozens of soft or harsh check-touches. I told them that if I
stayed on O, as it seemed I might be asked to do for a year
or so, I would come back next winter for another visit. On
the train going back through the hills to Ran'n, I thought
with a complacent gravity how I might return to the farm
next winter, finding them all just the same; and how, if I
came back after another eighteen years or even longer, some
of them would be gone and some would be new to me and
yet it would be always my home, Udan with its wide dark
roofs riding time like a dark-sailed ship. I always grow
poetic when I am lying to myself.

I got back to Ran'n, checked in with my people at the lab
in Tower Hall, and had dinner with colleagues, good food
and drink—I brought them a bottle of wine from Udan, for
Isidri was making splendid wines, and had given me a case
of the fifteen-year-old Kedun. We talked about the latest
breakthrough in churten technology, "continuous-field sending," reported from Anarres just yesterday on the ansible. I
went to my rooms in the New Quadrangle through the
summer night, my head full of physics, read a little, and
went to bed. I turned out the light and darkness filled me as
it filled the room. Where was I? Alone in a room among

strangers. As I had been for ten years and would always be. On one planet or another, what did it matter? Alone, part of nothing, part of no one. Udan was not my home. I had no home, no people. I had no future, no destiny, any more than a bubble of foam, a whirlpool in a current, has a destiny. It is and it isn't. Nothing more.

I turned the light on because I could not bear the darkness, but the light was worse. I sat huddled up in the bed and began to cry. I could not stop crying. I became frightened at how the sobs racked and shook me till I was sick and weak and still could not stop sobbing. After a long time I calmed myself gradually by clinging to an imagination, a childish idea: in the morning I would call Isidri and talk to her, telling her that I needed instruction in religion, that I wanted to give worship at the shrines again, but it had been so long, and I had never listened to the Discussions, but now I needed to, and I would ask her, Isidri, to help me. So, holding fast to that, I could at last stop the terrible sobbing and lie spent, exhausted, until the day came.

I did not call Isidri. In daylight the thought which had saved me from the dark seemed foolish; and I thought if I called her she would ask advice of her husband, the religious scholar. But I knew I needed help. I went to the shrine in the Old School and gave worship. I asked for a copy of the First Discussions, and read it. I joined a Discussion group, and we read and talked together. My religion is godless, argumentative, and mystical. The name of our world is the first word of its first prayer. For human beings its vehicle is the human voice and mind. As I began to rediscover it, I found it quite as strange as churten theory and in some respects complementary to it. I knew, but had never understood, that Cetian physics and religion are aspects of one knowledge. I wondered if all physics and religion are aspects of one knowledge.

At night I never slept well and often could not sleep at all. After the bountiful tables of Udan, college food seemed poor stuff; I had no appetite. But our work, my work went well—wonderfully well.

"No more mouses," said Gvonesh on the voice ansible from Hain. "Peoples."

"What people?" I demanded.

"Me," said Gvonesh.

So our Director of Research churtened from one corner of Laboratory One to another, and then from Building One to Building Two—vanishing in one laboratory and appearing in the other, smiling, in the same instant, in no time.

"What did it feel like?" they asked, of course, and Gvonesh answered, of course, "Like nothing."

Many experiments followed; mice and gholes churtened halfway around Ve and back; robot crews churtened from Anarres to Urras, from Hain to Ve, and then from Anarres to Ve, twenty-two lightyears. So, then, eventually the *Shoby* and her crew of ten human beings churtened into orbit around a miserable planet seventeen lightyears from Ve and returned (but words that imply coming and going, that imply distance traveled, are not appropriate) thanks only to their intelligent use of entertainment, rescuing themselves from a kind of chaos of dissolution, a death by unreality, that horrified us all. Experiments with high-intelligence life forms came to a halt.

"The rhythm is wrong," Gvonesh said on the ansible (she said it "rithkhom"). For a moment I thought of my mother saying, "It can't be right to have event without interval." What else had Isako said? Something about dancing. But I did not want to think about Udan. I did not think about Udan. When I did I felt, far down deeper inside me than my bones, the knowledge of being no one, no where, and a shaking like a frightened animal.

My religion reassured me that I was part of the Way, and my physics absorbed my despair in work. Experiments, cautiously resumed, succeeded beyond hope. The Terran Dalzul and his psychophysics took everyone at the research station on Ve by storm; I am sorry I never met him. As he predicted, using the continuity field he churtened without a hint of trouble, alone, first locally, then from Ve to Hain, then the great jump to Tadkla and back. From the second journey to Tadkla, his three companions returned without

him. He died on that far world. It did not seem to us in the
laboratories that his death was in any way caused by the
churten field or by what had come to be known as "the churten
experience," though his three companions were not so
sure.

"Maybe Dalzul was right. One people at a time," said
Gvonesh; and she made herself again the subject, the "ritual
animal," as the Hainish say, of the next experiment. Using
continuity technology she churtened right round Ve in four
skips, which took 32 seconds because of the time needed to
set up the coordinates. We had taken to calling the non-
interval in time/real interval in space a "skip." It sounded
light, trivial. Scientists like to trivialize.

I wanted to try the improvement to double-field stability
that I had been working on ever since I came to Ran'n. It
was time to give it a test; my patience was short, life was too
short to fiddle with figures forever. Talking to Gvonesh on
the ansible I said, "I'll skip over to Ve Port. And then back
here to Ran'n. I promised a visit to my home farm this
winter." Scientists like to trivialize.

"You still got that wrinkle in your field?" Gvonesh asked.
"Some kind, you know, like a fold?"

"It's ironed out, ammar," I assured her.

"Good, fine," said Gvonesh, who never questioned what
one said. "Come."

So, then: we set up the fields in a constant stable churten
link with ansible connection; and I was standing inside a
chalked circle in the Churten Field Laboratory of Ran'n
Center on a late autumn afternoon and standing inside a
chalked circle in the Churten Research Station Field Laboratory in Ve Port on a late summer day at a distance of 4.2
light-years and no interval of time.

"Feel nothing?" Gvonesh inquired, shaking my hand
heartily. "Good fellow, good fellow, welcome, ammar,
Hideo. Good to see. No wrinkle, hah?"

I laughed with the shock and queerness of it, and gave
Gvonesh the bottle of Udan Kedun '49 that I had picked up
a moment ago from the laboratory table on O.

I had expected, if I arrived at all, to churten promptly

back again, but Gvonesh and others wanted me on Ve for a
while for discussions and tests of the field. I think now that
the Directors' extraordinary intuition was at work; the
"wrinkle," the "fold" in the Tiokunan'n Field still bothered
her. "Is unaesthetical," she said.

"But it works," I said.

"It worked," said Gvonesh.

Except to retest my Field, to prove its reliability, I had no
desire to return to O. I was sleeping somewhat better here on
Ve, although food was still unpalatable to me, and when I
was not working I felt shaky and drained, a disagreeable
reminder of my exhaustion after the night when I tried not
to remember when for some reason or other I had cried so
much. But the work went very well.

"You got no sex, Hideo?"

Gvonesh asked me when we were alone in the Lab one
day. I playing with a new set of calculations and she
finishing her box lunch.

The question took me utterly aback. I knew it was not as
impertinent as Gvonesh's peculiar usage of the language
made it sound. But Gvonesh never asked questions like that.
Her own sex life was as much a mystery as the rest of her
existence. No one had ever heard her mention the word, let
alone suggest the act.

When I sat with my mouth open, stumped, she said, "You
used to, hah," as she chewed on a cold varvet.

I stammered something. I knew she was not proposing
that she and I have sex, but inquiring after my well-being.
But I did not know what to say.

"You got some kind of wrinkle in your life, hah,"
Gvonesh said. "Sorry. Not my business."

Wanting to assure her I had taken no offense I said, as we
say on O, "I honor your intent."

She looked directly at me, something she rarely did. Her
eyes were clear as water in her long, bony face softened by
a fine, thick, colorless down. "Maybe is time you go back to
O?" she asked.

"I don't know. The facilities here—"

She nodded. She always accepted what one said. "You read Harraven's report?" she asked, changing one subject for another as quickly and definitively as my mother.

All right, I thought, the challenge was issued. She was ready for me to test my Field again. Why not? After all, I could churten to Ran'n and churten right back again to Ve within a minute, if I chose, and if the Lab could afford it. Like ansible transmissions, churtening draws essentially on inertial mass, but setting up the field disinfecting it, and holding it stable in size uses a good deal of local energy. But it was Gvonesh's suggestion, which meant we had the money. I said, "How about a skip over and back?"

"Fine," Gvonesh said. "Tomorrow."

So the next day, on a morning of late autumn, I stood inside a chalked circle in the Field Laboratory on Ve and stood—

A shimmer, a shivering of everything—a missed beat—skipped

—in darkness. A darkness. A dark room. The lab? A lab—I found the light panel. In the darkness I was sure it was the laboratory on Ve. In the light I saw it was not. I didn't know where it was. I didn't know where I was. It seemed familiar yet I could not place it. What was it? A biology lab? There were specimens, an old subparticle microscope, the maker's ideogram on the battered brass casing, the lyre ideogram . . . I was on O. In some laboratory in some building of the Center at Ran'n? It smelled like the old buildings of Ran'n, it smelled like a rainy night on O. But how could I have not arrived in the receiving field, the circle carefully chalked on the wood floor of the lab in Tower Hall? The field itself must have moved. An appalling, an impossible thought.

I was alarmed and felt rather dizzy, as if my body had skipped that beat, but I was not yet frightened. I was all right, all here, all the pieces in the right places, and the mind working. A slight spatial displacement? said the mind.

I went on into the corridor. Perhaps I had myself been disoriented and left the Churten Field Laboratory and come to full consciousness somewhere else. But my crew would

have been there; where were they? And that would have
been hours ago; it should have been just past noon on O
when I arrived. A slight temporal displacement? said the
mind, working away. I went down the corridor looking for
my lab, and that is when it became like one of those dreams
in which you cannot find the room which you must find. It
was that dream The building was perfectly familiar: it was
Tower Hall, the second floor of Tower, but there was no
Churten Lab. All the labs were biology and biophysics, and
all were deserted. It was evidently late at night. Nobody
around. At last I saw a light under a door and knocked and
opened it on a student reading at a library terminal.

"I'm sorry," I said. "I'm looking for the Churten Field
Lab—"

"The what lab?"

She had never heard of it, and apologized. "I'm not in Ti
Phy, just Bi Phy," she said humbly.

I apologized too. Something was making me shakier,
increasing my sense of dizziness and disorientation. Was
this the "chaos effect" the crew of the *Shoby* and perhaps the
crew of the *Galba* had experienced? Would I begin to see
the stars through the walls, or turn around and see Gvonesh
here on O?

I asked her what time it was. "I should have got here at
noon," I said, though that of course meant nothing to her.

"It's about one," she said, glancing at the clock on the
terminal. I looked at it too. It gave the time, the tenday, the
month, the year.

"That's wrong," I said.

She looked worried.

"That's not right," I said. "The date. It's not right." But I
knew from the steady glow of the numbers on the clock,
from the girl's round, worried face, from the beat of my
heart, from the smell of the rain, that it was right, that it was
an hour after midnight eighteen years ago, that I was here,
now, on the day after the day I called "once upon a time"
when I began to tell this story.

A major temporal displacement, said the mind, working,
laboring.

"I don't belong here," I said, and turned to hurry back to what seemed a refuge. Biology Lab 6, which would be the Churten Field Lab eighteen years from now, as if I could re-enter the field, which had existed or would exist for .004 second.

The girl saw that something was wrong, made me sit down, and gave me a cup of hot tea from her insulated bottle.

"Where are you from?" I asked her, the kind, serious student.

"Herdud Farmhold of Deada Village on the South Watershed of the Saduun," she said.

"I'm from downriver," I said. "Udan of Derdan'nad." I suddenly broke into tears, I managed to control myself, apologized again, drank my tea, and set the cup down. She was not overly troubled by my fit of weeping. Students are intense people, they laugh and cry, they break down and rebuild. She asked if I had a place to spend the night: a perceptive question. I said I did, thanked her, and left.

I did not go back to the biology laboratory, but went downstairs and started to cut through the gardens to my rooms in the New Quadrangle. As I walked the mind kept working; it worked out that somebody else had been/would be in those rooms then/now.

I turned back towards the Shrine Quadrangle, where I had lived my last two years as a student before I left for Hain. If this was in fact, as the clock had indicated, the night after I had left, my room might still be empty and unlocked. It proved to be so, to be as I had left it, the mattress bare, the cyclebasket unemptied.

That was the most frightening moment. I stared at that cyclebasket for a long time before I took a crumpled bit of outprint from it and carefully smoothed it on the desk. It was a set of temporal equations scribbled on my old pocketscreen in my own handwriting, notes from Sedharad's class in Interval, from my last term at Ran'n, day before yesterday, eighteen years ago.

I was now very shaky indeed. You are caught in a chaos field, said the mind, and I believed it. Fear and stress, and

nothing to do about it, not till the long night was past. I lay
down on the bare bunk-mattress, ready for the stars to burn
through the walls and my eyelids if I shut them. I meant to
try and plan what I should do in the morning, if there was
a morning. I fell asleep instantly and slept like a stone till
broad daylight, when I woke up on the bare bed in the
familiar room, alert, hungry, and without a moment of doubt
as to who or where or when I was.

I went down into the village for breakfast. I didn't want
to meet my colleagues—no, fellow students—who might
know me and say, "Hideo! What are you doing here? You
left on the *Terraces of Darran'da* yesterday!"

I had little hope they would not recognize me. I was
thirty-two now, not twenty-one, much thinner and not as fit
as I had been; but my half-Terran features were unmistak-
able. I did not want to be recognized, to have to try to
explain. I wanted to get out of Ran'n. I wanted to go home.

O is a good world to time-travel in. Things don't change.
Our trains run on the same schedule to the same places for
centuries. We sign for payment and pay in contracted barter
or cash monthly, so I did not have to produce mysterious
coins from the future. I signed at the station and took the
morning train to Saduun Delta.

The little suntrain glided through the plains and hills of
the South Watershed and then the Northwest Watershed,
following the ever-widening river, stopping at each village.
I got off in the late afternoon at the station in Derdan'nad.
Since it was very early spring, the station was muddy, not
dusty.

I walked out the road to Udan. I opened the roadgate that
I had rehung a few days/eighteen years ago; it moved easily
on its new hinges. That gave me a little gleam of pleasure.
The she-yamas were all in the nursery pasture. Birthing
would start any day; their woolly sides stuck out, and they
moved like sailboats in a slow breeze, turning her elegant,
scornful heads to look distrustfully at me as I passed.
Rainclouds hung over the hills. I crossed the Oro on the
hump-backed wooden bridge. Four or five great blue orchid
hung in a backwater by the bridgefoot; I stopped to watch

them; if I'd had a spear . . . The clouds drifted overhead trailing a fine, faint drizzle. I strode on. My face felt hot and stiff as the cool rain touched it. I followed the river road and saw the house come into view, the dark, wide roofs low on the tree-crowned hill. I came past the aviary and the collectors, past the irrigation center, under the avenue of tall bare trees, up the steps to the deep porch, to the door, the wide door of Udan. I went in.

Tubdu was crossing the hall—not the woman I had last seen, in her sixties, gray-haired and tired and fragile, but Tubdu of the Great Giggle, Tubdu at forty-five, fat and rosy-brown and brisk, crossing the hall with short, quick steps, stopping, looking at me at first with mere recognition, there's Hideo, then with puzzlement, is that Hideo? and then with shock—that can't be Hideo!

"Ombu," I said, the baby word for othermother, "Ombu, it's me, Hideo, don't worry, it's all right. I came back." I embraced her, pressed my cheek to hers.

"But, but—" She held me off, looked up at my face. "But what has happened to you, darling boy?" she cried, and then turning, called out in a high voice, "Isako! Isako!"

When my mother saw me she thought, of course, that I had not left on the ship to Hain, that my courage or my intent had failed me; and in her first embrace there was an involuntary reserve, a withholding. Had I thrown away the destiny for which I had been so ready to throw away everything else? I knew what was in her mind. I laid my cheek to hers and whispered, "I did go, mother, and I came back. I'm thirty-two years old. I came back—"

She held me away a little just as Tubdu had done and saw my face. "Oh Hideo!" she said, and held me to her with all her strength. "My dear, my dear!"

We held each other in silence, till I said at last, "I need to see Isidri."

My mother looked up at me intently but asked no questions. "She's in the shrine, I think."

"I'll be right back."

I left her and Tubdu side by side and hurried through the halls of the central room, in the oldest part of the house,

rebuilt seven centuries ago on the foundations that go back
three thousand years. The walls are stone and clay, the roof
is thick glass, curved. It is always cool and still there. Books
line the walls, the Discussions, the discussions of the
Discussions, poetry, texts and versions of the Plays; there
are drums and whispersticks for meditation and ceremony;
the small, round pool which is the shrine itself wells up from
clay pipes and brims its blue-green basin, reflecting the
rainy sky above the skylight. Isidri was there. She had
brought in fresh boughs for the vase beside the shrine, and
was kneeling to arrange them.

I went straight to her and said, "Isidri, I came back.
Listen—"

Her face was utterly open, startled, scared, defenseless,
the soft, thin face of a woman of twenty-two, the dark eyes
gazing into me.

"Listen, Isidri: I went to Hain, I studied there, I worked
on a new kind of temporal physics, a new theory—
transilience—I spent ten years there. Then we began
experiments, I was in Ran'n and crossed over to the Hainish
system in no time, using that technology, in no time, you
understand me, literally, like the ansible—not at lightspeed,
not faster than light, but in no time. In one place and in
another place instantaneously, you understand? And it went
fine, it worked, but coming back there was . . . there was
a fold, a crease, in my field. I was in the same place in a
different time. I came back eighteen of your years, ten of
mine. I came back to the day I let, but I didn't leave, I came
back, I came back to you."

I was holding her hands, kneeling to face her as she knelt
by the silent pool. She searched my face with her watchful
eyes, silent. On her cheekbone there was a fresh scratch and
a little bruise; a branch had lashed her as she gathered the
evergreen boughs.

"Let me come back to you," I said in a whisper.

She touched my face with my hand. "You look so tired,"
she said. "Hideo . . . are you all right?"

"Yes," I said. "Oh, yes. I'm all right."

• • •

"And there my story, so far as it has any interest to the Ekumen or to research in transilience, comes to an end. I have lived now for eighteen years as a farmholder of Udan Farm of Derdan'nad Village of the hill region of the Northwestern Watershed of the Saduun, on Oket, on O. I am fifty years old. I am the Morning husband of the Second Sedoretu of Udan; my wife is Isidri; my Night marriage is to Sota of Drehe, whose Evening wife is my sister Koneko. My children of the Morning with Isidri are Latubdu and Tadri; the Evening children are Murmi and Lasako. But none of this is of much interest to the Stabiles of the Ekumen.

My mother, who had had some training in temporal engineering, asked for my story, listened to it carefully, and accepted it without question; so did Isidri. Most of the people of my farmhold chose a simpler and far more plausible story, which explained everything fairly well, even my severe loss of weight and ten-year age gain overnight. At the very last moment, just before the space ship left, they said, Hideo decided not to go to the Ekumenical School on Hain after all. He came back to Udan, because he was in love with Isidri. But it had made him quite ill, because it was a very hard decision and he was very much in love.

Maybe that is indeed the true story. But Isidri and Isako chose a stranger truth.

Later, when we were forming our sedoretu, Sota asked me for that truth. "You aren't the same man, Hideo, though you are the man I always loved," he said. I told him why, as best I could. He was sure that Koneko would understand it better than he could, and indeed she listened gravely, and asked several keen questions which I could not answer.

I did attempt to send a message to the temporal physics department of the Ekumenical Schools on Hain. I had not been home long before my mother, with her strong sense of duty and her obligation to the Ekumen, became insistent that I do so.

"Mother," I said, "what can I tell them? They haven't invented churten theory yet!"

"Apologize for not coming to study, as you said you would. And explain it to the Director, the Anarresti woman. Maybe she would understand."

"Even Gvonesh doesn't know about churten yet. They'll begin telling her about it on the ansible from Urras and Anarres about three years from now. Anyhow, Gvonesh didn't know me the first couple of years I was there." The past tense was inevitable but ridiculous; it would have been more accurate to say, "she won't know me the first couple of years I won't be there."

Or *was* I there on Hain, now? That paradoxical idea of two simultaneous existence on two different worlds disturbed me exceedingly. It was one of the points Koneko had asked about. No matter how I discounted it as impossible under every law of temporality, I could not keep from imagining that it was possible, that another *I* was living on Hain, and would come to Udan in eighteen years and meet myself. After all, my present existence was also and equally impossible.

When such notions haunted and troubled me I learned to replace them with a different image: the little whorls of water that slid down between the two big rocks, where the current ran strong, just above the swimming-bay in the Oro. I would imagine those whirlpools forming and dissolving, or I would go down to the river and sit and watch them. And they seemed to hold a solution to my question, to dissolve it as they endlessly dissolved and formed.

But my mother's sense of duty and obligation was unmoved by such trifles as a life impossibly lived twice.

"You should try to tell them," she said.

She was right. If my double transilience field had established itself permanently, it was a matter of real importance to temporal science, not only to myself. So I tried. I borrowed a staggering sum in cash from the farm reserves, went up to Kan'n, bought a 5000-word ansible screen transmission, and sent a message to my director of studies at the Ekumenical School, trying to explain why, after being accepted at the School, I had not arrived—if in fact I had not arrived.

I take it that this was the "creased message" or "ghost" they asked me to try to interpret, my first year there. Some of it is gibberish, and some words probably came from the other, nearly simultaneous transmission, but parts of my name are in it, and other words may be fragments or reversals from my long message—problem, churten, return, arrived, time.

It is interesting, I think, that at the ansible center the Receivers used the word "creased" for a temporally-disturbed transilient, as Gvonesh would use it for the anomaly, the "wrinkle" in my churten field. In fact, the ansible field was meeting a resonance resistance, caused by the ten-year anomaly in the churten field, which did fold the message back into itself, crumple up, inverting and erasing. At that point, within the implication of the Tiokunan'n Double Field, my existence on O as I sent the message was simultaneous with my existence on Hain when the message was received. There was an I who sent and an I who received. Yet, so long as the encapsulated field anomaly existed, the simultaneity was literally a point, an instant, a crossing without further implication in either the ansible of the churten field.

An image for the churten field in this case might be a river winding in its floodplain, winding in deep, redoubling curves, folding back upon itself so closely that at last the current breaks through the double banks of the S and runs straight, leaving a whole reach of the water aside as a curving lake, cut off from the current, unconnected. In this analogy, my ansible message would have been the one link, other than my memory, between the current and the lake.

But I think a truer image is the whirlpools of the current itself, occurring and recurring, the same? Or not the same?

I worked at the mathematics of an explanation in the early years of my marriage, while my physics was still in good working order. See the "Notes towards a Theory of Resonance Interference in Doubled Ansible and Churten Fields," appended to this document. I realize that the explanation is probably irrelevant, since, on this stretch of the river, there is no Tiokunan'n Field. But independent research from an odd direction can be useful. And I am attached to it, since it is the last temporal physics I did. I have followed churten research with intense interest, but my life's work has been concerned with vineyards, drainage, the care of yamas, the care and education of children, the Discussions, and trying to learn how to catch fish with my bare hands.

Working on that paper, I satisfied myself in terms of mathematics and physics that the existence in which I went to Hain and became a temporal physicist specializing in transilience was in fact encapsulated (enfolded, erased) by the churten effect. But no amount of theory or proof could quite allay my anxiety, my fear—which increased after my marriage and with the birth of each of my children—that there was a crossing-point yet to come. For all my images of rivers and whirlpools, I could not prove that the encapsulation might not reverse at the instant of transilience. It was possible that on the day I churtened from Ve to Ran'n I might undo, lose, erase my marriage, our children, all my life at Udan, crumple it up like a bit of paper tossed into a basket. I could not endure that thought.

I spoke of it at last to Isidri, from whom I have only ever kept one secret.

"No," she said, after thinking a long time. "I don't think that can be. There was a reason, wasn't there, that you came back—here."

"You," I said.

She smiled wonderfully. "Yes," she said. She added after a while, "And Sota, and Koneko, and the farmhold. . . . But there'd be no reason for you to go back there, would there?"

She was holding our sleeping baby as she spoke; she laid her cheek against the small silky head.

"Except maybe your work there," she said. She looked at me with a little yearning in her eyes. Her honesty of me.

"I miss it sometimes," I said. "I know that. I didn't know that I was missing you. But I was dying of it. I would have died and never known why, Isidri. And anyhow, it was all wrong—my work was wrong."

"How could it have been wrong, if it brought you back?" she said, and to that I had no answer at all.

When information on churten theory began to be published I subscribed to whatever the Center Library of O received, particularly the work done at the Ekumenical Schools and on Ve. The general progress of research was just as I remembered, racing along for three years, then hitting the hard places. But there was no reference to a Tiokunan'n Hideo doing research in the field. Nobody worked on a theory of a stabilized double field. No churten field research station was set up at Ran'n.

At last it was the winter of my visit home, and then the very day; and I will admit that, all reason to the contrary, it was a bad day. I felt waves of guilt, of nausea. I grew very shaky, thinking of the Udan of that visit, when Isidri had been married to Hedran, and I a mere visitor.

Hedran, a respected travelling scholar of the Discussions, had in fact come to teach several times in the village. Isidri had suggested inviting him to stay at Udan. I had vetoed the suggestion, saying that though he was a brilliant teacher there was something I disliked about him. I got a sidelong flash from Sidi's clear dark eyes: Is he jealous? She suppressed a smile. When I told her and my mother about my "other life" the one thing I had left out, the one secret I kept, was my visit to Udan, I did not want to tell my mother that in that "other life" she had been very ill. I did not want to tell Isidri that in that "other life" Hedran had been her Evening husband and she had had no children of her body. Perhaps I was wrong, but it seemed to me that I had no right to tell the things, that they were not mine to tell.

So Isidri could not know that what I felt was less jealousy than guilt. I had kept knowledge from her. And I had deprived Hedran of a life with Isidri, the dear joy, the center, the life of my own life.

Or had I shared it with him? I didn't know. I don't know.

That day passed like any other, except that one of Suudi's children broke her elbow falling out of a tree. "At least we know she won't drown," said Tubdu, wheezing.

Next came the date of the night in my rooms in the New

Quadrangle, when I had wept and not known why I wept. And a while after that, the day of my return, transilient, to Ve, carrying a bottle of Isidri's wine for Gvonesh. And finally, yesterday, I entered the churten field on Ve, and left it eighteen years ago on O. I spent the night, as I sometimes do, in the shrine. The hours went by quietly; I wrote, gave worship, meditated, and slept. And I woke beside the pool of silent water.

So, now: I hope the Stabiles will accept this report from a farmer they never heard of, and that the engineers of transilience may see it as at least a footnote to their experiments. Certainly it is difficult to verify, the only evidence for it being my word, and my otherwise almost inexplicable knowledge of the churten theory. To Gvonesh, who does not know me, I send my respect, my gratitude, and my hope that she will honor my intent.

Mitch turned to the door, then faced her again. "And don't worry about missing me while I'm busy. I've arranged for us to have a private dinner, here, in the apartment tonight."

Lila's breath froze. Private dinner? She remembered those thirty seconds when he'd yanked her against him on the dance floor. The sizzle. The confusion.

And the longing.

She fought the urge to squeeze her eyes shut. She'd had a crush on this man forever. When he'd pulled her so close...well, her thoughts had spun out of control and she'd felt so many wonderful things.

What if he'd felt them, too?

Oh, boy.

The words *private dinner* took on a whole new meaning.

But he opened the door and was gone before Lila could blink, let alone argue. She straightened her shoulders. She wasn't going to fall into the trap of thinking he intended to seduce her. They'd shared one "crackly" moment the night before. He hadn't instantly fallen in love with her. He probably wanted to have dinner alone so he could catch her up on whatever had happened at their family business meeting that day.

She was, after all, his a~~ssistant. BRAN~~

AUG 2018

Every once in a while a story comes along that doesn't follow the direction you'd intended. At every turn, Lila balked at the plans I had for her and her story.

To me, she was a simple girl with a crush on her boss who was going to get "her shot" at getting to know him—and maybe have him fall for her, too—by pretending to be his fiancée for two weeks. But her story was so much richer, and Lila herself was so much more than a typical girl finding love. And Mitch's response to that was always surprising. LOL! You've gotta love characters who step up on the page and take control of their stories.

Put all this in Spain, with a big, loving family and vineyard that sparkles in the summer sun, and Lila and Mitch's story comes to life in a vivid, wonderful way that will make you laugh sometimes, cry others.

I think you're going to love this book.

Happy reading...

Susan Meier